DIVINE MERIT

VIRGINIA CANTRELL

HOT TREE PUBLISHING

DIVINE MERIT

DIVINE
BOOK ONE

VIRGINIA CANTRELL

HOT TREE PUBLISHING

Also by Virginia Cantrell

Divine Merit

Divine Grace

For information, contact the publisher, Hot Tree Publishing.

www.hottreepublishing.com

Editing: Hot Tree Editing

Ebook ISBN: 9781925448023

Paperback ISBN: 9781925448030

SECOND EDITION

*To Deborah,
I wish you could've been here for the ending.*

ONE

"She is a child playing games, nothing more," she heard Caeden say from the other side of the doorway. His cold tone sent a shiver through her entire body and froze her mid step. Her handsome soldier was upset. This was a side of him she was not usually permitted to see. In her presence, he was always polite, if a bit distant and reserved. Everything about Caeden fascinated her, even his anger, and she couldn't help but stop to listen.

It would be extremely embarrassing for the Princess of Velius, the future ruler of the island of Cashile, to be caught eavesdropping at the door of the soldiers' keep, but Amira was willing to take a chance for the opportunity to glimpse the real Caeden. He was strong, determined, loyal, a pure warrior—her warrior... well, maybe not hers yet, but she could dream. She knew she spent entirely too much time focused on him, but despite his usual aloofness, there were times she would catch him watching her with an unguarded expression. She was inexperienced, but she would almost swear it was desire she read on his face.

That was the reason she now found herself sweaty and tired from their weekly self-defense lesson. It was against social etiquette for females, especially one of her stature, to participate in such a crude activity. She had originally asked him to train her solely for the chance to spend time with him, but she had actually grown to enjoy the physical activity as well. Unfortunately, they had just finished a particularly frustrating lesson on how to immobilize an attacker. She knew Caeden had been disappointed by her lack of attention and her unwillingness to take a swing at him, but she just couldn't force herself to hit him. She would look into his ice-blue eyes, feel herself melting inside, and be unable to think of anything else. The lesson had gone badly and she didn't want to end their encounter on a negative note, so she was using the excuse of returning a towel to the training room as an opportunity to see him one more time before they both went about their duties.

Standing in the hallway, she could picture the look of frustration in his intense eyes and the tension in his square jaw. She envisioned him carelessly pushing his honey-brown hair out of his ruggedly handsome face. She wished she were brave enough to run her fingers through his shoulder-length hair, brushing it away from his face for him. She'd let her hand rest on his broad shoulder before slowly sliding it down to explore and memorize his muscular chest and hard, flat stomach. Amira barely caught the sigh that nearly left her lips at the fantasy inspired by his masculine beauty and lethal grace. He had the build of a perfect warrior. As captain of the elite Royal Guard, which served her family directly, he was responsible for leading the army of Velius.

Legend said the people of Cashile were the descendants of the union between angels and humans, the fabled Nephilim. The angels had created the island as a sanctuary for their offspring to protect them from persecution by man for their strength, beauty, and longer life span. The island was located in the northern hemisphere and was hidden and protected by a shield. Amira had never seen any of the angels they were supposedly descendants of, but she imagined Caeden's powerful and flawless body rivaled that of the mighty angels. Just the mental image of his body was so enticing and distracting, she almost forgot where she was until the conversation beyond the doorway continued.

"True, she hasn't reached full maturity, but that hardly makes her a child," came the even response from Trevin, another member of the Royal Guard.

Their people reached full maturity at the age of twenty-five, when their aging process all but stopped and a type of near-immortality took over. After reaching full maturity, they became immune to disease, and although they could still be injured, their bodies healed quickly and with no marks. Their life span was more than ten times longer than a human's and they could live for near to a thousand years before their bodies settled into eternal rest. Before reaching full maturity, they were extremely vulnerable and fragile in comparison.

Amira rarely heard Trevin speak unless he was directly addressed. This was indeed a candid moment between the soldiers. Trevin was the quietest and most deceptively calm of all of the Royal Guard. His even manner often made others forget how absolutely deadly he could be. She had once witnessed his swift victory over a soldier who thought to challenge him; he had reminded her of a snake waiting for the exact moment to strike, and then it was all over.

"She reaches maturity in less than two years, but I'm not talking about her actual age," Caeden said, still sounding frustrated. "These training sessions are unbearable." A loud bang, like something hitting the wall, made her jump. "She is just so damn naïve, following me around, seeking my attention." He sighed. "The way she looks at me..."

Amira's whole body turned to lead. They were discussing her!

"What is wrong with it? She looks at you like a girl who has just received a gift from the angels."

"That's very poetic of you, Trevin," Caeden

responded dryly. "What's wrong with it is I'm her guard; she shouldn't look at me like that."

"And why not?" Trevin asked again.

After a slight hesitation, he answered firmly, "It chases off all of the other females; that's why not. They don't even want to be seen with me for fear of upsetting their beloved princess."

Child... naïve... *other females*!

She couldn't listen to another word. She could barely breathe. Hopefully, she would make it to her chambers before she made a complete fool of herself and broke down into tears in the hallway. The towel she had been returning fell silently to the floor as she turned and ran.

Trevin burst into laughter. "Glad to amuse you, Trevin," Caeden said sardonically. He could tell his closest friend was struggling to contain his enjoyment. It was rare to see him laugh, but that subject never failed to entertain him.

Typically, he'd smile enigmatically, but today it seemed he was in an unusually talkative mood as he said, "I didn't realize you knew this island had any other females."

"What is that supposed to mean?"

"When was the last time you were with a female?" Trevin asked knowingly.

Caeden had to admit to himself it had been a while. There were plenty of opportunities, despite what he said about the princess chasing them off, but the truth was, he just wasn't interested. Not that he'd ever admit that to anyone else.

"I've been busy with my duties," he said as an excuse. Caeden could still see the grin Trevin was trying to hide and knew he wasn't fooling his friend. Trevin was the type of person who often saw far more than you wanted anyone to see. His stoic nature made him easy to confide in and the fact he rarely spoke made him a great listener.

"Yes, your duties—guard rotation, soldier training, and, of course, your personal hands-on lessons with Princess Amira," Trevin pointed out with a smirk. He was the only other person who knew Caeden had been secretly instructing the princess. "If you're overwhelmed and she is really a burden, I could take on her weekly lessons."

"No," Caeden answered instinctively. A full smile split Trevin's face. "I mean, she found the courage to ask me and it is not a huge burden," he tried to explain. He couldn't admit there was a part of him that craved this time spent with her. His princess was usually so poised and polite, but in the training she was unguarded and excited; she had a fire in her eyes he rarely saw, like a dormant part of her was coming to life. Give that up? Not a chance.

"Technically, I shouldn't even be teaching her. I'll

face the consequences if we're found out, no need for you to be involved further. The rule is archaic, but it's still a rule; although, it hurts nothing for a female to learn a few basic moves to protect herself. Not that the princess will ever have need or opportunity."

That was the Royal Guard's job. His job.

"You don't have to defend it to me. My point being, you have sanctioned the time spent with our princess and have enjoyed her attentions. What male wouldn't?" Trevin said with a wicked glint in his eyes.

Indeed, what male wouldn't? He could picture all the males who would gladly stand in line just to have a conversation with his princess or even a touch of her hand. The thought of another male touching her made him want to snarl with fury. And that was exactly the problem. She wasn't his, would never be his, so he had no right to feel possessive of her. He was Princess Amira's guard, nothing more.

"As I said, she plays a childish game with me; flirting and trying to get my attention. I know it's all innocent, and I highly doubt she would know what to do with my attention anyhow. I'm sure she simply feels it's safe to behave this way with me because nothing can come of it. But I am a male, Trevin. I only have so much self-control. She'll get over this infatuation soon, but until then..." He sighed.

It was difficult for him to admit this weakness, even to his closest friend. Caeden prided himself on his control and hated not being able to let go of this all-consuming attraction he felt for his princess. There. He'd admitted it, at least to himself; he was attracted to the princess. She drove him to distraction with her delicate frame, her big gray eyes that flashed silver when she was excited, and the sweet scent of vanilla that seemed to trail after her. Her waist-length, rich, dark brown hair was an incredible sight. At 5'4, she was unusually short for their kind and his 6'4 frame dwarfed her. Princess Amira was so small and looked so delicate, it was no wonder he felt overly protective of her. She was in truth delicate and vulnerable, at least until she reached her maturity.

While he was being honest with himself, he had to admit her age scared him most of all. He feared all of the possible things that could happen to her. What if she were injured or became ill? Caeden was unused to the cramping fear in his stomach at the thought. He couldn't let himself even consider such an incident. It was his job to protect her and he would, even from himself.

"What if it's not a game?" Trevin asked quietly. "Not to her. Stop fighting it and stop trying to control it. Let things take their natural course."

Caeden felt like he had been sucker punched as his breath caught in his throat. What if... No, he couldn't allow himself to even entertain the idea for a single moment. Thoughts like that were dangerous.

"No." Caeden shook his head.

"Why not? I've seen the way she looks at you, like you're the reason the sun rises each morning."

He had seen that look, too. He loved that look.

"That is exactly what I mean. She is so innocent and doesn't know what is best for her. She's naïve enough to think I'm safe to practice her wiles on."

Trevin didn't bother to respond, but gave his friend a look that told him how much of an idiot he thought he was.

"I'm a soldier; she's a princess. My father was a low-ranking soldier, and my mother and sister tend the fruit orchard. I grew up in a modest cottage, and she was born into a palace. I have no social graces." Caeden explained, as if their social status would clarify everything.

"You are the highest-ranking soldier in the entire kingdom, hell, on this entire island. You somehow think your humble upbringing makes you unworthy of her? You've struggled and worked hard for everything you've achieved." Trevin continued before Caeden could respond. "Tell me, do you think one of the lazy aristocratic males from another territory would be better suited for her? Worthy of her? Could protect her and meet her needs? Let alone take command of the kingdom?"

No! "Yes," Caeden said through gritted teeth.

Trevin sighed, shook his head, and headed for the door. Caeden felt like punching something or someone. He'd like to start with all of the aristocratic males parading themselves around his princess, which happened more frequently as her maturity approached. He couldn't count how many formal dinners he had been forced to stand guard at, watching as the weak aristocrats tried to win favor with his princess. She was beautiful and sweet, never saying an unkind thing about anyone. She went out of her way to make every guest feel welcome and she genuinely cared about everyone in her kingdom. Princess Amira had a vibrant spirit she kept hidden behind her sense of duty, but that wasn't why they tried so hard to impress her. They pursued her because with her hand came the Kingdom of Velius and rulership of all of Cashile.

Thus far, she had shown no sign of favoritism toward any of her suitors, but Caeden knew someday that would change. It was his princess's duty to marry and continue the royal bloodline. So far, she was poised, polite, the perfect princess... but she was bored out of her mind by all of them. *Will tonight be different?* He dreaded the constant thought. Tonight was another formal dinner with the leaders of the three other territories of Cashile, and the most persistent of her suitors, Sorin of Ammon, would be present. The thought of Sorin and his princess together made his vision red with fury. He really needed to hit something. Thank the angels it was time for training.

～

"Amira, may I come in?" The soft words accompanied a light tap on her closed chamber door. "It's an hour until supper. Would you like me to help you prepare?"

Amira smiled through her still blurry eyes. Inaya always knew when she was upset and was there to lend her unwavering support. Inaya had been brought to live in the palace as Amira's companion sixteen years prior, when Amira had been seven and Inaya had been nine. The girls had bonded immediately and had been near inseparable for over half their lives. Amira took a deep breath and let it out slowly before opening the door.

"Yes, I do believe I could use your help tonight."

"Oh, dear...," Inaya breathed softly as she pulled Amira close for a comforting hug, closing the door firmly behind her.

Amira would not allow anyone else to see her like this. She knew her duty as the Princess of Velius. She was always to be cheerful, polite, and gracious. She wasn't allowed to show sorrow, hurt feelings, or pain. She was the hope and future of the Kingdom of Velius and the island of Cashile, a responsibility she could never forget. Through her choice of consort and her blood, the royal bloodline would continue, and thus the security of Cashile would be ensured.

Legend told, when the angels first created the island as a safe haven for their offspring, the royal family was created and entrusted with the duty to preserve the shield surrounding the island. The most sacred of bonds, a blood bond, was forged by the angels between the royal family and the island itself. Soon it would fall on Amira's shoulders to uphold that covenant. Therefore, in the privacy of her chambers she had given herself only until suppertime to feel her heartache. Now it was time to put it away and do her duty.

"I've brought a cold compress. Here, hold this on your eyes to help with the swelling while I redo your hair," Inaya said, immediately taking charge.

Amira noticed Inaya had already gotten herself ready for the formal dinner they would attend. She looked beautiful in her formfitting turquoise gown, which accentuated her generous curves and matched her eyes perfectly. She had clipped her long golden-blonde hair in an intricate knot, but left a few strands to frame her face. She looked flawless and well put together as always. At 5'8, Inaya loomed over Amira's small form, and her beauty at times made Amira self-conscious about what she considered to be her plain, mousy looks. But she couldn't be resentful of her friend. Inaya was as kind and generous as she was beautiful. Amira also knew Inaya didn't feel as confident as she looked, and was uncomfortable with her curvy body.

Amira had never been as grateful for her friend as she was at that moment. "You are such a blessing. How did you know?"

"Oh, that's easy," Inaya said as she worked. "I heard

you sneak up to your chambers through the hidden servants' entrance. When you didn't come back down, I knew it must be something awful, if it kept you confined to your rooms for half of the day." She paused, and then she asked hesitantly, "Are you ready to talk about it yet?"

Amira shared what she had overheard. "I'm just so embarrassed!" she finished. "I have been in love with him for years and he sees me as nothing but a nuisance." Inaya was shaking her head. "What?"

"That just doesn't make sense. I've seen you two together and there are definitely sparks on both sides." Inaya tried to explain. "I think you rattle him. Males, especially soldiers, like to be in control. I think Caeden does want you, but deep down you scare him senseless. He knows he cannot control you; you're the princess, for crying out loud."

"He said he wanted other women!" Amira couldn't get past that point; the pain cut deep.

Inaya started laughing.

"What's so funny?" Amira didn't find the thought of Caeden with another female the least bit funny.

"I just remembered a conversation I heard between Murdock and a couple of the other guards."

Murdock was Inaya's oldest brother and a member of the Royal Guard. There were six in all. They usually paired off and rotated shifts between guard duty and training the other soldiers. Caeden was the captain and Trevin was his second-in-command.

Levi and Murdock were usually the guards during the day. Levi liked to keep his nights and evenings free for female companionship, for which he never lacked. Murdock, on the other hand, could usually be found at home spending time with his wife Maryse, who was expecting their first child. He was a good soldier, but Amira thought he was one of the more arrogant and bossy of the guards, probably because she and his sister had spent so much time together that he now treated her much like a sister as well.

Dalek and Osmond were the guards usually on the night shift. Amira was told Dalek was playful and had a wicked sense of humor when he wasn't on duty, but unfortunately, she was never able to see that side of him. Osmond, on the other hand, was the most formidable and unapproachable of her guards. She was thankful he was usually assigned to her father. It was Amira's opinion that he didn't much care for women, although she knew he was married to a robust and sturdy female named Francine.

"I swear, the soldiers gossip worse than females," Inaya continued with another giggle.

"What did they say?" Amira's interest was fully piqued. She couldn't help but grin at her friend's amusement.

"I heard Dalek telling the other guards that he thought Caeden must be going daft because he saw that hussy, Sadie"—she said the name with a shudder and a comical look of distaste—"all but strip naked and throw herself at Caeden's feet in the middle of the courtyard, yet Caeden barely spared her a glance."

Amira released the breath she hadn't realized she'd been holding. She tried hard not to think badly of anyone, but just then she couldn't help the unkind things she was thinking about Sadie.

"Murdock said Caeden was just showing good sense by staying clear of that viper, but Levi seemed to think Caeden was developing an aversion to females. Then the conversation digressed into crude jokes and caveman-like behavior, which would scald your inno-cent little ears," Inaya said with revulsion.

Amira would have loved to have been a witness to the rest of their conversation. Having been sheltered most of her life, she would have found it thrilling; unlike Inaya, who had grown up with two older brothers.

"That doesn't mean anything; maybe I should just give up and accept that he doesn't want me," she said dejectedly.

"Or maybe you should show him what he is miss-ing." Inaya eyed Amira calculatingly.

"Holy hell, you almost took my head off!" Murdock panted.

"Just checking your reflexes," Caeden replied, barely winded.

"This is supposed to be friendly sparring," Dalek added.

After the soldiers had finished training, the other members of the Royal Guard had decided to help Caeden out of his apparently dark mood by challenging him to a three-on-one sparring match. Now they were regretting their decision. Dalek, Murdock, and Levi had their asses handed to them by Caeden.

"How am I supposed to explain to Murdock's pregnant wife that he died while in a friendly competition?" Dalek questioned.

"Easy. You say, 'Maryse, your husband was slow as shit,'" Levi provided helpfully. "Better yet, I'll tell her, and then I could comfort her."

He'd barely finished his sentence before Murdock launched himself at Levi. Dalek and Caeden were between the two males before any blood could be shed.

"I'm sure Maryse doesn't like that shade of lipstick on her man," Dalek said, staring at Levi's lips. Caeden, Dalek, and Murdock all roared with laughter as Levi shot them each a look of contempt while wiping his mouth.

"You let me go all this time with cosmetics on my face?" he accused. "What kind of friends are you?"

They all laughed harder.

"So, Levi, tell us again how you were late for practice because you were helping repair a fence in the northern field," Caeden said once he was able to catch his breath, which stirred another round of laughter.

Levi couldn't stay angry and had to agree, it had been a fitting punishment. "Well, the fence did break, I just didn't mention how it broke," he said with a wicked grin.

"Sadie?" Dalek questioned.

"Nope; her sister, Rebecca," Levi answered with a wink.

"I don't know how you do it," Dalek said in awe.

Levi definitely had a reputation with the females. He was known for being elusive, but instead of being deterred, females seemed to find him all the more appealing because of that. Each hoped she would be able to keep the alluring warrior. Most women found Levi's shaggy, blond-streaked hair, lean muscular build, and big green eyes irresistible. He could almost be described as pretty, except for the hard look that rarely left his eyes.

"All your promiscuity is going to come back to haunt you," Murdock predicted with a shake of his head.

"You have been trapped too long, my friend," Levi answered, slapping Murdock on the back, all of their earlier hostility forgotten.

"If the ability to climb in bed with Maryse each night, to hold her in my arms and feel our child growing within her is a trap, then I pray to never break free. I only hope one day you will be as lucky as I am, my friend," Murdock told him seriously before walking away.

Caeden couldn't help but agree and secretly envied the bond Murdock and his Maryse shared.

They all began to make their way back to the soldiers' keep.

"Lucky Osmond and Trevin, to be on duty this afternoon. I'm glad he isn't usually this moody. I thought for sure he was going to dismember at least a couple of the trainees," Levi murmured to Dalek.

"Yeah, I'm pretty sure a few of the newer recruits left in need of clean underpants." Dalek smirked.

"We could always take advantage of his dark mood to weed out the weaker males," Murdock suggested logically.

Caeden glared at the three soldiers as they continued to talk about him as if he weren't walking right beside them.

"Maybe he needs to get laid," Levi added helpfully, shooting Caeden a pointed look.

"Sex is not the answer to all of life's problems," Murdock retorted.

"Hey, it works well for me." Levi smiled.

"Except when your female friends have a catfight in the courtyard," Dalek reminded him gleefully.

"Hey, that was only one time, and have you noticed how well Ruth and Kaitlyn get along now?" Levi defended, smirking.

"Not sure how you accomplished that," Murdock grumbled.

"I told you it worked well for me." Levi wiggled his eyebrows suggestively.

"You're a god," Dalek said in awe at the same time Murdock muttered, "Someday..." with a shake of his head. Caeden just rolled his eyes.

"To each his own." Levi laughed.

"Maybe it's the stress of extra guard duty, due to our guests' arrival," Dalek said, returning to the previous topic, clearly not done teasing Caeden. "Maybe he is cracking under the pressure," he added, shooting Caeden a sly look.

Any time there were visitors from the other territories, the Guard was on high alert. The royal family was not usually guarded inside the palace, except when they had foreign guests. The leaders of the three other territories and their entourages were not to be trusted. Each leader was a distant relative to the royal family, assigned to govern their specific part of the island. For the most part, they were good men and women, but greed and squabbles over territory borders were not unheard of—hence the need for each territory to have its own military and defense—but each territory was under the rule of the royal family that governed the territory of Velius.

Caeden shook his head, not taking the bait.

"Pfft," Murdock scoffed. "More like he is cracking under the pressure not to kill that rat bastard Sorin."

"I'd like to have a go at him myself," Dalek said, suddenly very serious.

"If you ladies are finished gossiping, maybe you could go about your duties," Caeden interrupted, wanting to end the thread of conversation before his "dark mood" returned in full force.

"Yep, needs to get laid," Caeden heard Dalek mumble as he walked away.

"Amira, darling, the guests are arriving," her Aunt Marcelle's husky voice interrupted through the closed door.

Amira's mother, Queen Maryam, had died weeks after giving birth to her. She'd had a hard time conceiving and never regained her strength after Amira was born. Her mother's sister, Marcelle, tried to fill the role of surrogate mother as best she could, but it definitely did not come naturally for her.

"Good evening, Aunt Marcelle," Amira said in greeting, admitting her into her chambers.

"Don't you look just lovely, darling? Your gown will surely make an impression on our guests. You know Lord Sorin of Ammon will be here," she said in a falsely conspiratorial tone.

Marcelle loved to use a person's full title, as if having a title made someone more important than those without. The gown Inaya had picked out for Amira was a little more daring than usual. It was a long, sleeveless champagne-gold silk gown, which hugged her slender curves to perfection. Amira had never worn anything quite so revealing, but she had to admit it made her small breasts look much more ample than they really were and she felt kind of beautiful for once.

"Yes, one must always try to impress Lord Sorin," Inaya said with disdain.

"You look lovely as well, Aunt Marcelle," Amira said quickly, trying to divert her aunt's attention.

It was no secret that Inaya and Marcelle didn't get along; in fact, Marcelle didn't get along with many. Although Marcelle was the second born and would not be able to inherit the throne, she had grown up as royalty and often thought those without royal blood to be beneath her. She hadn't thought Inaya a good companion for Amira and to this day rarely acknowledged her existence.

The flattery worked to distract Marcelle from making a biting retort, just as Amira knew it would. Marcelle had chosen a bright red dress that was almost the exact color of her tinted red hair. Her brown eyes were darkly outlined, making them appear small and beady, and her generous mouth was shaded in the same bright red as her gown.

As most second born children of the royal family, Marcelle had been trained to be the Supreme Healer. It was the Supreme Healer's duty to safeguard the ancient traditions and ceremonies passed down from their first ancestors. She presided over all sacred ceremonies, such as the marriage ceremonies in which the couple undertook the sacred bond. It was also her duty to care for the injured and the vulnerable young ones who hadn't yet reached full maturity. Although she hadn't taken an apprentice in over half a century, it was her responsibility to train other healers as well.

Marcelle had never been married, and as far as Amira knew, she had never been seriously involved with any male. At times, Amira felt guilty that her aunt had sacrificed her chance at happiness to help care for her.

"Thank you, darling. It is very important to make the right impression," she advised Amira, as she had her entire life. Marcelle wrapped her arm around Amira's shoulders and walked her a few steps away from Inaya. "I'd like you to keep in mind your duty tonight, Amira. Soon it will be your turn to lead our people. You will need a strong, worthy male at your side as your consort and king. Keep an open mind about our guests tonight. For me?"

"She is aware of her duty, Marcelle. Why must she dwell on it tonight? She hasn't even reached her full maturity and cannot join into a bond of marriage until she does," Inaya interrupted.

"This does not concern you, girl," Marcelle snapped.

"Aunt Marcelle, this is a formal dinner to celebrate the launch of the new scout. This dinner has nothing to do with my future consort," Amira weighed in.

Every century a new scout was sent out to travel the Earth to evaluate the condition of humanity. It was their job to report the circumstances, changes, and advancements. Upon the scout's return every decade, the leaders of Cashile would meet to determine if it were time to return to the world of man. The last scout had made his final return the previous month. At his debriefing, it was decided humanity was still on a path of self-destruction with war, pollution, and, most harmful, their indifference. It was determined the people of Cashile would remain within their protective shield.

This had been the first time Amira had been present at a scout's debriefing and she had found the scout's report fascinating. Humanity reminded her of a rebellious teenager without the guidance of a loving parent, struggling to find its way but subjugated by volatile emotions.

In her opinion, humanity was capable of great things, as was illustrated by their many technological advancements and ability to persevere regardless of their self-destructive nature.

Amira worried that the counsel in charge of arbitration had made their decision before hearing the scout's report and insisted upon refusing to acknowledge any positive aspects, so sure in their own superiority. The new scout, trained since birth for her duty, would be embarking on her mission in the morning. Tonight would be her farewell. This would be the first time in their history that a female would be sent out.

"Foolish girl," Marcelle began, venom still within her husky tone. "Any situation can be used as an opportunity to achieve one's goals. That female, that nobody, doesn't deserve a celebration in her honor. Scout or not, she should not be seated at the table of royalty. Good riddance to her; we'll all be better off once she is gone."

Amira was taken aback by the hatred pouring from Marcelle. Her shock must have registered to her aunt, because Marcelle's tone became sweet and she abruptly returned to her original topic.

"With Lord Sorin in attendance tonight you have the perfect opportunity to secure a strong match for the future of Cashile."

Amira could see the disgust on Inaya's face and tried to hide her own negative feelings at the thought of being bonded to Sorin.

"I'm not sure Sorin is the right choice...," Amira began hesitantly.

"Lord Sorin is the perfect choice for the future King of Cashile," Marcelle said with conviction. "He has the purest blood ties to the royal family of any other male. He is a strong leader in Ammon and you will require a consort of such strength to counteract your... delicate nature."

Amira knew that in her need to please others, she was widely considered to be passive and weak. It hurt to be judged as lacking when all she wanted was to do her duty.

"Darling, you know I only have your best interest in mind," Marcelle said in her lovingly sweet tone.

"Yes, Aunt, I will do as you counsel and keep the possibility in mind throughout the evening," Amira promised.

"That is all I ask. Do not be late," she said, sounding appeased, as she kissed Amira's cheek and left the room.

"I don't believe the nerve of that woman! Advising you as if you aren't already burdened down by the weight of your duty." Inaya fumed as she began pacing the room.

"Maybe she is right. Maybe I'm not strong enough to rule," Amira suggested solemnly.

"You cannot be serious! Amira, look at me," she said, stopping directly in front of her friend. "I know you better than anyone. You are not weak. You lack confidence, but that will come with experience and wisdom. You have a heavy burden to carry and, at times, I believe your fear of failure overwhelms you, but you have the heart of a true queen. Follow your heart in all things and Cashile will benefit."

The confidence Inaya showed brought tears back to Amira's eyes. "Thank you," she whispered, once again embracing her friend.

"As for *Lord* Sorin, let that arrogant ass share his

affections with those worthy of it, like the swine that wallow in the mud."

Amira couldn't help but giggle at Inaya's absurd suggestion, which in turn caused Inaya's own giggles.

"Come, let us not keep Lord Sorin waiting," Inaya said when she could finally catch her breath.

"Caeden will be there tonight. Do I look presentable?" Amira asked, nervous about seeing him and a little disappointed with herself for caring about his opinion.

"Beautiful, as always. You'll definitely catch his attention in that dress, and as long as no one looks too closely, they'll never know you've been crying."

Linking arms, they walked to dinner together.

TWO

Something was wrong. Caeden knew it the moment Amira entered the room. She was as beautiful as always, her silky hair slightly curled and left hanging free to caress her slender bare shoulders. Tonight she was wearing a gown he had never before seen. Just looking at the way it encased her small frame made his mouth go dry and his heart race. But her smile was a little too forced, her shoulders too stiff, and her usually glowing skin was pale.

"Princess?" he questioned, and took a step forward as she started to walk past him.

"Captain," she said formally with a nod, not making eye contact or slowing her steps.

Captain? She never addressed him by his title while speaking privately; he was always "Caeden" to her. What had happened?

"May I have a word with you?"

She nodded to Inaya to continue on without her before addressing Caeden.

"What is it you need, Captain?" Amira asked, finally meeting his eyes.

Caeden sucked in a hard breath at the pink circles around her puffy eyes.

"Are you unwell?" His concern was clear.

"I am well, thank you," she said in her overly polite princess way, making it clear the subject was not open for discussion. Her impassive tone reminded him of his place. He nodded, and she turned to enter the dining room. He watched as she crossed the room and placed a kiss on her father, King Vidar's, cheek in greeting.

Caeden couldn't help but silently agree as he heard her father say, "You look splendid, my dear." In return, she gave him a dazzling smile that almost reached her eyes.

"Sorry to keep you waiting," she apologized.

"Not at all, you are right on time," her father reassured her.

Caeden watched even closer as she turned to greet their guests. King Vidar was seated at the head of the table. On the king's left was the guest of honor, the new scout, Kearney, followed by Marcelle and Sorin. Seated on the king's right were Lord Donovan of Kimi, Lady Ferrara of Zefania, and Inaya. Amira would sit opposite her father at the end of the table, with Lord Sorin on her right and Inaya on her left. Everyone stood in front of their seats, waiting for the princess to reach her chair.

Amira greeted the guest of honor first. "Kearney, it is a pleasure seeing you again."

"Princess Amira," Kearney responded with a small nod, but said nothing else. The scout wasn't very friendly, but Amira seemed determined to win her over. At their first meeting, Amira had worried she had somehow offended Kearney, but they all quickly discovered the female was standoffish with everyone.

Amira nodded a greeting to her aunt, and then circled the table to greet Lord Donovan and Lady Ferrara. They exchanged pleasantries, but when she couldn't avoid the end of the table any longer without appearing rude, she went to her seat and nodded a greeting to Sorin. He promptly took hold of her hand and brought it to his lips.

Caeden's jaw clenched so tightly his teeth began to hurt, and didn't release until he noticed her smile slip a little as she quickly pulled her hand away. His fists clenched. He hated that her duty forced her to accept unwanted touches from that arrogant, slimy male. He had to remind himself she was not in any real harm and, therefore, there was nothing he could do.

This is going to be a long evening, Amira thought. She wished she were seated at the other end of the table, where Kearney and her father were discussing the launch and what would be expected in the human world. All Nephilim were educated and kept up to date on the development of the humans in preparation for possible integration, but Amira was fascinated by the human world of the twenty-first century. She loved learning about their technology, behaviorism, and discoveries. The differences between their island sanctuary and the rest of the world were so vast, but she didn't think either was better than the other. Her people had learned so much from them and there was so much they could learn from her people if ever given the chance.

Amira struggled to hear their conversation.

"They have a complete disregard for our planet," Lord Donovan was saying. "Just look at the depletion of natural resources and the damage they are doing to their environment. Always needing bigger and better, never satisfied, and never thinking about anyone but themselves."

"Exactly," Lady Ferrara cut in. "They even compete over who has the most 'weapons of mass destruction,' as if one wouldn't be sufficient; such crude weaponry. What is wrong with facing your opponent with strength and bravery, as we do, instead of this 'mass destruction'? No need for petty wars and innocents being harmed by ignorance."

"I mean, they have the ability to create clean-burning fuel, such as we use..." Donovan was saying.

"Precisely like the fuel you will be using in the transport that will take you to their world," King Vidar told Kearney, interrupting the rant and complaints he had repeatedly heard from Donovan and Ferrara. "Are you comfortable with the controls?" he asked. It wasn't that Amira's father didn't care or understand Donovan and Ferrara's viewpoint; he just knew some things weren't under his control.

Movement to Amira's right brought her attention back to her end of the table. Sorin not only sat closer than was proper, but to her frustration he also took every opportunity to touch her. And it seemed he only knew two topics of conversation—his superiority and everyone else's inadequacies. Even Kearney's brusque manner, which bordered on rudeness, would be better companionship. Amira was trying to be polite, but her patience was wearing thin.

To top it all off, she was having a difficult time concentrating, knowing Caeden was in the same room, standing guard. Her mind kept replaying the conversation she had heard earlier, and she struggled to keep the hurt locked deep inside.

Even Inaya seemed to be distracted and was little help at making the night pass pleasantly. Amira was trying to keep her promise to her aunt and look for the good qualities in Sorin, but her usually generous nature seemed to be lacking. Her head throbbed from her earlier tears, and she wished to just go to bed with the hope the next day would be better.

Her mind wandered back to Caeden. She refused to look directly at him, but she could see him out of the corner of her eye. He appeared to be watching her more closely than usual. *It's probably just wishful thinking*, she thought with a sigh.

"What's the problem, doll?" Sorin asked, grabbing her free hand before answering his own question. "Not liking the soup?"

Amira hadn't even realized she had been eating her soup, her actions completely automatic. She tried to pull her hand free, but was unable to without creating a scene.

"It is a little bland," Sorin continued, as if he didn't notice her struggle to free herself. "You really must replace your chef. My own chef, whom I've had for the last decade, is quite splendid. But it is difficult to find good help. They sometimes forget their place," he said, the last in a sneer as he looked across the table at Inaya.

Inaya's eyes narrowed, yet she said nothing. Amira was momentarily shocked at the rudeness shown to her friend.

Sorin quickly resumed his charming smile and looked at Amira once again. "The chef I had before that didn't last long. I'm sure he was trying to poison me, so I had his hands removed," he said calmly, his smile never fading. "That is the only way to ensure true loyalty: swift and just punishment. Being a ruler, you must show strength and not be afraid to act," he finished.

Amira had taken all she could for one day; she felt as if something inside of her had snapped. She pasted a sweet smile on her face for her father's benefit, as he was giving her a questioning look from across the table.

Amira leaned closer to Sorin and spoke in a voice so low she hoped only he could hear. "Speaking of hands, please remove yours from my person before I have my guards do it for you."

Sorin's eyes traveled between Trevin and Caeden, the two guards on duty, before releasing her hand and swallowing deeply. Amira couldn't help but lock eyes with Caeden for a heartbeat. He had been watching closely and stood menacingly. It gave her the courage she needed to continue.

"For future reference, and so there will not be any more confusion, the Lady Inaya is not a servant but an honorary part of the royal family and will be addressed with the respect she deserves. Furthermore, since I must instruct you on what is proper, you will address me as 'Princess,' not 'doll.' Is that understood?"

If looks could kill, she feared she would not live through this night.

"I apologize for any offense, Princess," he said, struggling to mask his expression.

Amira glanced toward Inaya and saw her sitting in openmouthed shock. Apparently she hadn't been speaking quite as quietly as she'd thought. Inaya's shock soon turned to open excitement and giggles. Unfortunately, Amira could not find humor in the situation, and judging by the look Sorin was now giving Inaya, neither could he.

Inaya's mirth gathered the attention of the entire table; Marcelle, who had been listening intently to the king, was now glaring at Inaya, but the rest of the guests seemed to find her gaiety infectious and were broadly smiling.

"Inaya, sweetheart, would you like to share your amusement with the rest of us?" the king asked with interest.

"Oh no, I couldn't," she said, trying to control her giggles. "Amira was just sharing with us her outlook. You know how charming and entertaining she is. I apologize for interrupting your conversation," Inaya said, still smiling broadly.

King Vidar looked fondly at Inaya, and then turned his attention to his daughter, his smile dimming a bit.

"My dear, are you feeling all right?" he asked with concern.

Amira wasn't sure what he had read on her face, but she was grateful for the opening.

"Father and dear guests," she began as she stood from the table, "I'm going to have to excuse myself for the rest of the evening. I find that I am feeling a little unwell."

She again kissed her father's cheek, softly assured him she would be all right, and turned to leave the dining hall.

Caeden had tried to remain indifferent as he watched all the interactions during dinner. The king and the new scout, Kearney, spoke about her upcoming adventures while Lord Donovan and Lady Ferrara joined in occasionally to add their insight, though they seemed happier complaining among themselves about the downfall of humanity. Caeden made a mental note to watch the two leaders. He had a feeling there was more to their relationship than it seemed.

As usual, Marcelle hung on the king's every word, trying to insert herself into the conversation anytime she could. Caeden almost felt sorry for her. Although she sat between Sorin and Kearney, she never addressed either of them or them her. One would think they weren't aware the others existed at all. Neither Marcelle nor Sorin even looked toward the other all evening. Sorin's attention seemed to be caught between trying to impress Amira and staring daggers at Inaya.

As for Inaya, she seemed distracted, only occasionally answering a question or returning a spiteful look in Sorin's direction. It was one of the most awkward interactions Caeden had ever witnessed. He might have found it amusing if it weren't for the fact that Amira was so clearly distressed and the bastard Sorin didn't know how to keep his hands to himself.

Caeden kept trying to catch Amira's eye, not sure if he was trying to lend her support or seeking reassurance, but she never once looked his way. Caeden could tell that Trevin, who stood guard at the other side of the room, was not amused by the evening's happenings either. He kept giving Caeden questioning looks, which he could only decipher as asking, *Can we please just rip his head off his damn shoulders already?* Unfortunately, Caeden had to answer with his own look that said, *Not yet, too many witnesses*, but man, that was one request he'd like to accommodate.

Caeden saw something unusual flash in Amira's eyes. If he hadn't been watching her so closely, he was sure he would have missed it. But he had seen it, and it was enough to bring Caeden to full attention. Trevin, following his lead, prepared to act. Caeden watched as Amira leaned close to Sorin and began whispering into his ear. Caeden wasn't close enough to hear what was said, but Inaya was and whatever she heard shocked her and engaged her full attention.

Sorin's head shot up and he looked first to Trevin, and then to where Caeden stood. Caeden saw Sorin quickly release Amira's hand. Caeden couldn't control his overwhelming satisfaction. Then Amira, too, looked his way, and their eyes connected and held for a long moment. Everything else ceased to exist and time stood still, but all too quickly the moment was lost.

Amira took a deep breath and seemed to gather herself before she once again addressed Sorin. A look of pure rage crossed Sorin's face before he could mask it. Caeden wasn't sure exactly what had passed between the two, but it triggered every one of his protective instincts. Amira was still speaking quietly, but Caeden had unconsciously taken a couple steps closer and was able to make out enough words to understand that she was taking him to task for his behavior and lack of respect.

Caeden felt a fierce sense of pride at his princess's actions, but he also understood the danger she was putting herself into by making an enemy of Sorin. Sorin was known for his temper and cruelty toward those who were weaker than himself or foolishly crossed him. They would need to watch him even closer.

By this time, Inaya had attracted the attention of the other guests and her indomitable laughter wasn't helping the situation. Caeden heard Amira ask to be excused and he felt a huge lump at the base of his throat. The predicament with Sorin would have to wait for now. His first objective was to find out what was wrong with Amira.

His instinct had told him when she first entered the room that something was not right with her, and now she was asking to be excused. She never left a function prematurely; she was the epitome of social etiquette and would usually fake it until she literally dropped from exhaustion. Yes, something was definitely wrong.

~

"May I escort you to your chambers, Princess?" Sorin said, directly behind her. The sneer in his voice could clearly be heard as he said her title. Her shoulders sagged in despair. She had almost made it out of the dining hall and to safety before he had stopped her.

"That won't be necessary," she began, at the same time Caeden said, "That honor belongs to her Guard." His tone invited no argument. Sorin had no choice but to back down and return to his place at the table; the look on his face said he wasn't pleased.

"Thank you," she whispered, watching Sorin's retreat. From the corner of her eye, she saw Caeden send Trevin a meaningful glance, which must have communicated his expectations, because Trevin nodded in response.

With escape her only thought, Amira walked away quickly, but Caeden's long legs had no problem matching her steps.

"Are you all right, Princess?"

She used to pretend the term "Princess" coming from his lips was an endearment, but now she knew it for what it was, simply her title.

"I will be just fine, Captain. I thank you for your concern," she said politely as she reached the foot of the stairs that led to her chambers, her safe haven.

Caeden grabbed her arm, stopping her, and turned her to face him. It was the first time he had ever touched her outside of her self-defense lessons. Amira was shocked. She was sure her mouth was hanging open.

"I guess this is a night for both of us to act out of character," she said, almost amused.

"Are you ill? Or hurt?" he asked, ignoring her statement.

He held on to her arm as if he were afraid she'd run from the room before answering his questions. Her arm tingled from his touch, warming her. She had to remind herself of the conversation she had overheard earlier, lest she melt into his touch and make an even bigger fool of herself.

"No, Captain, I am not," she answered, straightening her back and shoulders.

"Why are you calling me that?" he asked, looking genuinely confused.

"Calling you what?"

"Captain. Why are you calling me captain?" he asked in exasperation.

"It's your title, is it not?"

"Yes, Princess," he said, remembering his place.

Amira looked pointedly at where his hand connected with her arm. "Please release me. I've had enough unwanted hands grabbing me today."

He dropped his hand as if she'd burned him, and Amira felt an immediate chill at the loss of contact. What was wrong with her? Why did only this one male affect her so strongly?

As what she'd said penetrated, fury crossed his face.

"Did he hurt you?" Caeden asked in a deadly calm tone that didn't match the look in his now frigid blue eyes.

Amira's heart began to race. "I have taken care of the problem," she tried to reassure him.

His show of protectiveness caused excited butter-flies to flutter uncontrollably in her stomach. *He's doing his job*, she reminded herself in an attempt to kill them.

"Princess," he began.

"Caeden," she said on a sigh, "I've had a terrible day, and wish for nothing more than to go up to my rooms, climb into bed, and pretend this day never happened." She should have left it at that, but she couldn't seem to stop herself from adding, "I'm sure you'll have no problem, with me out of the way, finding another female to naïvely follow you around and look at you like you are a gift straight from the angels. As for me, I just don't have it in me right now."

"Oh hell," Caeden muttered to himself as he watched her race up the stairs and into her chambers.

Later that night, there was a tap on her bedroom door.

"My dear, can we talk?" her father asked, poking his head into her room.

"Of course, Father. Is everything all right?"

"Everything is fine, dear. I wanted to see how you were feeling."

Amira felt guilty for making her father worry, until she looked into his eyes and saw a twinkle there. He actually looked amused.

"Father?" She hesitated.

A huge grin broke across his beloved face. "I'm so proud of you, my girl. I saw the confrontation you had with Sorin."

Amira's face turned bright red. "Father, I apologize for insulting your guests," she began.

"Nonsense. I'm sure he deserved everything you said and much more. He is pompous and has a callousness to him that, I'm sad to see, he has not outgrown. It was delightful to see you show such spirit while you reminded him of his place." King Vidar beamed.

"But a princess must never—"

"A princess must take care of her people," her father interrupted, "and to do so, she must be able to take care of herself and use good judgment. Why do you think I've allowed your training with Caeden?"

"You know about that?" She was shocked and more embarrassed than before.

"I am king, of course I know," he said with an enigmatic smile.

Amira couldn't help smiling with him. She always enjoyed her father's confidence and commanding presence. Although her father had many duties as king, he had always taken the time to be her father, too. He made sure Amira didn't carry any guilt for her mother's passing. He often reminded her that she was a blessing and a gift to both him and her mother.

"Father, if you're aware of Sorin's true character, why have you allowed him to continue leading Ammon, and why have you allowed his presence here?"

Her father considered this for a moment before answering. "It is his birthright to lead Ammon. But more importantly, I believe no person is all good, or all evil. We all have our assets and character defects. With the proper motivation or willingness, I believe anyone can change. As for why I have allowed his pursuit of you, he is *your* suitor, not mine. Therefore, it is your decision, your judgment that must matter. It is your right as princess to decide the future king of our people. Together you shall lead them. With your maturity approaching, I know this is a heavy weight to bear, but take comfort in knowing you are not alone. Every other firstborn child in the royal family has been faced with this same responsibility, including your mother. It is your legacy. It is a great honor as well as a harsh responsibility." He couldn't help adding, "But you have chosen well and I couldn't be prouder."

"What do you mean? I cannot choose. I have not yet reached my maturity."

"Have you not chosen the Captain of the Royal Guard?" he arched his eyebrow in question, looking her directly in the face. Her eyes widened and her cheeks went hot. "I am king, of course I know," he said once again as he tapped her on the nose with his index finger.

Amira couldn't hold her father's gaze, so she looked away as she admitted, "He doesn't want me."

"Of course he does!" Grabbing her chin, he forced her to look into his eyes. "Males are stubborn and thickheaded, soldiers more so than others. You will have your work cut out for you with that one," he said with another enigmatic smile before winking. "But once he comes around... give him hell, my girl."

King Vidar turned to Osmond, who had awaited him outside Amira's chambers. "Any idea as to where we can locate your fearless leader at this hour?" Vidar asked, feeling more lighthearted than he had in years.

Osmond couldn't help but share his king's excitement; this had been coming for a while. "He's most likely still pacing the lower courtyard," he said with a chuckle.

"Yes, she does seem to have him chasing his own tail of late. It has been most entertaining to watch. I have no doubt things will take their natural course, but let us see if we can't nudge nature along a little."

Caeden was found right where Osmond predicted. His hair, which had always reminded Vidar of a great lion's mane, was sticking out in all directions. He could tell Caeden had run his fingers through it many times.

Vidar found it difficult to hold in his glee. He had seen the possibility of a relationship between Amira and Caeden for years and had decided to let things develop as they would, but now that it was coming to fruition, he found himself becoming impatient. He couldn't be more pleased with his daughter's choice of consort. He knew his tired body would be able to rest in peace with such a strong and honorable male there to look after his precious girl.

He had been devastated when his beloved wife had died, and through his marriage bond he had been pulled to join her in the afterlife. Their people had been blessed with the ability to create a blood bond between true mates. This bond ensured the two halves would be tied together for all eternity. Vidar hadn't been born royalty, but the marriage bond had allowed him to honor the covenant of the angels, which maintained the protective shield around Cashile. Yet his body grew more tired with every year that passed and he longed to join his beautiful Maryam. He held on only for the sake of his daughter and for the fate of Cashile, because Amira was not yet strong enough to support the bond. With Amira nearing her maturity and with things progressing nicely with Caeden, he saw an end in sight. Within a few more years, he would be able to relinquish his duty and finally find the peace his weary mind and body craved.

If he could just help his young friend overcome some of his foolish stubbornness...

"Ahem." Vidar cleared his throat to announce his presence.

It appeared Caeden had been too lost in his own thoughts to realize he was no longer alone. Caeden's hand instantly fell to his sword as he swung around to discover who had invaded his privacy.

"If I were a threat, I doubt I'd have tried to gain your attention before I cut you down." Vidar smirked, looking pointedly at Caeden's sword arm.

"Yes, my king." Caeden grinned, duly chastened. He placed his right fist over his heart and bowed his head in respect.

"Come now, you are not on duty this night and I find my thoughts unable to rest. Care to join me in a game of chess? You, too, look like you could use the distraction," he said with a knowing expression.

Many times Caeden had found himself in this chair in the king's study late into the night, keeping the king company. The Royal Guard changed every two hundred years, and Caeden had only taken command a little over a decade ago. In the last ten years, he'd had the honor of becoming a sounding board and confidant to the king.

Being Captain of the Royal Guard, Caeden was

present at all important functions and private meetings, and therefore was privy to all the affairs of Cashile. The king claimed Caeden's feedback kept his mind "young and fresh." Caeden was proud to call the king his friend, but he never forgot his place.

For the first couple of moves, both males were relatively silent, content to be lost in their own thoughts.

"I've always enjoyed the game of chess," Vidar said, interrupting the stillness. "You are indeed a worthy opponent, Caeden. Your strategy and tactics are flawless, which is part of the reason you are captain at such a young age."

"Thank you, sir," Caeden said, honored by the unexpected praise.

After another moment of silence, the king began again. "The knight has always been my favorite game piece. He has the ability to move and think in unexpected ways, unlike the other pieces, which must remain linear. Also unlike the other pieces, he has the power to leap over any obstacle in his way." Vidar paused and met Caeden's gaze with his unyielding gray steel, so much like his daughter's. "I believe this makes him the best qualified to care for the most important and powerful piece in the whole game, the queen," Vidar continued. "In fact, when the two come together, they can defeat any opponent."

Caeden wasn't sure if he completely grasped what the king was trying to communicate, but his heart pounded. He knew this went deeper than the game they played.

"Chess also has the ability to teach us an important lesson every male must learn. It teaches us how to admit when capture is inescapable and how to graciously surrender to the inevitable," Vidar finished with a grin.

The room grew quiet for a long moment as they continued their game and Caeden considered the king's words.

"Did you know that I, too, was part of the Royal Guard? Centuries before your birth, of course," the king began, his expression now thoughtful.

The shift in the conversation caught Caeden off guard. The king rarely spoke about his past or his personal affairs.

"Unlike you, I was not the captain, but I loved being a soldier. I loved the feel of my sword in my hand, the adrenaline pumping through my body in the heat of battle as I bested my opponent. I lived for the challenge, the adventure, the competition... it was all I ever wanted. Until the day I looked into the most beautiful blue eyes, when everything changed and my whole world shifted. When I met Maryam, I realized I'd had a giant hole inside my chest that I had been trying to fill with all of the things I had thought I wanted. I realized all the things I tried to fill it with just made the hole bigger. But with Maryam, I didn't need the thrill of adventure or to prove my dominance."

Vidar paused once again to look Caeden in the eye. "My hole was not only filled, it was completely gone."

The king's expression was somber as he continued. "I would have given my life in exchange for Maryam's. We struggled to conceive a child, not only because it was our duty to continue the royal bloodline, but because Maryam had so much love to give and wanted a child more than anything." Caeden pretended not to notice the tears in Vidar's eyes. "I could deny her nothing. If she had requested the sun and the moon, I would have made it my personal mission to acquire them for her. Amira was our miracle and Maryam was the proudest momma ever to live." His voice cracked and Caeden felt the pressure behind his own eyes.

The king swallowed and pulled himself together by force of will. "She hung on for two weeks after Amira's birth before her heart finally gave out. Marcelle used all of her healers' knowledge, but nothing could be done. We couldn't save her. Now, not a day passes that I don't feel like I'm going to be swallowed up by this massive hole in my chest. I live only to safeguard my miracle, like I promised Maryam I would, but soon my shift will end and a new guard must take my place." He gave Caeden another pointed look.

Caeden felt a bit overwhelmed by his king's impassioned speech. Although their game had continued during their conversation, he had barely given his moves any thought, so caught up in what Vidar was saying. Therefore, he was surprised when the king stated, "Checkmate. You'll have to learn to guard your queen better than that, son, but I have complete faith in you."

Caeden looked down and discovered the king had in fact taken his queen and placed him in checkmate.

"I think my weary mind will be able to rest now," Vidar said as he stood to take his leave. "Good night."

"Good night, sir." Caeden smiled as he watched the king exit. "Well, that was interesting," he muttered to himself, more than a little stunned.

"Do you think he understood what you were trying to tell him?" Osmond asked as he escorted King Vidar to his chambers.

"Not fully, but he will in time," he predicted with a satisfied grin on his face.

THREE

I'm sorry," she squeaked in pain as the hand tightened in her hair.

He pulled harder as he watched the tears rapidly fall from her eyes. Finally, a sense of calm began to clear away the red haze of rage. *How dare I be treated in such a way?* Sorin replayed the injustice he had been dealt that day. He would make them pay, he assured himself as his focus began to return, and he would start right now, with her.

"Yes, my dear, and what are you sorry for?" Sorin asked through gritted teeth as he yanked her to him. He needed to see the fear in her eyes, feel her trembling body pressed against his.

"My lord, I tried to do only as you instructed," she stammered.

Hands still tangled in her hair; he shook her roughly until she fell to her knees before him. He held her head down so she could look only at the floor. *Much better.*

"Did I instruct you to disrespect me at dinner? Did I instruct you to be a stupid whore and lust after another male in my presence?" His voice rose and he punctuated every question with a vicious shake.

He used her hair to pull her head back so she could look him in the face and fully appreciate his anger. The tears were streaming uncontrollably down her cheeks now.

"No, my lord, I tried only to protect your plans by not letting our relationship be known. Please, my lord, I'm sorry. I want only to please you."

She looks so earnest and she's such a useful little slut; I can afford to be generous. Not loosening the grip on her hair, he caressed her face with his other hand to comfort her. "You look so beautiful like this," he praised. "I will forgive you," he then reassured her softly as he brushed his thumb over her swollen bottom lip. Her whole body shuddered as she released the breath she had been holding and he felt a deep satisfaction. Slowly, he trailed his hand down her slender throat to where he could feel her pulse hammering, and he let his fingers tighten, digging into her tender flesh just enough to make her breath catch. "But only this once," he threatened before releasing her throat and hair.

"Thank you." She sobbed her gratitude and clutched the hand that had been tangled in her hair.

She tried to rise, but he restrained her with a hand on her shoulder.

"Stay just as you are. It pleases me," he told her softly as he began to stroke her hair out of her face. "In a moment, I will allow you to show me just how grateful you are." He tilted her head so she was staring directly at the straining zipper of his pants. "But first we have business to discuss."

She licked her lips and nodded eagerly, her eyes never leaving the bulge in his pants.

"The princess is proving to be less than accommodating toward our goal," he stated calmly, now completely back in control.

"I have tried, my lord," she stammered repentantly.

"Shh, my pet, I know you have," he assured, once again absentmindedly petting her hair, "but now is the time, we must force her hand."

"Vidar will not force her to bond with you."

Sorin felt a flare of irritation at hearing her say another male's name, but forced himself not to clench his fist into her hair once again.

"No, he is too weak to do what is best for this kingdom; therefore, we must do it. What if something were to happen to King Vidar? Say he had an accident; what then?"

"What... what do you mean?"

Sorin arched his eyebrow at the woman still kneeling at his feet, and noticed that although her tears had ceased, her face was stained and blotchy. Her skin tone almost matched her red hair and her body trembled. He couldn't help but smile; she was such a lovely creature. "With King Vidar out of the way, Amira would have to turn to me."

The woman's brown eyes widened in shock. "But the shield would fall. Amira is not strong enough to support it."

"Not alone, but tied to me... I have more royal blood in my veins than any other male; I can keep the shield intact and we can have our kingdom. She will have to turn to me. We won't give her any other options."

"But she can't bond with anyone until she reaches maturity." She was too astounded by the turn of the conversation to worry about offending him by arguing.

"True, she cannot join into a marriage bond, but surely you, being the Supreme Healer, know of the binding ceremony."

Marcelle looked up into Sorin's handsome face in astonishment. "The binding ceremony... but that hasn't been used in centuries; the consequences are too unpredictable."

"But it would work," Sorin interrupted her. "If you bind her life force to mine, I can support the shield and then we will finally have all we have worked so hard for. Amira will be easy to control until she reaches her maturity, then we'll complete the bond. Once we have the kingdom secure, we'll have no further use for the princess and the kingdom will be ours, my pet."

"But... Vidar?"

"Don't be stupid, Marcelle. He will never make you his consort."

As much as he enjoyed the flinch that crossed her face, he knew he needed her cooperation. He forced his fists to unclench and stroked the backs of his fingers down her soft cheek to her vulnerable neck.

"But I will make you a queen, my love. We will finally have everything we deserve. I will give you the world, but Vidar stands in our way. Will you help me?" he finished softly.

Marcelle looked up into Sorin's eyes and was unable to deny him. "Yes," she whispered.

"That's my good girl. Now show me," he said as he held the back of her head with one hand and unfastened his pants with the other.

Four

Amira watched the sunrise from her bedroom window. Morning had always been her favorite part of the day. She loved to sit at her window and watch the brilliant colors that came with the sun to chase away the darkness of night. She would listen to the sounds of the soldiers preparing for training in the lower courtyard and little by little hear the palace come to life as her people went about their daily tasks. The predictability and routine usually brought her comfort, but today she was very much aware of how disconnected she was from it all.

She could hear the maids in the hallway gossiping and most likely flirting with whichever guard was posted outside her door, but she knew she couldn't be a part of that life. The moment she made her presence known to them, they would immediately quiet and go about their duties until she was gone. *What would it be like to be normal and carefree?*

With a deep cleansing breath, she reminded herself there was no point in wishing for things that couldn't be changed. She had barely slept the night before, with the day's events replaying in her head over and over again. Despite her father's reassurance, Caeden's words to Trevin echoed the loudest. He still saw her as a child and didn't return her feelings. It hurt her pride knowing her affections and attempts to get his attention had annoyed him. Amira angrily brushed a fallen tear away. Maybe she had been acting childish, dreaming of a happily ever after with Caeden starring as her hero.

But why had he acted so strangely at dinner? Did it matter? Her duties had to come first. Her father had been right about one thing: it would be her responsibility to protect her people, yet she barely knew how to stand up for herself. How could she do her duty if she spent all of her time trying to be the "perfect princess"? Amira straightened her shoulders as she recalled how freeing it had felt to stand up to Sorin last night.

Shouting from the hallway interrupted her thoughts. Opening the door to peek out, she saw Trevin and Inaya standing nose to nose.

"Who do you think you are?" Inaya yelled directly into Trevin's face.

"Sweetheart, you know exactly who I am," he growled back at her.

Amira gasped in shock, drawing their attention. The two broke apart quickly and Trevin's expression shuttered. Inaya was much easier to read. She was livid, her green eyes bright with fury, and it showed in every tense muscle. Amira would have sworn her best friend didn't have a mean bone in her body, but at the moment Trevin looked in real danger of receiving one of her fists to his face. Amira was much too shocked to speak and could only stare between the two. What was going on in her orderly world?

"Good morning, Princess," Trevin said, breaking the long silence. He never took his eyes off Inaya, his tone as detached and formal as always. Amira could almost believe she had imagined his outburst.

"Trevin," she answered with a nod.

Inaya refused to even look his way as she marched past him and into Amira's room.

What had upset her so much? Amira was about to demand an answer from Trevin, but halted when she saw his pained expression as he watched Inaya walk away. He briefly closed his eyes and when they opened, his detachment was firmly back in place.

Interesting.

"The send-off is in an hour, Princess," he reminded her before returning back to his post beside her door.

Inaya was furiously pacing the room, mumbling to herself. "The nerve! Arrogant man! Who does he think he is?" she asked, abruptly looking at Amira.

"Apparently you know exactly who he is." Amira

couldn't resist quoting him, suddenly finding the humor in the situation.

Inaya held her serious expression for as long as she could before succumbing to giggles with Amira. "Can you believe he said that?" She laughed.

"What was that about, anyway? I've never seen either of you so angry before."

Inaya shrugged. "I guess we rub each other the wrong way. He thinks he has a right to tell me what to do and I know I have a right to tell him where he can go with his opinions. But, oh man, he can make me crazy."

Amira settled in for Inaya's usual rant about "male delusions of grandeur due to the appendage between their legs and their belief of entitlement that came with their greater physical strength." Amira had heard it many times before and had always written it off as a much-needed release from having grown up with two dominant older brothers who possessed an excess of testosterone, but today it seemed more emotional.

"What exactly is he trying to control?" Amira couldn't help but interrupt.

"Me!" Inaya exploded. "He thinks he can dictate whom I talk to and what I say. He jumped all over me last night and you saw how mad he was this morning." She sighed and the anger seemed to melt away. "I guess he's just trying to protect me. He's worried we made Sorin angry last night. He can't yell at you"—she smirked—"so I guess I get to take the brunt of it. He's just doing his job." She now sounded dejected.

"That seemed more personal to me. I've never seen Trevin angry before. Heck, I didn't even know he had emotions," Amira said half-jokingly, trying to lighten the mood once again.

"Oh, he has them all right, but let's not talk about Trevin anymore. I can't believe what you said to Sorin last night! That was the best political function I've ever been to!" Inaya's grin was infectious.

"My father found it amusing as well." Amira couldn't help but share proudly.

She told Inaya about the conversation she'd had with her father, excluding the part about Caeden. She wasn't ready to think about him yet; her emotions were still too raw, so she focused on the other parts of the discussion. The approval and pride she had seen in her father's eyes had been a shock, but recalling it now brought her peace. That day would be a new beginning.

A knock on the door reminded her that duty awaited and her new resolve would surely be put to the test.

Patience was definitely not one of Sorin's virtues. He much preferred things be done when and how he directed. The fact he was left waiting for that pathetic little girl to make an appearance was pushing him to breaking point. He tried to wipe the scowl from his face, but the effort was making his dark eyes twitch. His inner self ranted the words he begrudgingly suppressed.

Does she really think being a princess makes her so much better than me that she can just keep me waiting? Or worse... what if the little bitch decides not to show up at all? That was a sobering thought. No, she would come; it was her duty to bid farewell to all important dignitaries such as himself. *Of course she will want to see me before I leave*, he reassured himself.

He looked around, but no one else seemed to notice the slight the princess was giving him. The other dignitaries seemed content yapping amongst themselves, but the brainless twits usually were oblivious. He couldn't wait until the day he could force their eyes to open.

The sound of the gate opening roused Sorin from his thoughts in time to watch Amira enter the clearing through the side entrance.

Finally.

He couldn't help but admire the way the sun brought out the auburn glints in her long hair. His hand twitched to have it wrapped around his fist as he brought her to her knees, the way he had Marcelle the night before. Amira was quite beautiful and he loved how, with her smaller build, he effortlessly towered over her. They would make a very attractive couple.

Maybe he would train her and keep her for a little while.

Before he even made the decision to move, he found himself standing in front of her. *Today it's my turn to instruct her on manners.* As he reached out to grab her arm, a tall and very muscular figure stepped up from behind her.

Ah yes, her ever-present Guard. How could he have not seen Trevin skulking in the background? Sorin brought his arm back to his side before he made contact. Trevin looked just past Sorin's left shoulder and gave a slight nod. Sorin knew what he'd see if he turned around, yet he looked anyway. Just as expected, the Captain of the Royal Guard was piercing him with his icy glare. Sorin briefly met his gaze so the soldier wouldn't think he could be intimidated, but he could only hold it for a moment before quickly looking away.

Fine. He was adaptable, he reminded himself.

Sorin brushed away imaginary wrinkles from his immaculate clothes to buy himself a minute to regroup. When he once again felt centered, he put on his most charming smile and turned back to address the princess. She had stood quietly during the brief exchange between the males, unable to pass with Sorin blocking her path.

"My lady, I am so pleased I was able to see you again before I take my leave," he began. He reached to take Amira's hand, this time moving slowly and trying to look as innocent as possible. He wanted to see how her guard was responding, but refused to let him know he was even aware of his presence.

Sorin brought her hand to his lips for a chaste kiss and didn't let it go afterward. "I feel I owe you an apology for last night; you simply must forgive my behavior. You see, I am so overcome by your beauty and wish only to make a good impression with you that sometimes my words run away from me. I feel deep remorse for offending you by addressing you so informally; it's just I feel a deep connection with you and don't feel the need for such formalities. I am sure you can understand. We are friends, are we not?" Sorin paused to inspect Amira's features for her reception of his words. Her gray eyes were flashing silver and her small body was held stiffly, but she was too skilled at hiding her emotions for him to be able to tell exactly what was going on inside her head.

"Your apology is accepted, Lord Sorin. I, too, am glad to be here to see you take your leave," she said in return, avoiding his question.

Sorin refused to be deterred by her rigidity or by the way she tugged her hand free of his grasp. "I wish I could extend my stay; I hate for us to part on bad terms, but unfortunately, I have important obligations to attend. I will return soon, though. It is my greatest wish for you to know me better and for you to see the welfare of this kingdom is always my first concern. I wish to only be at your service, Princess."

"The kingdom appreciates your dedication," she

began diplomatically, but he cut her off before she could finish her thought.

"I wish to be dedicated to you personally, Princess," he whispered, so passionately he almost believed it himself.

Amira looked shocked, her mouth slightly open and her eyes wide. It was the first time he had bluntly stated his intentions to her.

"In my absence I hope you will consider an alliance between the two of us. Our strengths and weaknesses balance the other's well, and I can be a great asset at your disposal."

"Sorin—" she began, but again he cut her off.

"Please, do not answer now. Let us put this visit behind us and start fresh when next we meet. For now, I must bid you farewell." Sorin brushed a kiss to her cheek, but retreated before she or her guard could respond.

Sorin heard Trevin's growl as he made his exit and couldn't help but feel euphoric about the success of the conversation. For the time being, he would use honey to catch this fly and when the time came, he would crush her.

He had almost made it out of the clearing when he felt the weight of eyes watching him. He looked up and was immediately caught in an icy glare, which he swore could see right through him. He almost tripped over his own feet as the murderous look brought him to a sudden stop. A chill slipped through his entire body and his smirk quickly disappeared. The Royal Guard would be a problem; hell, the captain alone was a problem. How could one insignificant soldier inspire so much fear in him? Sorin refused to let himself be controlled by his emotions. He broke eye contact and hurried out of the clearing. Clearly, something must be done to remove this obstacle.

Caeden glanced at the time again; she was late. Amira was never late. He'd only seen her in passing for the last two days and he'd been unsuccessful at finding a time alone with her. He needed to make sure she was okay. He needed to explain.

Five more minutes; he'd give her five more minutes, and then he was going to go get her. It had become apparent she was avoiding him. Every time he'd tried to speak with her, they had been interrupted or she was unavailable. He'd finally given up and decided to wait until their next lesson to broach the situation again, and now that the time had arrived, she had yet to show up. He had tried to be patient and give her space, but he was finished with that. She would hear him out; he was tired of waiting.

Caeden found her in the main fitness room. She was alone, other than Murdock, who was in the middle of his weight-lifting routine. It was apparent she had decided to work out by herself instead of with him. Unacceptable. He wasn't going to allow her to hide from him any longer.

Caeden approached Murdock quietly; Amira had yet to notice his presence. They watched silently for a moment as Amira repeatedly struck the punching bag that hung from the ceiling.

"Who knew the girl had such a wicked right hook? She has perfect form," Murdock said quietly to Caeden.

"Yeah, she's something, all right," he mumbled noncommittally, his eyes never straying from Amira. "You about finished here?"

Murdock quickly glanced between Caeden and Amira before saying, "She's still young."

"I know."

"You're..." Murdock began.

"Leave us," Caeden whispered firmly.

Murdock set down the weight he had been lifting, grabbed his towel, and stood. "I was just on my way out."

Caeden nodded distractedly, his eyes still on Amira. She definitely seemed to be working out some frustration with the punching bag. Caeden followed Murdock to the door and locked it after the other guard exited. He'd be damned if they would be interrupted again today.

Amira must have heard the door close, because when he turned she was watching him cautiously.

"What are you doing here?" she asked hesitantly as she wiped the sweat from her brow.

"What are you doing here, Princess?" he countered.

"I was just finishing up," she began as she walked over to her belongings, preparing to leave.

"We had a lesson scheduled; you didn't show up."

"I apologize," she said, her natural politeness taking over. "I should have informed you I was canceling. I appreciate all of the time you've expended in my training, but your services are no longer necessary."

She was trying to hide from him. *Not going to happen*, he told himself. He couldn't help but notice she wouldn't meet his eyes.

"You've been avoiding me," he stated.

"Yes."

"Why, Princess?"

Amira tried to push past him. "I need to be going."

Caeden refused to let her pass. He ran one hand through his hair in frustration and gently grabbed her arm with the other, stopping her. She looked pointedly at his hand, just as she had the last time he had touched her. This time he wasn't going to let her get away.

"We have to talk about what you heard—" he began.

"No, we don't," she interrupted, but he continued to speak over her.

"You heard at least part of a conversation I had with Trevin, and I need to explain. Hear me out." He paused and her eyes met his briefly. She nodded slightly for him to continue. "I hurt you and I'm sorry. I know you have a... fondness for me. I understand you are young and will grow out of this adulation; but, Princess, you need to understand that I am only a male. You are a beautiful woman and it's difficult not to respond to you. What you heard was me speaking from frustration. I never meant to hurt you and I want you to know you have nothing to worry about from me. I understand it's my job to protect you, even from myself."

"Are you finished?" she asked, her voice cracking a little and her face flushed. At his nod, she continued, "I appreciate your apology, but it seems you have misjudged my feelings. Although you still see me as a child, I assure you I am a grown female and I am fully capable of being responsible for my feelings and actions. I don't need you to protect me from yourself or any other male to whom I give my affections."

Caeden clenched his jaw, but it seemed Amira was too wound up to notice.

"I will not apologize for 'tempting' you and causing you frustration. I had meant to tempt you. I am only sorry you are not interested enough to return my affection, but I am glad that I overheard your conversation. It has opened my eyes to your feelings, and now I can stop wasting both of our time," she said tightly as she pulled from his grasp, finishing her speech.

He had gotten what he wanted, for her to realize

there could be nothing between them, but Caeden couldn't let her walk away.

"You don't need me to protect you, then prove it," he challenged.

"Caeden," she began.

"Prove to me you can protect yourself from the next man you decide is worthy of your affection," Caeden demanded as he invaded her personal space. "Show me you can defend yourself if he doesn't respect that you're a lady or doesn't honor your innocence."

He had advanced on her until he'd completely backed her against the wall, but he was beyond caring. The idea of her offering herself to another had driven him beyond reasoning.

"Caeden, stop."

He was satisfied to hear the tremble in her voice. "Show me," he demanded through clenched teeth.

"Fine!" she yelled into his face as she put both hands on his chest and pushed.

He didn't budge; instead, he grabbed her by both wrists and pulled her closer, crushing her body to his.

Amira found herself in the one place she had been trying to avoid. For the last two days, she had done everything in her power to prevent being alone with Caeden. She had known there was no way she could have a conversation with him and not let her feelings show. She didn't want him to know how deeply she felt for him or how much his words had affected her. She refused to engage in this unrequited love any longer, and had hoped distance would lessen her feelings for him. Unfortunately, it hadn't helped.

Now she found herself practically in his arms. Days ago, this prospect would have thrilled her, but today it angered her. Why, when she had given up on him and was working on letting him go, did he decide it was the time to touch her or try to engage her in something beyond polite conversation? Fine, if he wanted her to fight him, she'd give him a fight.

She hooked her right leg behind his left knee and let the weight of her body fall against him, knocking him off balance and tumbling both of them to the ground. Caeden had enough time to wrap his arms around her and curl his body around hers to protect her from the impact with the floor. Amira began to wiggle out of his embrace, which only made him tighten his arms further. She was so furious she clenched her fists and pounded against his chest, releasing all of her hurt feelings and disappointment into the action.

"Let me go and stay away from me!"

"No, it's my duty to protect you," he answered through gritted teeth, finally restraining her flailing arms.

"I don't need your protection," she said, sounding

unreasonable even to herself. "I'm not a child, nor am I as weak as everyone seems to think."

"You do need me, and you are weak." He grunted, flipping them over and trapping her body under his to prove his point. "You haven't reached full maturity yet and your body is still vulnerable. You could be hurt so easily and I refuse to let that happen. We'll both just have to deal with your crush until you grow out of it. Until then, you're stuck with me, so no more of this avoidance."

"Let me up," she said as calmly as she could. She felt as if he had struck her. The ease with which he so readily disregarded her feelings for him burned a path through her insides, leaving her in physical pain.

"No, not until you submit to me and admit you need my protection."

Amira knew she didn't have the strength to force him off her, so she did the only thing she could think of; she lifted her head from the floor and brought her lips to his. She kissed him with all of the anger, frustration, hurt feelings, and above all, the love she couldn't help but feel. His whole body turned to stone above hers, but he didn't pull away. He stayed very still and seemed to stop breathing.

Amira knew it might be her only chance to ever kiss him, so she decided she would allow herself to savor it for the moment. She opened her mouth and caressed his closed lips with her tongue invitingly. At his low growl, she did it again, only this time he opened his mouth in acceptance and began to kiss her back, his whole body relaxing into the kiss. She brought her hand up and ran her fingers through his long hair like she'd always wanted to. She had planned the kiss only to be a distraction, but it turned out to be something far more.

Before she was completely lost, she reminded herself of her original purpose. Easing back, she brushed her lips against his and whispered, "I'm sorry."

She brought her right knee up quickly and made contact with the sensitive juncture between his legs. Using all of her strength to push him off, she rolled out from beneath him, made it to her feet, and stood over him.

"You taught me that because I'm smaller, I need to use any means necessary. I'm sorry, but that was necessary. If you don't need me in return, then I won't allow myself to need you."

Watching her walk out of the room, Caeden had to admit she was tougher than he gave her credit for and he was oddly proud of her. As a way to keep his own desire in check, he had refused to see her as she really was and had been hiding behind her age and title. He had kissed many females in his lifetime, but never had he been kissed with that much passion and longing; never had a kiss felt so right. That had not been a kiss from someone with a passing fancy. There was no doubt in his mind she really did care for him. He wasn't good enough for her, but if she could accept him as he was, he vowed to never let her regret her feelings for him.

He hoped he hadn't messed things up with her too badly, but he had time to fix it, he assured himself. She would be unable to take a consort for almost another two years and he vowed to earn back her trust and affection. He had been mistaken; now he only wished there could have been a less painful way for her to open his eyes.

FIVE

Later that night, King Vidar was murdered by a coward who snuck into his chamber and stabbed him to death in his bed. The piercing screams still echoed in Amira's head hours later. It had been the sound of her own fear and pain manifesting throughout the walls of the palace, upon waking to the intense burden of the blood bond to the shield being passed down to her. She had felt it the moment of her father's death. It was a tangible, yet indescribable entity now within her. She could close her eyes and actually envision the bindings connecting her to Cashile and the protective shield. Upon the transition from father to daughter, the island itself reacted with a violent shudder, shaking with a terrifying earthquake.

So many questions circled in her head. *How did this happen? How* could *this happen?* It didn't make sense and her brain refused to believe any of it was real.

Her father had hundreds of years left; he couldn't be gone. So lost in thought, it took her a while to realize someone was calling her name. She looked up to see Inaya's haunted turquoise eyes fixed on her.

"You should get some rest," Amira told her friend.

At the sound of her flat, toneless voice, all whispers ceased and eyes turned to her. It was only then she realized there were other people in the room. Many people, in fact, and all of them staring at her as if they had never seen her before.

She looked around to find Inaya, Aunt Marcelle, and the Royal Guard all crowded in her chamber. For the life of her, she couldn't remember how they had all gotten in there. In truth, she couldn't remember how she had gotten to her sitting room either. She looked around the room, again feeling something wasn't quite right. What was it? A distant part of her knew her mind was focusing on small details to distract herself from the reality of her grief, but she was okay with that.

In the distance, she heard Marcelle's uncontrollable sobbing and Inaya speaking to her again, but she couldn't bring herself to pay attention. Her eyes found Caeden's. His ice-blue gaze seemed to be trying to convey something to her, but her brain was foggy and she couldn't understand. She allowed herself the comfort of his strength, and the safety his presence provided. Caeden and the Royal Guard were there, everything would be... wait... that was it! That was what was wrong. She quickly scanned the room again; someone was missing.

"Where is Levi?"

All other eyes quickly looked away as she again made eye contact with Caeden.

"He's missing," Caeden answered. He paused and she saw him swallow hard before he continued. "It was his weapon found in your father's chamber."

"Why would he leave his weapon in my father's room?" Amira asked in confusion.

"Because he used it to kill King Vidar," Marcelle wailed, clutching Amira's arm.

"No," Amira said instantly, jumping to her feet and knocking Marcelle's hand away. "That can't be. Levi didn't do this. He's Royal Guard."

In Amira's mind, that settled the matter. There had to be another reason. She pleaded with her eyes for Caeden to have another explanation.

Caeden took two steps toward her before stopping himself. "We'll find him, Princess, and we'll find who killed your father," he promised fiercely.

At her nod, the Royal Guard exited her chamber, as if they'd only been awaiting her order to seek out the traitor.

Caeden couldn't believe one of his brothers could be responsible for the king's murder. He would have never believed it were possible, but the evidence was there. The possible betrayal ached far worse than any pain he'd ever experienced; then to see the complete devastation in Amira, he had never been so hurt and furious at the same time.

He was responsible; he should have known the king was in danger. He should have been there to protect him. There was no bringing the king back from the dead, but seeing Amira so lost and hurt, he made a vow to himself that he would make it right for her. No matter how long it took or what he had to do, he would fix it.

Walking from the room was one of the most difficult things he'd ever done. Everything in him demanded he go to her, hold her in his arms and make her believe everything would be okay. However, he wasn't sure of the reception he would receive. Things were still unsettled between them and the last words she had spoken to him didn't suggest she would accept his comfort. Besides, he had a job to do.

The Royal Guard stopped just outside the bedroom door. They had much to discuss, but could not leave the Princess unguarded, even for a moment. Therefore, business would have to be conducted in the hallway.

"How could he have betrayed us like this?" Murdock began.

Suddenly they all spoke at once.

"Quiet," Caeden demanded when he couldn't take

anymore. "This isn't helping. Did anyone notice anything odd, any changes in his behavior? Anything that would lead you to believe he might be hiding something?"

Caeden studied the men before him, his brothers. Every one of them he would give his life to protect and felt confident they would do the same for him. They all shook their heads in answer to his questions.

"Let us review the evidence against him," Trevin said reasonably.

"Levi's bloody dagger was found next to the king's dead body and Levi is nowhere to be found," Osmond stated factually.

"Why would he leave his weapon?" Dalek asked. "A soldier never loses his weapon."

"It doesn't add up," Murdock mumbled.

"No, it doesn't," Caeden agreed. Things were not as they appeared. "Murdock, I want you to search the king's chambers again and find out if the village healers are finished examining the body. Dalek, you go to Levi's quarters, see what you can find. Osmond, you question everyone who was in the palace last night, and I'll search the keep and talk with all the guards who were on duty. Someone has to have seen something. Trevin," he said, making eye contact, "keep our princess safe."

Everyone nodded and left to do their duty, leaving Trevin standing guard and Caeden staring at the closed door.

Trevin grabbed his arm to get his attention. Dark brown, almost black eyes met cool ice blue. "By my blood, my life," Trevin vowed.

Only then did Caeden nod and walk away, confident Trevin would indeed give his life for Amira. It was time to work.

The fog that had been clouding Amira's brain was finally lifting. The overwhelming grief needed to be pushed aside, as there was much to be done, but it was a struggle to even breathe, the pain in her chest was so great. She looked at the women in the room with her. Inaya's hip-length blonde hair was still in the braid she had put it in to sleep. Her eyes were swollen and red, but she seemed to be handling everything okay for the moment. Amira turned her eyes to Marcelle. She looked as if she had aged a hundred years overnight and now carried the weight of the world on her shoulders. Marcelle had been one of her father's closest companions and she was obviously struggling to keep herself together. Both women were hovering over her, but looked ready to drop where they stood.

"Ladies, please have a seat while I dress for the day, and I'll order up lunch and hot tea," Amira instructed them in her most take-charge tone.

"Oh, let me," Inaya began.

"Sit; you're both exhausted and we have much to take care of."

Amira wasn't hungry, but it was a small distraction they all needed. She pushed her food around her plate until the other ladies were finished.

She couldn't put it off any longer, so she said with a reluctant sigh, "We need to make arrangements for Father's memorial."

At her words, Marcelle again dissolved into hysterics, leaving Amira and Inaya to make plans.

The body was to be prepared by morning. At dawn, they would all make the long trek to the Meadow of Spirits, where King Vidar's body would be burnt, as was their custom; from dust to dust. Afterward, the memorial feast would commence upon their return to the palace. It felt good to Amira to be making arrangements; it gave her a sense of control in an uncontrollable situation.

All good feelings faded as Marcelle briefly roused herself from her grief. "Amira, we must discuss the fate of Cashile now that your father has passed," she said, her voice breaking at the end. "The shield was constructed from the blood of the royal family. With you not at full maturity, you cannot possibly support it on your own."

"What are you saying?" Amira asked, confused.

Of course, she knew how the shield was constructed, in theory at least, but she didn't know how that would affect the situation. Legend said the angels took the strongest and most worthy of their offspring, a female named Niome, and used her blood to create a sacred bond connecting their people to the island and creating a shield for their protection. Her blood, passed down through the generations, became the royal family, and the bond was held through the oldest offspring and their chosen consort.

"I'm saying you are not strong enough to hold the covenant. It will drain you until there is nothing left... Oh heavens, there's nothing left... he's gone... nothing left..." Marcelle's dark eyes darted wildly around the room and she began to mumble incoherently.

"Aunt Marcelle! You must calm yourself and explain how that can be. I am the next descendant; the shield cannot fail with me."

Marcelle visibly brought herself back under control, and released a heavy sigh before reiterating, "Yes, but you have not yet reached your full maturity; you are not strong enough."

Hearing the words, Amira knew they were true; she could already feel the weight of the bond bearing down on her.

"How long do we have?" Amira questioned, fear creeping up her spine.

"There is no way to be certain as there is no known record of this happening before. I would guess you have no longer than one week before it completely fails, but... I may know of another way."

"What is it?" Amira prompted when Marcelle hesitated and seemed to struggle with the answer.

"If you have a mating bond," she said, as if that were explanation enough.

"But I can't support that bond either until I reach maturity." Amira despaired. Her heart raced and it became a struggle to breathe. She began to panic.

"No, but..." There was a heavy pause, then a sigh. "We could do a binding instead. We could temporarily bind your life force to a male of strength and nobility, someone with strong royal blood in his ancestry. That should sustain you and the shield until you are able to do so for yourself."

The world began to spin for Amira; it was all too much and she felt her knees give out. Inaya was there instantly, wrapping her arms around Amira and helping her into a chair.

"You don't have to decide at this moment, Amira," Inaya spoke up for the first time, wiping a tear from her own eye.

"This has to be settled and it is not your business, girl," Marcelle said angrily.

Inaya gave her a confused look. "No, we have some time. She doesn't have to decide right now. The king hasn't even been laid to rest yet. Why are you pushing this now? Can't you see the princess is overwhelmed and grieving?"

"But..."

Seeing an impending argument, Amira quietly

stepped in. "Inaya's right, let us get through the memorial; then we will do what we must. But my father comes first."

Caeden arrived at the palace at dawn, just in time to meet with the Guard and to take his place in the procession to the Meadow of Spirits. None of them had found any sign of Levi and no one had seen him leave the palace. After questioning the guards who had been stationed at the gate, Caeden had learned there had only been the usual village workers and their trade carts passing through. He had spent all night trying to track down and discover the identity of each one, but so far, his efforts had proven fruitless in finding anything suspicious. Conferring with the other Guard members, he knew there had been no forced entry into the king's chambers and there had been no sign of struggle. The king had slept peacefully while the murderer crept inside.

The murder weapon, Levi's bloody dagger, had been found lying on the floor beside the bed. Levi had been on guard duty at the gate until dusk, where he had mentioned to his replacement his eagerness to leave. He'd had plans with Rebecca, but never arrived at her room that night, nor did he return to his own. His room was as neat and clean as always, nothing missing or out of place. Caeden wasn't sure what had happened to Levi, but his gut told him his friend didn't commit the crime, regardless of the evidence.

King Vidar's body was burnt as the sun rose into the sky and the ashes scattered across the meadow. For Amira, it passed like a dream. People and things moved around her and she watched herself interacting with others from afar, it seemed. She witnessed her father's body burn until nothing was left and felt empty, hollow... nothing. She looked around at the large group gathered. So many faces, all sharing her grief and fear. It was her duty to lead these people, to give them hope for the future, but right now she had nothing to give.

Her chest tightened; her vision blurred, and it became hard to breathe. As panic consumed her, a warm hand slid across the small of her back. Startled, her eyes shot up and met intense ice-blue eyes. He acknowledged her with a brief nod before returning his attention to the crowd, but his hand remained where it was. Warmth filled her and she was finally able to catch her breath. She wasn't alone. She could do this. Her father had instructed her well in her duties and she would do him proud. She slipped on her facade of serenity and hid her shaking hands in the folds of her skirt.

Caeden stood behind his princess, slightly to her right, guarding her while he scanned the crowd. He worried for her safety as never before. Was the murderer amongst the large crowd? Amira looked so small and frightened. Caeden noticed her hands were trembling and her breathing had become labored. Was she worried he couldn't protect her?

Although he knew it wasn't his right, he couldn't keep his hands to himself. He placed his hand on her back as a reminder to her that she wasn't alone and, hopefully, provide any comfort he could. He made sure his touch was discreet, not wanting to embarrass her.

Her shoulders squared; her chin lifted and her breathing returned to normal. She would lead by example for her people. Caeden was so damn proud of her. It was time to return to the palace for the memorial feast in honor of the king. He couldn't wait for it to be over; Amira was too exposed in this crowd. When the feast was over, he would make sure she was secure, then he'd once again go out in search of the murderer; until he was found, she wouldn't be safe.

The mourners, led by Princess Amira, were met in the courtyard by a contingent of armed soldiers. The group stopped in shock.

"What is the meaning of this?" Amira demanded,

trying to push through the Royal Guard that suddenly surrounded her.

"Thank the heavens you are safe, my princess," came a sickeningly sweet voice from the group of soldiers. "I was so worried about your safety after hearing the terrible news."

Sorin strolled from the group. Her guards closed in even more as he approached.

"Why are your armed soldiers in my courtyard, Sorin?" she asked, sounding shocked and confused even to herself.

"Why, for your protection of course." He almost looked sincere as he said it. "Your Guard has been compromised. Therefore, I take it upon myself as my duty to see to your protection. Secure the princess," he addressed the last to his soldiers.

Her Guard raised their weapons and readied themselves as the group of soldiers approached. The crowd was eerily quiet, waiting to see what would happen.

"Stop!" she screamed into the quiet, panic once again rising and her mind beginning to race. "I appreciate your concern, Sorin, but I assure you this is not necessary. I already have my Guard, as you can see," she said with a sweep of her hand, striving for diplomacy.

"Your Guard can no longer be trusted; surely even you can understand that. Was it not a member of your own Guard who killed our dear king?" Sorin couldn't hide his smugness at being able to deliver this news to the crowd. It seemed like everyone drew in a sharp breath. The crowd stirred and murmurs of Levi's absence could be heard.

"Where did you hear that lie?" Amira asked defiantly.

"Lie? Was it not your guard Levi's own weapon that killed our king? Where is Levi, by the way?"

Sorin posed his questions as if he were on a stage delivering lines. But who wrote the script? How did he have the details of the murder and Levi's disappearance? The crowd was buying into his act and was becoming increasingly louder.

"The murderer has yet to be identified. As for my guard's whereabouts, that is not your concern," Amira said confidently, trying to convey a calm and strength she didn't feel.

"It is all of our concern, Princess. Your safety is vital to us all," he countered. Turning to address the crowd once again, he fairly shouted, "Our princess is in danger from her own Guard. This is unacceptable. While her loyalty is admirable, it is misplaced. Grief clouds her thinking. We cannot know how many of the Royal Guard were involved in the murder of our dearest king. We must insist on the princess's safety!"

Sorin had riled the crowd into a frenzy; people were now pushing and yelling. Pleas from the crowd could be heard, along with outrage at the Guard. Things were quickly getting out of hand.

"All right, quiet, please," Amira addressed the crowd. "Please listen to me!" She had to raise her voice to get their attention; she wasn't used to shouting, but it was vital that she gain their attention and find a way to calm them. After a couple of seconds, the crowd began to still.

"Arrest the Royal Guard!" Sorin commanded into the quiet before Amira could continue.

"No!" Amira screamed, finally pushing herself between Sorin's soldiers and her Guard, much to their frustration and attempts to keep her surrounded. "No one touches my Guard!"

Exhausted and completely panicked, she struggled to find an amicable solution. Her people were grieving, making their reaction unpredictable. In addition, an altercation between her Guard and Sorin's soldiers would only serve to antagonize them further. Even outnumbered, her Guard had a good chance at defeating the soldiers, but considering the circum-stances, she couldn't take that risk.

She took a deep breath and tried to sound reason-able and in control. "Sorin, for my people's peace of mind, I will allow your soldiers' protection for the time being. That will free my Guard for the more important task of bringing my father's murderer to justice."

She could hear her guards' anger and displeasure, but she ignored them, except to give a shake of her head as they once again approached trying to surround her.

She turned to address the crowd. "Levi and the rest of my Guard are not responsible for the death of the king and will not be treated as such or punished in any way." She made sure her tone was commanding and clear.

Sorin nodded once to his soldiers to stand down. "Come along, Princess," he commanded, completely ignoring her Guard now that he felt he had won.

"I will have a private word with my Guard before they are relieved of duty."

"I don't think—" Sorin began.

"That was not a request," Amira snapped, completely out of patience. She pushed through the group, no one daring to get in her way, and took her Guard into a private chamber.

"No," was Caeden's immediate response as the door closed.

"You must." She tried to sound firm, but her voice wavered. They all began to speak at once.

"We are loyal to you, Princess!"

"This is not acceptable."

"We can take them all."

And all sorts of angry grumbling could be heard.

"I know you are not responsible," Amira began with complete confidence. "This is actually a good thing. Now you will have time to find Levi and clear his name."

"Your safety comes first. Always," Caeden said adamantly.

"Please," she whispered to Caeden alone, looking into his eyes. She took his hand and continued softly. "I need your help. Find my father's killer. This is important to me and if you aren't wasting time babysitting me, you'll have more time to devote to the search. Please, Caeden."

He had never heard Amira beg for anything; his guts knotted and pain filled his chest. He was torn between wanting to bring her justice and not wanting to leave her side.

"I don't trust Sorin or his men." Caeden made one last objection.

"Neither do I, but since he has sworn to my safety in front of everyone, he cannot afford to let anything happen to me." She hoped, at least. Amira knew her Guard was not pleased, but she could tell by the men's grim expressions they would do as she asked. When Caeden started to pull his hand from hers, she felt a stir of panic and tightened her grip. He met her eyes as she whispered, "Hurry back to me."

"Always," he vowed. Caeden leaned in to Amira until their bodies were almost touching. He no longer cared if they were alone. "Amira," he whispered, using her given name for the first time.

She couldn't let him finish whatever he was going to say. "Please, Caeden. This is the only way. I can't allow you to be imprisoned. I lied. I do need your help... I need you."

Seeing her fight back the tears in her beautiful grey eyes filled him with an impotent rage and a deep ache in his chest; he felt damn near out of control. He took a deep breath to steady himself; losing control wouldn't help her. He brought his forehead down to rest against hers and caressed her cheek gently with his calloused fingers, wiping away the single tear that had finally fallen.

"When this is over, you and I are going to have another discussion about needs." He kissed her lips softly. "I'll make this right," he swore to her, "then we'll talk."

She gave him a smile that didn't reach her eyes, and nodded. It nearly crushed him, but Caeden turned away from her, signaled to his men, and left her in the hands of another.

Amira's legs collapsed from under her as the door clicked closed behind the last of her Guard. She had used all of her remaining energy standing up to Sorin and then pretending to be strong while sending her Guard away. She knew if they had any idea how weak she felt, she would never have been able to persuade them to leave her. She fell to her knees in despair. Lost and alone, her tears flowed freely.

She was startled by the sound of a throat clearing. Wiping her face quickly, and breathing slowly to calm herself, she looked up and discovered one of Sorin's soldiers slowly approaching her.

"I'll escort you to your chambers," the soldier said

in a neutral tone that matched the emotionless expression on his face, but his hands were gentle as they lifted her off the floor and carried her to her room.

She tried to struggle out of his arms, not wanting to appear as weak as she felt, but it was useless. She didn't have the strength and all the effort only amounted to him tightening his hold on her. She quickly gave up her wiggling, deciding to make things easier on the soldier; after all, he was only doing what he was instructed. Amira was extremely thankful the hallways proved empty of anyone to witness her shame.

She noticed the soldier wouldn't make eye contact with her, nor did he respond when she tried to engage him in polite conversation by asking his name. After reaching her room, he sat her on the bed and turned to leave.

"Thank you," she called out to him.

He paused briefly and gave a stiff nod, but he still refused to look her way. Just as the door was closing behind him, Amira thought she heard him whisper, "I'm sorry." Then she heard the lock on the outside slam into place.

For a brief moment, she was terrified, but exhaustion soon overcame all else and her eyes drifted closed as she slumped onto the bed.

Amira was awakened by the sound of angry voices. Despair immediately overwhelmed her as her mind strained to come to terms with everything that had happened. She felt drained and confused. It was a struggle to open her tired eyes and her head was heavy as she turned to look toward the open doorway where the voices were coming from.

Sorin and Aunt Marcelle stood close together. Something wasn't right about what she saw, but her mind refused to acknowledge exactly what it was. Their bodies were so close they were touching, and Sorin's hand was tangled in Marcelle's red hair, tilting her head to the side. They almost looked as if they were in a lover's embrace, except it was clear they were both far from happy.

"You will wake her now!" Sorin shouted directly into Marcelle's face.

"I've tried everything, she—" Marcelle's husky voice trembled as Sorin cut her off.

"You are the Supreme Healer so heal her! Don't give me excuses!" he demanded.

"This is not my fault. If y-you—" Marcelle stammered.

"Enough!" He jerked Marcelle's head back by her hair. "Now is not the time. We must finish this," Sorin growled at her.

Amira couldn't watch any longer. "What is going on?" she tried to demand forcefully, but her words barely croaked out. Her throat felt as if sandpaper had been generously rubbed around the inside.

Marcelle made a startled sound as the two quickly jumped apart. Sorin pushed Marcelle forward while growling, "Finish this."

Marcelle's face softened, a trembling smile on her thin lips as she approached. "Thank the angels you are awake! We have been so worried about you."

Amira noticed Marcelle's dark eyes darted around the bed, but didn't settle on her. Marcelle handed her a glass of water and Amira drank it gratefully.

"What? What do you mean?" Amira asked, her voice now a little stronger.

Marcelle's eyes met Amira's accusingly. "You have been asleep for two days and we are running out of time!" Her husky voice sounded angry again.

"What do you mean?" Amira asked again, her mind still having trouble catching up. Marcelle paced along the side of the bed, her hands tangling in her own hair.

"I told you. I told you this would happen! Now he's dead... he's dead! Why? Why, why, why..." Her voice had risen to a frantic screech. Amira could only stare in shock.

Sorin moved for the first time since the conversation began. He quickly made his way to Marcelle, grabbing her by the arms and giving her a jarring shake. "Not now, Marcelle. Keep it together," he hissed.

Amira held her breath as they stood there frozen, eyes locked, not moving. It took a few minutes, but

Marcelle seemed to gather herself. She nodded to Sorin and he released her, but didn't move from her side. Marcelle turned slowly and sat next to Amira on the bed.

"I'm sorry, darling. I'm just upset. The shield is failing and we are running out of time. The entire island has been affected." Her voice was eerily calm and it caused goose bumps to spread across Amira's arms.

She felt herself catching Marcelle's previous panic. Her heart began to race and fear threatened to steal her breath, but she forced herself to ask, "How?"

Marcelle bit her lower lip and looked to Sorin.

Sorin stared back at Marcelle for a long moment. It was becoming increasingly obvious to him he had broken his toy. It seemed as if the last task he had assigned her had been more than she could handle. He had put decades into her training; it was a pity to lose her. *Oh well*, he sighed to himself; she had almost outlived her usefulness anyhow. He just had to keep her together for a little bit longer, and then he'd have his new toy.

He looked toward Amira, propped up in the bed. She'd been unconscious for two days, but still managed to wake up looking as beautiful as ever, and for some unknown reason that pissed him off. Soon that beauty would belong to him, he reminded himself, and he had to fight a smile at the thought.

He was standing directly behind where Marcelle sat on the edge of the bed. He placed his hand on her shoulder to help steady her when he noticed her eyes begin to dart wildly around the room once again.

Princess Amira wanted to know how the island and her people had been affected by his actions, and he would take great pleasure in explaining it to her.

"As Marcelle said, the shield is failing. The island is no longer being protected from the harsh weather of the northern hemisphere. The core temperature has dropped drastically. Plants and animals are dying. Your people are dying."

He paused to savor the pained devastation on her face. Yes, that had cut deep, which would serve his purpose well.

"For the first time in our history, the island of Cashile has snow. The entire eastern side of the island has been ravished by a winter storm and is completely covered in ice. Most of the residents there have lost their homes, and earthquakes have begun to devastate the island. Your people have been leaderless and afraid while you have lain weakly in this bed, and we can only expect worse to come."

Sorin found great joy in Amira's reaction. Her face paled, her eyes closed, and she looked like she was trying not to vomit on her pretty pink-and-yellow bedspread. He was greatly disappointed when she took a deep breath, released it slowly, and looked at him.

Her gray eyes were cloudy with concern, but she seemed in complete control of herself.

"What has been done to care for my people?" she asked in a steady voice.

"In your absence, Princess," he said, having difficulty holding back his sneer, "I have taken the liberty of dispatching your army to the aid of those in need."

"Thank you, Lord Sorin, for your assistance." Amira tried to rise from the bed, but fell back after only being able to sit up halfway.

"Careful!" Marcelle said as she reached out to help Amira back down. "Your health is failing along with the shield. Let me get you something to help you feel better."

Marcelle started to rise, but Amira quickly stopped her.

"No, I'm fine for now. Where are Lord Donovan and Lady Ferrera?"

Marcelle's eyes darted toward Sorin before she answered, "There has been no sign of them; we fear they have been lost in the storm."

Amira paused as if to accept that and gather her thoughts before continuing. "I need full reports on all areas affected. I need details on what is being done to secure food and shelter for those in need. My people must be taken care of first. Who has been leading my army and where is the Royal Guard? I would like them to report to me immediately."

Sorin had had enough. It was time the princess realized she was no longer in control. He once again placed his hand on Marcelle's shoulder, this time to steady himself. It wouldn't do to lose complete control of his temper, not yet. He squeezed, and Marcelle's indrawn breath brought him a small amount of comfort.

"Princess, I am now leading your army and can assure you all details are being taken care of. As for your Royal Guard, no one has seen them." *And no one will see them again*, he silently added, his lips quirking in a small smile he had to work to contain. "It seems they are cowards and are hiding from the justice they deserve."

Amira looked as if she would interrupt, so he quickly continued. "But worry not for your safety, as my army now surrounds the palace. No one gets in or out and no one will get near you."

That's right, Princess, you're all alone. Sorin smirked to himself. He saw in her eyes when that fact registered to her.

For a moment, she almost looked defeated; then she turned to Marcelle and calmly asked, "What can we do to repair the shield?"

Sorin was greatly disappointed with Amira's reaction. There were no tears, no begging. Hell, she didn't even argue with him. He clenched his fists in frustration but held his tongue. It was time for Marcelle to do her part. Her husky voice was now answering Amira, and he took a second to be grateful she was at least keeping her shit together.

"Darling, I tried to tell you. There is only one way to save us all. You must allow me to bind your life force to that of a strong male in order to be able to support the bond to the shield without it killing you. Binding yourself to Lord Sorin is the only way."

"To Sorin? No, there must be another way."

Amira's world was crumbling around her. Her people were suffering and dying, and she was useless to help them. She was alone for the first time in her life and her body was too weak to even get out of bed. Now her aunt was demanding she bind herself to this cruel excuse for a male. More than anything, she wanted to hide under the covers and cry herself back to sleep, but she couldn't do that. She knew instinctively she couldn't afford to show any more weakness in front of Sorin or Marcelle.

From the corner of her eye, she saw Sorin's jaw clench. She no longer cared if she offended him or not.

"There is no other way! It must be Lord Sorin!" Marcelle was once again visibly agitated.

The solution felt wrong to Amira. The thought of tying herself to him left a heavy feeling in her chest and made her sick to her stomach.

"Why must it be Sorin? You said I must bind

myself to a male of strength. I have in my acquaintance a line full of males with more strength than Sorin." But only one pair of icy blue eyes came to mind when she pictured herself being bound to another.

"You ungrateful wretch!" Marcelle screeched before launching herself at Amira.

She was too shocked to defend herself, even if she had had the strength to move. Luckily, Sorin was able to grab Marcelle by the waist and drag her away from Amira before she made contact. The entire time, she screamed indecipherable words at Amira.

Sorin physically restrained Marcelle until she calmed.

"That's enough, my pet," he crooned to her when she settled enough to understand. "The princess is unwell. Go fetch her something to help her relax and regain her strength."

Marcelle nodded and left the room without looking Amira's way. Once she was gone, Sorin pulled a chair close to the bed and settled in it, propping his feet up on the bed next to her hips.

"So, doll, you think you have someone more suitable than me? Well, where is he? I don't see anyone else here offering to save you or your people." He paused for effect and looked around the room. "Where is this line? Or is it just one male you have in mind?"

Amira lifted her chin in defiance and refused to answer, but something in her face must have given her away because he said, "Ah, you do. Let me guess, it's one of your precious Royal Guard you are so worried about." When she again wouldn't engage in the conversation, he continued. "Which one is it? The murderous man whore? No, not him. The dark silent one? No, I bet it's the Captain of the Guard. Am I right? You silly girls always make up these unrealistic fantasies about who you foolishly consider the 'alpha male.'"

Amira schooled her expression and tried her best to give him nothing. She didn't know how he had figured out her feelings for Caeden, but she refused to give him any more leverage over her.

A soft scraping sound followed by a slight click could just barely be heard from the adjoining room, which served as her sitting room and wardrobe. Amira recognized the noise and had to fight against a sigh of relief. Unfortunately, Sorin heard it as well; she realized this as he tilted his head, as if listening intently.

"Any of my Guard would serve as a better substitute than you," she said to distract him.

"Your mighty Guard is nowhere near as great as you think they are." Amira could see the joy in Sorin's face as he readied himself to continue. Whatever he was about to say was bad and he was going to find great pleasure in telling her. She braced herself for the worst. "In fact, it took hardly any effort to capture them all."

"What have you done with them?" Amira tried to once again jump from the bed, but was still unable to do so.

"Tsk, tsk. What a temper. Careful not to injure yourself there, Princess," he sneered. "Your Guard are currently my... guests, until they can be punished for their part in the murder of King Vidar."

"Sorin," she began in the most reasonable tone she could muster, but he wouldn't let her continue.

"My dear, you should be thrilled I am bringing justice to your father's murderers; I know the people of Cashile will be. But you're too selfish to care about the people, aren't you? They are suffering and you lie here thinking about yourself and your wants and refuse to do the one thing that will save the people. If the people don't matter to you, how about I trade you for what does matter to you? How about I give you the life of your Captain? I can't give you them all—someone must be punished—but I would be willing to exile the Captain in place of the death sentence, for your cooperation in the binding ceremony."

Marcelle chose that time to come back into the room, giving Amira another minute to think. She decided the best course of action was to play along, because she knew something they didn't. She wasn't alone, and there was still hope.

"Well, darling, what have you decided?" Marcelle asked.

"I think Lord Sorin and I have come to an agreement," she said, her eyes never leaving Sorin's.

"Excellent! Drink this herbal tea; it will help you feel better." Marcelle watched closely while she drank every drop. "Good. Now rest a while and we'll prepare for the ceremony."

Just after the door clicked shut behind Marcelle and Sorin, Amira saw Inaya's head poke around the corner of the connecting doorway. She stood frozen, tears streaming down her face until Amira whispered, "Oh, honey."

That seemed to unlock her and she rushed over to Amira, practically leaping onto the bed to hug her close. "I was so worried," Inaya sobbed.

Amira petted her long golden hair for comfort before saying, "Shh... it's okay, but we don't have much time." Inaya did her best to stifle her tears and sat up, but grabbed on to Amira's hand, refusing to let her go completely. "Marcelle drugged the tea she gave me, and I'll soon be asleep, so this will have to be quick. Did you hear what Sorin said about the Guard?"

Inaya sniffed and nodded.

"Is it true? Have you heard from Murdock or any of the Guard?"

"There is no sign of them. My brother Alyx is the only soldier I have been in any contact with, and he says no one knows anything about their whereabouts, but they have scouts out searching. Maryse had her baby last night. Murdock wouldn't have been absent for that unless he had no choice." Her voice cracked.

The world began to spin and Amira raised her hand to her forehead, willing herself to focus for a little while longer. "Okay, then we assume it's true; Sorin has the Guard locked up."

"That son of a bitch!" Inaya said through clenched teeth.

"Inaya, I need to know if everything else he said was true. Is the shield really failing? Have there really been extreme changes to the island?"

She looked at her lap and answered in a small voice, "Yes... it's bad."

Amira took a deep breath to calm herself; giving in to tears wouldn't help anyone. "What is being done?"

Inaya shook her head. "I'm not sure. All the servants, including myself, were removed from the palace and replaced with Sorin's. I've been staying with Maryse and sneaking back in here to check on you. Apparently Sorin doesn't know about the hidden servants' entrances." She tried to smile, but it came out halfhearted. "Our army was sent out yesterday morning when most of the devastation was reported. It's too soon to know all of the details, but we do know Velius has been affected the least. I guess that is because you are here. Refugees from the other territories are making their way here, but are getting little help and are not even permitted within the palace walls. Sorin has the palace locked down with his soldiers. They are spreading rumors of your death." Her tears were now flowing freely again.

Amira couldn't contain her tears any longer. "I'm going to be fine." She tried to sound confident. "Marcelle has—"

"Marcelle is in league with Sorin to take your kingdom!"

"Shh... I know something isn't right between them, but Marcelle has the only solution we know of."

"Tying yourself to Sorin! You can't really be considering that!"

Amira's eyes were getting heavy and she was losing the battle to stay awake. "No, not to Sorin, but if binding myself to someone will save Cashile, then I'll do it. Surely Sorin isn't the only person it will work with. But I'll need your help."

"Anything."

"Find where Sorin is keeping the Royal Guard. See if you can get some of our army back here to release them. But Inaya, do not take unnecessary risks," Amira said, trying to make her voice firm. She hoped Inaya would listen and take care of herself.

"I'll get them free, but come with me," Inaya begged desperately.

"I can't. I'm not strong enough and you can't support me. Plus, I need to be where Marcelle is. She is the only one who can perform the ceremony. I'll try to hold them off until you return with help, and then we'll force her to perform the ceremony using someone else."

"But what if I don't return in time? Please just come with me now. I'll—"

"Honey," Amira interrupted, "you need to go now."

"But—"

"Please."

Inaya pulled Amira in for another hug. "I love you. I'll send help," she whispered in her ear.

"I love you, too. Be safe."

Both women were crying uncontrollably as Inaya left. Amira was asleep before the hidden door clicked closed.

Six

The cellar was musky and damp and the smell of dirty bodies and urine immediately offended Sorin's nose. The stairs creaked as he descended, and a shiver crawled up his spine. He'd always hated places like that. His imagination would try to torture him with the monsters waiting for him in the darkness, but today he knew the monsters in his imagination couldn't compete with what the cellar actually held: Amira's Royal Guard. If freed, he knew these males would cause him more pain and torment than any monster possibly could, and hell, they would probably enjoy it more, too.

He had taken a risk by locking them in this makeshift prison, but he couldn't place them in the real prisoners' holding cells and chance having them discovered; the people might riot. They needed to believe the Royal Guard had abandoned them, so that when he produced evidence they were responsible for the murder of the king, he would have their complete support as he executed the Royal Guard one by one. Only a few of his most trusted soldiers knew they were being held there, and they were trying to keep the cellar looking as discreet as possible; only one light and one guard posted just beyond the bottom of the stairway.

Sorin held a small light in front of him; only enough illumination to see the next step ahead. He heard a creak on the stairs above him and his heart thumped. He turned quickly, almost losing his balance on the stairs. Catching himself against the wall, he scanned the area as far as his light would allow. There was no one there, he assured himself. He took a minute to collect himself, all the while berating himself for his irrational fears. He was the new ruler of Cashile and all of its people; he would not allow himself to be afraid of the dark or what could possibly be hiding within it.

With chin up, shoulders squared, and snarl firmly on his face, he descended the last of the stairs. At the bottom, the cellar split off into two sections; the dark area to the right held the stored produce and to the left was the makeshift prison.

"My lord." The senior soldier on duty, Heath, stood and bowed in respect.

"Report," Sorin barked in return. He was in no mood to even pretend civility.

"All is quiet and the prisoners are subdued, my lord."

"Yes, well I can imagine being kept in the dark with little food for days would subdue any weak male."

Sorin felt a burst of pride at his accomplishment of besting the infamous Royal Guard. It hadn't even been that difficult. He had set a trap for them and they'd easily fallen in it. Of course, he'd lost thirty-two soldiers and had a dozen or so wounded, but that was an acceptable loss. Those soldiers could be replaced, and besides, he now controlled Velius's army as well. Yes, he was the best male on this playing field, hell, on any playing field; no one could stop him.

"I will speak to the former captain alone," Sorin instructed, but as Heath moved to leave, the feeling of trepidation returned. "You will wait at the bottom of the stairs," he quickly amended his command, "and leave your light with me."

Heath set his light down, bowed again to his leader, and stumbled through the dark to the staircase.

Sorin was told Caeden had been the hardest to capture and he'd fought like a demon possessed; therefore, he had been placed in seclusion from the other guards and was being held in the small closet toward the back of the cellar.

As he passed the room holding the other Guard members, he eagerly peeked through the small window. They looked so pathetic. Sorin didn't try to hide the smirk that curved his lips. Dirty and chained to the walls, they sat with dried blood covering their torn clothing. Damn them their speedy healing; their wounds were almost gone. Sorin made a mental note to send someone to replace them. *Can't have the prisoners enjoying their stay too much*, he joked to himself.

His eyes caught on the only body lying prone on the ground, and he paused to wonder if that one still lived. It was the pretty one, the one they had captured first, Levi. His wounds had not yet healed, but Sorin could see the rise and fall of his chest. *So he still lives*, Sorin thought in near amazement. Of course, he hadn't been present for any of their captures, but the report stated this Guard member had been prepared to fight to the death and nearly had. Sorin refused to feel an ounce of admiration for the strength of the males, because it frustrated him that theirs was not a strength he could command. Therefore, they were no better than rabid animals in his opinion, and they deserved to be put down.

He continued on to the small closet and opened the door slowly. He peeked in, prepared to slam the door shut if there were any surprises awaiting him inside, but all was as it should be. Caeden was leaning against the back wall with his legs crossed in front of him, actually looking relaxed. His head was bowed and his long hair blocked his face from view. Unlike the other prisoners, who were only chained to the wall by one ankle cuff, the captain had been deemed too dangerous and had been chained by wrists and ankles with only two feet of chain to allow for movement.

"Ah, and how are we faring today, Captain?" Sorin asked in condescending politeness. "Not in the mood to chat?" he added, when his prisoner refused to answer. Hell, Caeden hadn't even twitched in acknowledgement. The disrespect infuriated Sorin, and if he'd been speaking to anyone else he would have yanked them by their hair and commanded their full attention, but he knew it wouldn't be wise to get within reach of this particular male, even if he was chained to a wall. Therefore, he had to use his words instead.

"That's okay. I don't really care to hear anything you have to say anyway. I just thought, since you were used to being in command around here, I'd throw you a bone and keep you in the loop of what is going on. I'm a generous person like that."

He paused to calmly brush a smudge of dirt off the sleeve of his otherwise immaculate clothing, as if they were discussing the weather and he hadn't a care in the world.

"I now command your army, but no worries, I have sent them far from here, so don't concern yourself with them accidentally seeing you in this humiliating condition. I can understand how embarrassing that would be for you." Sorin paused to gauge Caeden's reaction. Nothing.

"As for your friends, their accommodations are

slightly better than your own." He paused to glance around the closet for effect. "Worry not; they will be released in the morning, just in time to attend their execution." He smiled wickedly and continued. "I'll save yours for last. I'd hate for you to miss out on all of the fun."

Still no change. Sorin's simmering anger was turning to rage. What would it take to provoke this male? Time to use his last resort.

"I just left your female. I wonder... can you smell the princess on me, the sweet scent of vanilla that lingers on her skin?"

That did it. Caeden's head popped up and his usual icy blue gaze was now as cold as glaciers, promising a slow and torturous death. Sorin stumbled back and tasted blood in his mouth from biting his tongue. He was unable to stop the wince of pain before he gathered himself and once again stepped forward. He cursed himself for his reaction and vowed to make Caeden pay for it.

"She sends her regards," he said as casually as he could manage.

Caeden's head had been the only part of his body that had moved. His stare was so intense, Sorin couldn't bring himself to meet it. So, he struck again with his words.

"The first day, she was convinced you were going to come save her. How brave she pretended to be, but by nightfall, she knew you had abandoned her. Her weeping and begging were quite pathetic, actually. Luckily, I was there to comfort her, to show her what a real male can do. Seems you haven't been taking good care of the poor girl. Tsk, tsk."

Sorin forced himself to meet Caeden's eyes; it would make his lies more believable, and he didn't want to miss Caeden's reaction to his next words. "I gave her exactly what she needed. I fucked her so hard and long she couldn't remember her own name, let alone yours."

The fiery rage in Caeden's eyes and his clenched jaw were his only reactions, and that wasn't enough to satisfy Sorin. He leaned against the doorjamb, well out of reach, and said with mock boredom, "That's why I have been so neglectful in my duty to visit you. You must forgive me. I couldn't get the girl off my cock."

That was what it took. Caeden lunged forward and if Sorin hadn't been expecting it, the suddenness would have shocked him. He'd gauged his safety distance well, though, and was able to control his natural instinct to flee.

"No need for tantrums, Captain. At her persistent begging, I have decided tonight I will make an honest woman of her," he said calmly, pretending to inspect his fingernails.

Caeden's voice was controlled and deadly calm, but Sorin felt the dark promise whispered in his ear. "You will die slowly by my hands."

Sorin's mouth went dry and his heart slammed

against his ribs, but he refused to let it show. He forced himself to laugh.

"Now, Caeden, that was rude, and here I was going to invite you to the ceremony. I guess you'll have to stay here." Sorin shut the door as calmly as he could and hoped his shaking hands weren't obvious.

Heath stood as Sorin approached.

"You'll stay on duty for another shift," Sorin instructed.

"But, my lord, I've already served a twelve-hour duty without food or rest."

"Then you'll serve another twelve," Sorin said with a shrug as he ascended the stairs.

Caeden struggled with the chains holding him bound to the wall until blood oozed from the abrasions around his wrists and ankles. After Sorin left him, he'd worked himself into a frenzy trying to get free, but only succeeded in causing more injury and wearing himself out. Sweat dripped into his eyes and his breathing was labored, but he refused to give in. His brain refused to release the image of Amira in Sorin's arms, which caused a far greater pain in his chest than any wound caused by his restraints. He couldn't let her down when she needed him most.

He took a moment to rest, and his mind began to play tricks on him; he thought he heard her voice. Was he losing his mind? No, he definitely heard a woman's voice. He held his breath to listen closely. He heard the mumbling of the guard and a feminine response, but it wasn't Amira; he'd recognize her voice anywhere. The only other female it could be... Inaya.

"Enjoy your dinner, I'll keep you company while you eat. You must get terribly lonely down here all by yourself," Caeden heard her say.

Why is she here? Surely she isn't here willingly... but of course she is, he thought ruefully. That female had more guts than sense of self-preservation. She must be up to something. In the years she had been Amira's companion, those two females had come up with some harebrained ideas to get into mischief, but never before had they been this reckless. He knew Amira had to be involved somehow. Where there was one female, the other was usually plotting as well.

Caeden felt more helpless than before, but knew all he could do was wait and see how this would play out. The minutes passed as hours. He could hear the soft murmur of voices, but with the closet door closed, he couldn't hear what was being said. Suddenly there was a shriek, a loud crash, and the sound of chaos as the rest of the Royal Guard began yelling.

After an eternity, the closet door opened. Dalek stood there, bruised but grinning. "Now, if you promise to be a good boy, you can come out of time-out."

"I'm going to hurt you."

"Can we take back the kingdom first?"

"Absolutely," Caeden growled.

Dalek made quick work of unlocking the chains, and Caeden took a moment to stretch and return proper blood flow to his limbs, all the while taking stock of his surroundings and assuring himself of the status of his men.

He spotted the soldier who had been guarding them. He was lying facedown by the foot of the stairs, unconscious. Inaya stood a few feet away, sandwiched between her brother Murdock and Trevin. Her hands were up in the air in a placating manner, but he could tell by the males' expressions, they weren't appeased by whatever explanation she had given them. Caeden quickly made his way over.

"Stop yelling at me so I can tell you that you have a son, Murdock," he heard her say as he approached. Amazement plastered Murdock's face as he quit ranting midsentence. She turned to Trevin next and shouted, "I should have left you chained to the wall!"

"When this is over, I'm going to give you the spanking you deserve," he promised.

She looked from Murdock to Caeden with an expression that screamed "are you going to let him say that to me?"

"I have a son," Murdock answered with a goofy grin on his face, as if the fact he had just been held captive for two days no longer mattered.

"And you can meet him after we have escaped and Sorin is dead," Caeden reminded him. Murdock's expression turned serious and he nodded his agreement.

"Tell me everything," Caeden demanded of Inaya.

SEVEN

Consciousness came slowly. The pounding in her head was a major deterrent against wakefulness. Unsure how long she had been unconscious, Amira thought it would be wise to take stock of her body before even attempting to open her eyes. She ached everywhere but didn't feel any real pain besides the throbbing in her head. That was good, right? She felt more drained and weaker than before, which was to be expected.

She lifted her hand to rub her temple in an attempt to alleviate the headache, but realized she couldn't move her arm. She panicked, her eyes popping open, and three things occurred to her: One, she was no longer in her room. Two, she was tied down. And three, she once again had awoken to Sorin and Marcelle standing over her. The recurring situation was getting tiresome.

"Perfect timing, Princess. We're about to begin."

"Be-begin what?" she stuttered around the lump of fear in her throat.

"Don't tell me you've already forgotten the special relationship you and I are going to embark on." The cheer in Sorin's voice and the wide grin on his face didn't match the fierce determination in his eyes. "It's time for you to make a commitment. We're going to save our world and then you're going to give me your kingdom."

"No, I'm not," she denied, more out of shock than belief.

The world around her became clear. She was in the Ceremonial Chamber and she had been strapped to the stone altar in the middle of the room. The chamber was dark, save for the light from the ring of white candles surrounding the altar, trapping Sorin, Marcelle, and herself in its circle. The smell of burnt sage and almond oil was thick in the air.

Amira looked to Marcelle where she stood at the foot of the altar, humming to herself while she mixed ingredients in a small bowl.

"Aunt Marcelle, untie me! We will do this another way. Please."

Marcelle seemed too absorbed in her task to hear Amira's plea and didn't acknowledge her in any way. Trying again, Amira began to fight against her restraints while demanding, "You will release me at once. I will find another way!"

"Don't deceive yourself, Princess," Sorin snarled. "Marcelle wants this as much as I do."

"I won't do it!"

"Unluckily for you, we don't need your agreement."

"It is ready."

Amira froze at Marcelle's cold tone. Time seemed to slow as she watched Marcelle glide around the altar and make her way to Sorin's side. In complete shock, she watched her beloved aunt press her body against Sorin, coil herself around him, and kiss him passionately. They kissed fiercely and the bitterness of betrayal burned in Amira's chest.

Her hope died quickly and strength drained from her already worn-out body. A sob rose in her chest, but she refused to allow it to escape. She may be defeated, but she would not give them the satisfaction of thinking they had broken her. She was the Princess of Velius and the new ruler of Cashile; she would keep her dignity.

"Let's do this, love," Sorin whispered, breaking the kiss and nuzzling Marcelle's ear. He stepped back and playfully slapped her on the backside while winking at Amira, causing Marcelle to giggle like a young girl.

Amira couldn't reconcile what she was witnessing with reality; confusion and despair warred within her.

Marcelle popped up on her toes and gave him one last peck on his lips. "As you wish, my lord."

She turned her attention to the altar and all expression left her face as she dipped her thumb into the ingredients she'd prepared. First she smeared the herbal mixture onto Sorin's forehead, leaving a gray streak, and then repeated the action on Amira. Amira tried to turn her head, but it was futile.

Marcelle seemed to recognize Amira for the first time. "Shh," she cooed, "this is for the best, you'll see, darling."

The gentle and loving tone Marcelle used was Amira's undoing. "Please, Aunt Marcelle, please don't do this!" she begged as the tears fell rapidly down the side of her face and into her hair. "Please." Her voice broke on an uncontrolled sob.

Marcelle shook her head slowly. "I told you, you aren't strong enough."

It had been said gently, yet still felt like a slap to the face. Amira recoiled, her breath catching.

Marcelle made her way to the front of the altar and began in an almost cheerful voice. "Sorin and Amira, please join hands."

"No, no, no...," Amira chanted, sobbing, and tried to wrench her hand away as Sorin took hold. She wanted to close her eyes and wish it all away, but was afraid of what they might do if she looked away for even a moment.

She watched as Marcelle raised both arms to the heavens and in a clear voice began.

"Spawn of Angels,
Womb of Woman,

Power be thy blessing."

She brought her arms down and lit the three candles sitting in front of her; first the green, then the red, and last the brown.

"Your strength to me,
By the power of Three,
My will be done,
This to you I am requesting."

The air felt thicker and Amira's heart pounded, her tears falling uncontrollably. Her begging and pleading were now even incoherent to her, but she couldn't make herself quiet.

Marcelle picked up a leather strap and tied Sorin's wrist to Amira's right above the restraint that held her to the altar. Her entire body was shaking violently.

"By Creator made,
By Creator changed,
Binding be thy blessing.
Cord go round,
Strength be bound,
Power revealed,
Now be sealed."

Lightning raced through Amira's body, bringing every nerve to life. She could no longer make a sound and in the silence, she heard Sorin's heavy breathing and moan of pleasure. She felt the currents of electricity flowing from her body into his. Through her tears, she recognized the expression of complete bliss on his unguarded face; it disgusted her.

She began to retch and her body shuddered with dry heaves. Suddenly, she felt a burning sensation on her wrist, distracting her from the nausea. She turned her head to find that Marcelle had slashed a superficial cut across both her and Sorin's bound wrists with a ceremonial dagger. Black spots floated in her vision and it became increasingly more difficult to comprehend her surroundings.

"Blood is shed,
And then combined,
By blood and spirit,
These two I Bind,
With the power of Three,
This is my will,
So mote it be."
Then there was darkness.

Reality returned with a loud crash. Amira's mind was instantly clear and she felt stronger than she had in days. Totally aware of her surroundings, she knew she was no longer bound to the altar and the circle of candles had been extinguished. The room was now illuminated by the glow of lanterns and she saw Marcelle and Sorin were once again arguing on the other side of the room. She made a vow to herself to never again wake up in a room with the two of them. Taking advantage of their distraction, she silently rolled off the altar and crouched behind it.

The binding ceremony had been completed and the lingering effects still tingled throughout her body. The consequences of what had been done were unknown to her, but she wasn't going to hang around to find out from the two of them. On bare feet, she darted from the chamber as quietly as she could.

The euphoria from the connection with the Princess sang through Sorin's veins, making it difficult to concentrate. It was overwhelming to the point of pain, but instantly addictive, leaving him desperate for more. Instinctively he knew the binding was just the beginning. A true bonding was needed to receive the full impact of the power that now slowly crept within him. He forced himself to concentrate beyond the exquisite pleasure so he could achieve his ultimate goal.

"You will now complete the mating bond!" he demanded of Marcelle once again, picking up the nearby candleholder and slamming it against the wall beside her head for emphasis.

"No." To his astonishment, she refused once again. "I have given up everything for this kingdom, and I will not help you take it from me! We will rule it together, the way I was meant to rule it with Vidar, or I will give you nothing more."

With foreign sensations passing through him, he couldn't contain the added burst of rage burning within him at her opposition. This time it was her head he slammed against the wall. Anger clouded his vision and he lost control of his own actions.

Eerie cackling brought him back. He looked to the floor where the sound was coming from to find Marcelle's bloody and bruised body crumpled there and the wicked laughter passing through her lips. Sorin couldn't remember abusing her into that state, but the evidence was on his cracked and bloodied knuckles. Her beady eyes seemed to look right through him as she continued to make that awful noise. He couldn't help but take an involuntary step back, his heart racing.

"Marcelle?" he softly questioned.

The laughter suddenly stopped and she had a far-off, unfocused look in her eyes. Her usually husky voice was childlike as she began to sing. "Choices, choices... We all make the wrong ones." Her black eyes rose to meet his. "Vidar suffered the consequences for choosing the wrong woman; don't repeat his mistakes."

Still rattled, he tried to reason with her. "It's not the woman, but the power she contains. This exquisite force"—he closed his eyes, savoring the feeling—"it pours into me from our connection. There is more; I can feel it, but I can't reach it. I need it! I have to have it."

He was desperate for it. He looked down at her and struggled to concentrate. "My pet, the pain you feel now is of your own making. You will help me get what I desire and when I do, I will not only have this kingdom. I will rule the entire world."

Her cynical sneer cut through his hum of pleasure, sparking his indignation. "I care not for the world," she informed him as she slowly lifted herself off the hard floor. "You promised me the kingdom of Velius and the island of Cashile, and I intend to collect. You will give me what Vidar never would or you will meet his fate." She stood and wiped the blood from her chin defiantly.

"Are you threatening me, my love?" he asked incredulously. Shock and anger once again controlling him, he stepped forward, latched on to her hair, and raised his fist to strike her, but her next words froze him.

"I can undo what has been done. In fact, I think I will."

The eerie cackling began again, this time echoing inside his skull. It surrounded him, overwhelmed him. It started to drown out all of the euphoria that had passed through him since the binding ceremony. The creepy laughter consumed him; his breathing matched the rhythm; his heartbeat stuttered at each change in pitch. Jaw clenched and body tensed, he prepared to fight whatever magic was pouring out from her madness. With a horrendous cracking sound, the world fell silent.

He took a deep cleansing breath, thankful for the blessed silence, before slowly opening his eyes. Finding Marcelle's head still in his hands, her neck broken, was a bit disturbing. After all, he hadn't made the conscious decision to kill her, but he found he didn't regret doing so. He was adaptable and intelligent; he could find another way to achieve his goal. Surely someone else could perform a simple mating bond.

"Well, it's just you and me, Princess," he said, turning to the altar. It was empty. His enraged roar shook the room and an assemblage of soldiers raced into the chamber.

"Find the princess," he ordered. To his astonishment, they hesitated.

"My lord"—the leader approached slowly—"the Velius army is returning. They have been spotted in the distance in force. They look to be assembling to reacquire the kingdom, and..."

"And what?" Sorin asked through clenched teeth.

"Your prisoners... the Royal Guard... they have escaped."

Sorin nodded and calmly asked, "Anything else I need to be made aware of?"

The soldier visibly relaxed at Sorin's accepting demeanor and shook his head.

"Excellent."

Before the soldier could even flinch, Sorin grasped

his sword with both hands and swung it at the soldier's vulnerable neck, severing his head from his body.

"Anyone else have something to add?"

They collectively had taken a step back and were shaking their heads emphatically.

"Great. Now gather my army and bring me the princess!" he ended in a roar.

Amira raced through the hallways as fast as she dared, trying to remain unseen. Foreign emotions and strange sensations flashed through her consciousness, distracting her and making her stumble over her own feet. Before she could hit the unforgiving ground, a strong arm circled her waist and she found herself pressed against a hard muscular body. She sucked in a breath to scream, but a warm hand quickly covered her mouth. She was carried out of the hallway and into a nearby sitting room.

"Shh, Amira, I've got you."

She instantly recognized that rough voice. As her body relaxed into his, the hand dropped from her mouth. She turned her head and found herself staring into beautiful ice-blue eyes. Her heart raced and her eyes filled with tears. She turned in his arms and clutched him to her as tight as she could, pressing her face into his neck, her body shaking with her quiet sobs.

"I've got you," he whispered over and over, stroking her hair and back, trying to reassure her. She began to calm and he held her silently for a couple minutes, both of them savoring the closeness, before they were interrupted.

"We can't stay here long, we need to keep moving."

Amira was startled to realize they were not alone. She peeked around Caeden's shoulder to see Osmond, Dalek, and Trevin standing close by. She tore herself from Caeden's embrace and threw her arms around all three of them as best she could. "You're okay!"

Her uncharacteristic affection had taken them by surprise, but they quickly recovered and embraced her in return. Osmond even went as far as awkwardly patting her on the back and grumbling a gruff, "It's good to see you, girl."

Even considering the danger they were all in, she couldn't help but giggle a little at that. She stepped back and once again found herself pressed against Caeden, his arm around her waist. She surveyed her Guard; they were dirty and bruised, but they were whole.

"Where is Murdock? Did you find Levi?" she asked, scanning the room for them and beginning to panic at their absence.

"They're both safe," Caeden quickly assured her. "Levi is injured. Murdock is taking him and Inaya somewhere safe for now."

"Inaya?" she asked, still panicked.

"That crazy girl came to free us," Trevin said, shaking his head in exasperation.

"I knew she'd find you. Was she injured?"

"She's daft but unharmed," Osmond grunted, and Trevin shot him an irritated look.

Amira took a deep breath and tried to accept that her loved ones were safe and she was no longer alone.

Caeden turned her to face him and examined her from head to toe and back. "How are you? Inaya said you have been ill," he questioned with obvious worry.

"I'm better right now." She couldn't look him in the eye as she continued, staring at her bare feet as she spoke. "They did something to me."

A sob threatened to break free and she swallowed hard to contain it. She felt the men turn to stone around her, waiting for her to continue.

"They performed a ceremony..." She paused again to gather her courage, her whole body shaking, tears sliding down her face. She wouldn't be a coward; she made herself meet Caeden's eyes as she finished. "I am now bound to Sorin; we are joined through a binding ceremony. I'm so sorry," she told him on a sob.

Once again, Amira found her face pressed into the crook of his neck. His fingers tangled in her hair and he kissed wherever he could reach as he murmured words of comfort and encouragement. "It's okay, Amira. It's all right; we'll fix this," he softly whispered. She breathed him in and let his strength comfort her.

"We need to know what happened," he said when she was calm.

Amira explained the best she could and was grateful for Caeden's reluctance to let her go. It was easier to relive and accept the truth while wrapped in his arms. Her Guard listened intently without interruption until she had finished, then questioned her in detail. She did her best to provide them with the information they needed. The last question was the one they were all eager for her to answer.

"Where is he?" Caeden growled. She knew he was trying to control his anger for her benefit, but she also knew he was barely holding on.

"I left Sorin and Marcelle in the Ceremonial Chamber."

"Were they alone?" Dalek interrupted.

Before she even finished nodding, Caeden was already giving orders. "Check it out. Take him if you can," he instructed Trevin and Osmond.

As they waited, Caeden sat with Amira cuddled in his lap, stroking her, while Dalek stood guard. She questioned him and he reluctantly told her about their capture and imprisonment, but refused to give details, explaining it would only upset her and there was no need; it was over and they were all safe. She decided to let it go and tried to relax in the safety of his arms.

Trevin and Osmond returned quickly with the news that the chamber was empty except for Marcelle's dead body, which had been left on the floor.

Amira couldn't help but grieve, even knowing Marcelle had betrayed her. She closed her eyes and tried to sort through her conflicting emotions as the Guard discussed strategy around her. She realized part of what she was feeling didn't belong to her, but was coming from the connection she now had with Sorin. If she concentrated, it was easy to distinguish his emotions from her own. His were tainted with something she couldn't define, but whatever it was, it terrified her. She could feel his anger, his frustration, his desire... her eyes popped open and she tried to focus on her surroundings, no longer wishing to acknowledge what was going on inside of her.

"We have to meet up with our army. The five of us are good, but even we cannot defeat Sorin's army on our own," Dalek was saying.

"Agreed. Inaya has sent word with her brother Alyx to have our army return and await us to join them. We can trust him to have them assembled and prepared for what must be done," Trevin informed him.

"The problem is our army is on the outside. Velius's walls are damn..." Osmond paused to give Amira a contrite look for swearing in her presence before continuing, "Our walls are near impenetrable. The only reason Sorin was able to take the kingdom was because he did it from within. He has the advantage here."

"Yes, but we know Velius's secrets better than

anyone. We'll get her back," Caeden stated confidently as he absentmindedly rubbed Amira's back and neck.

If anyone thought it odd that she was cuddled in his lap, no one showed any indication. It felt natural to Amira and she allowed herself to take comfort in it.

"Sorin's army is distracted right now, but we're unsafe here. We need to leave," Dalek reminded them nervously.

"Amira, can you walk?" Caeden asked her gently.

"I'm fine," she reassured him, trying for a smile but failing. "But I can't leave the palace without knowing exactly what they've done to me. Did you see any indication in the Ceremonial Chamber?" she hopefully asked Trevin and Osmond.

At the negative shakes of their heads, her hopes began to crumble. Dalek must have noticed because he quickly suggested, "I'll search Marcelle's chambers to see what I can find. I'm sure there will be answers there." Caeden nodded his approval as Amira thanked him with a genuine smile.

"Osmond, you will accompany Dalek. Join us at Murdock's cottage when you're finished," Caeden further instructed.

EIGHT

Murdock's small home was located on the western border of Velius. Amira had never been there before, but she found the warmth of it extremely comfortable. The trip from the palace had been terrifying, although uneventful. Sorin's army had, indeed, been distracted, preparing for the return of Velius's army. Caeden hadn't been two feet from her side the entire time. Even now, standing in Murdock and Maryse's living quarters, he stood beside her with his warm hand resting on the small of her back, as if he were afraid she would disappear if he moved away or let her go. She was grateful for his constant attention after feeling so alone while she was at the mercy of her aunt and Sorin.

Night had fallen and they were still awaiting Osmond and Dalek's return. Levi was resting peacefully in one of the spare rooms; his injuries were severe, but thankfully, not life threatening. Osmond's wife Francine, who had a similar personality to her husband, had taken over his care and if he had any sense at all, he'd be too afraid of her to do anything but thrive back to health quickly.

Murdock was the proudest papa in existence. He held his son, Elijah, contentedly, and repeatedly kissed his wife at every opportunity. Watching them together, she was happy for them, but selfishly it caused a heaviness in her chest. She felt guilty for her envy and had to turn away from the happy family.

She found Caeden staring at her and, as she met his eyes, he nodded as if he knew exactly what she had been thinking. He leaned forward and softly brushed her lips with his. Feeling self-conscious, she looked around to see if anyone had noticed his unexpected show of affection, but only Inaya and Trevin seemed to be paying them any attention. Inaya grinned, but Trevin had the nerve to wink at her before he looked away, giving them privacy. Her mouth must have dropped open in shock because Caeden chuckled softly beside her. She was unaccustomed to this kind of interaction and decided the best course of action was to ignore them all and focus on baby Elijah.

~

Amira was no longer standing in Murdock's home. She turned quickly to survey her surroundings and found herself back in the Ceremonial Chamber. How had she gotten there? The altar in the middle of the chamber drew her attention. There was a body lying lifelessly upon it. She approached slowly, her heart pounding, and only as she stood directly over it looking down did she recognize it as herself lying unconscious there. Her racing heart stopped mid beat. This couldn't be real. She closed her eyes to make it all disappear. Opening her eyes slowly, she hoped it would all be gone, but it wasn't... it was worse. Sorin was now in the room with them.

He sat directly across from her, his hip resting on the side of the altar, half lying on the altar himself. He was leaning over the prone body and his soft hand was caressing her cheek. She could feel his lust and arousal as he pressed himself against her still form. His hand began to travel the body, touching her intimately. Amira felt the touch as if he were actually touching her and not the unconscious version of her.

She tried to stop him, tried to wake her sleeping self, but her screams went unheard and her hands passed through the body fruitlessly. What was going on? Was she dead? The more she struggled and fought, the more aggressive he became. His breathing was hard and she heard him growl, "Yes, doll, fight me. It makes my victory all the sweeter."

Amira froze, the body on the altar hadn't stirred and he didn't seem to notice her. How did he know she was fighting him?

"I can feel you, just as you can feel me," he answered her unasked question. "We are one."

He passionately kissed her sleeping form, leaving her lips swollen and bruised, covered in his stinking saliva. Amira's stomach rolled as she began to panic. She looked away, but it didn't stop her from feeling his touch. She tried to calm herself, telling herself it wasn't real. *It can't be; none of this is happening.*

"Oh, but it can and it is," he answered her thoughts, his husky voice slithering through her, making her shiver. "Come to me, Princess. Let us consummate our union."

"Never!" She tried to sound fierce and defiant, but her voice came out shaky and weak.

Sorin's head snapped to face her. He slowly climbed off the altar and approached her as her other form began to fade into nothing.

"There you are," he said as if only now able to locate her. She stumbled back, but he continued to pursue her, the wild look in his eyes making her tremble. "You will come to me and we will truly join as one, as we are meant to be."

She shook her head in denial, unable to speak.

"You want this as much as I do. You need it. I can feel your need to belong, to be held, to be loved." He reached out and caressed a lock of her hair, letting his fingers trail through it.

At his touch, the hints of his emotions she had glimpsed became overwhelming. She felt his sick and twisted need, his obsession to possess her, to dominate her, to violate her, and to hurt her. She felt his pleasure at her fear, the excitement of near victory, and the extreme pleasure he received from the power exchange of their connection. All of it sickened and terrified her, but the worst was what lay hidden under the surface. Inside him was a dark, cold emptiness reeking of rage, hatred, and a bone-deep terror.

Having his darkness brush against her stole the breath from her body. Her legs could no longer hold her and she collapsed to the unyielding ground. Spots clouded her vision and she knew she would lose consciousness soon. Amira felt as if she were dying and was so grateful for the reprieve it would bring. She prayed to the angels that her death would come quickly.

Amira watched the strange expressions cross Sorin's face. She was thankful he was no longer touching her and she wasn't experiencing those emotions with him. His initial look of shock shifted to what she thought might be shame, but that couldn't be right. His face finally settled in an expression she had no problem reading at all. Murderous rage. *This is the end,* she thought as her eyes closed for the last time and blessed oblivion finally overtook her.

Sorin was frozen in shock. He had never felt so exposed in his life and hadn't meant to reveal so much of himself to her; he'd only meant to frighten her and make her cower. He needed her to know the danger he represented so it would be easier for him to control her. Using the Supreme Healers' journals, he'd called Amira into this dream-like rendezvous for that purpose.

He had been able to draw her back to the Ceremonial Chamber, but being inexperienced, he'd been unable to force her to fully manifest and reveal herself. Nevertheless, he was an expert at compelling others to do his will. With what little control he was able to wield over her subconscious, he'd produced the image of her on the altar and connected her to it. It had been exhilarating to feel her distress and panic as he took his pleasure with her helpless form, until she willingly exposed herself to him by addressing him directly.

What he hadn't counted on with this encounter was their connection opened him completely to her. She had been given access to the furthest depths of his soul, and what she discovered there, it didn't inspire fear in her—it was disgust; he'd read it clearly in her face. And for a moment, he'd been completely overcome with shame. Shame for the way he'd behaved, what he thought, how he felt, but most of all... shame for who he was. That shame quickly turned to anger. How dare she! How dare she judge him and find him lacking! He would teach her. She would pay.

"Amira, wake up!" Caeden's urgent voice breached her unconsciousness.

Startled, she sat up in bed, gasping for air, her heart racing, her body covered in sweat. She scanned the room quickly, looking for any sign of danger, and realized she was surrounded. Scurrying to the far side of the bed, she pressed herself against the wall, trying to make herself as small a target she possibly could. She eyed the people around her wearily, but no one made a move to attack her. Fighting her disorientation, the faces around her slowly began to register. She was surrounded by her Guard and Murdock's wife, Maryse. They all wore various expressions of fear and anxiety as they openly stared at her.

Memories of being with Sorin in the Ceremonial Chamber flashed back to her. She heard a whimper and only realized the sound had come from herself when Caeden suddenly gathered her into his arms, holding her tightly, and whispered to her, "It's okay, Amira, it was a dream."

"No, no it wasn't." She shook her head for emphasis. "I was with him. Our connection brought us together. I was back in the Ceremonial Chamber with him and I couldn't wake myself up! I tried, but I was like a ghost and had no control! Then he was there... he spoke to me... he t-t-touched me... I could feel everything! Oh heavens, I'm going to be sick." Covering her mouth, she struggled out of Caeden's arms and scrambled off the bed.

Luckily, Maryse moved quickly and brought a wastebasket to her. She was even kind enough to smooth the hair from her face and hold it out of the way while Amira emptied her stomach and the soldiers looked on helplessly.

When she was finished, Maryse helped her settle and cooed to her, "You're all right now, honey. Just lie back and rest for a minute."

She then proceeded to order the soldiers around as if she were their captain instead of a tiny slip of a female. Under different circumstances, Amira would have found it hilarious to watch her big, strong Guard scurry to her bidding.

"Osmond, take care of the receptacle. Trevin, fetch me a warm wet cloth to wipe her face. Dalek, bring the princess some water to rinse her mouth. Murdock, the princess needs bread to settle her stomach."

Caeden then gathered Amira back into his arms. Maryse gave him a look that said she was about to demand something from him too, but was wise enough not to push her luck after seeing the determination on his face. Maryse would make an excellent drill instructor for their army.

The soldiers seemed relieved to have something to do. They probably would have preferred to have someone to kill, but at least these small tasks helped them to not feel so useless in the face of their princess's fear and distress. They did as they were told and Maryse dismissed them so Amira could get some rest.

"Captain, she'll be fine now. Princess, please assure him you're all right before he has a fit and starts breaking things," she said with a playful grin. "Get some rest and call out if you need anything." She gave Amira a reassuring pat before leaving them alone.

Caeden was sure he looked as shaken as he felt. He should never have left her side. She had been sleeping peacefully when he left the room to discuss Osmond and Dalek's findings with the rest of the Guard. He'd only gone fifteen feet from her, into the living quarters, but it had been far enough to allow Sorin's evil to intrude and hurt her again. Caeden burned with the need to destroy Sorin, but the coward had locked himself down in the palace, surrounded by his army. *There is no way to get to him at the moment, but the time will come*, he assured himself.

Amira's hesitant hand touched his chest, interrupting his thoughts. "Will you lie with me for a while?

Hold me?" she asked in a soft voice, sounding unsure of the reception her request would receive.

"Always," he reassured her and gathered her closer as they got comfortable on the bed. After a moment of silence, he needed to ask. "Tell me?"

She knew exactly what he wanted to know. Body trembling, she relived her "dream" encounter with Sorin. As he listened, he had to keep his body firmly locked down to prevent himself from tensing with rage, knowing she would misunderstand. She needed his comfort, his strength, not his need for vengeance.

"I'm such a coward." She sobbed at the end. "I prayed for death. I prayed for an easy way out so I would never have to face him again; so this would no longer be my reality."

"Death cannot have you, I won't allow it," he told her firmly. A strangled laugh came through her tears; she must have assumed he wasn't being serious. He'd let her believe that if it made her feel better. He hated how there were no words to change how she felt or what had been done to her, but at least he could offer her some hope. "Osmond and Dalek found Marcelle's journals. They may hold the key to severing the connection between you and Sorin." Amira looked like she was going to interrupt, so he added, "Without causing any more damage to Cashile. We'll find a way."

Her tears had ceased for the moment and she listened carefully as he explained Marcelle's chamber had been filled with journal after journal containing

not only her personal information, but many ceremonies and rites that had been considered long
forgotten.

"That is why it took them so long to join us. They
were trying to locate the one that would help you, but
there were too many. Finally, they decided it was best
to bring them all. The more recent ones are more
difficult to follow and will take time to fully
understand."

Amira nodded in understanding. "I'm afraid Aunt
Marcelle had slowly been spiraling into madness for a
while, but I failed to notice." The guilt she felt was
clear in her voice.

"We all did. This isn't your fault." Caeden hoped
he could make her believe that. "It's late and you've
barely slept. Let's get some rest and start fresh in the
morning."

He could tell the idea of sleeping and possibly
opening herself back up to Sorin's invasion frightened
her, but she'd been struggling to keep her eyes open
and he knew it wouldn't be long before sleep claimed
her.

She sounded anxious and self-conscious as she
asked, "You'll stay with me?"

His heart constricted with pain that she had any
doubts he would, and pure elation that she wanted
him to.

"Amira, we still haven't had our talk and now is
probably not the time either, but know this: I need to

be with you. I need you. You're mine and I'm yours. Always. Forever."

"Always. Forever," she echoed in her soft sweet voice, and for once his heart felt whole.

Caeden cuddled her close and breathed in her beautiful scent of vanilla mixed with pure Amira. Their world was in chaos around them, but they both slept peacefully wrapped in each other's arms.

NINE

"By the angels, Marcelle was cracked! How did we miss this?" Dalek asked in astonishment.

"Simple. We had no reason to question our Supreme Healer. She could be a vicious hag, but she was a member of the royal family and a person of stature," Osmond answered in his gruff manner.

"My question is, how do we protect Princess Amira from this?" Murdock asked solemnly.

They'd been scouring Marcelle's journals since sunrise and it was now midafternoon. Amira had taken a break to help Inaya, Francine, and Maryse make the midday meal. Caeden was sure she had never done such domestic work in her life, but from the sounds coming from the kitchen and the sporadic bursts of giggles, it seemed like she and the other ladies were enjoying themselves. Content to listen to her happiness, he smiled, thankful for this brief respite. The things they were unearthing in Marcelle's journals would be very difficult for Amira to face. He wished he could spare her the pain to come, but it was her right to know.

"We can't. She is the rightful ruler of Cashile and must be fully informed," Caeden said regretfully.

"But she is so young and has been through so much..." Murdock trailed off.

After a brief silence, where each man was lost in his own thoughts, Osmond surprised everyone by stating, "She is stronger than you give her credit for."

For Amira to have grumpy Osmond's respect gave Caeden a sense of pride in his female. She was stronger than even she gave herself credit for. She would deal with this and be better for it, but he still wished to spare her the immediate pain.

The ladies chose that moment to bring in the platters of food. Caeden didn't even try to hide his delight when Amira naturally took her place beside him.

"What has you smiling?" she asked sweetly.

"You," he answered, bending down to press a kiss against her temple, causing her to blush beautifully.

Caeden had never been one to show his feelings, but he realized that recently he had smiled more than he had in his entire life. Looking at his men, he would have never guessed they had recently been beaten and held captive or that the world they lived in had drastically changed and suffered an enormous loss. Those men and women were survivors who remembered to be grateful for their blessings.

"Find anything yet?" Inaya asked, interrupting his thoughts. She wasn't eating any of her food, only pushing it around on her plate, and by the disgruntled looks Trevin kept sending her peas, Caeden knew he wasn't the only one who'd noticed.

"Nothing regarding reversal of the binding ceremony," Caeden answered vaguely, unwilling to ruin their meal by bringing up what they had discovered.

"When will Levi be able to travel?" Dalek asked Francine, eager to change the subject.

Francine had watched over him through the night and Levi seemed to be progressing, but the soldier was still in and out of consciousness.

"Not being a trained healer, I don't know for sure, but it seems as if his body is beginning to fight off and dispel whatever poison they gave him. His physical wounds need more time to heal. With proper rest and nourishment, he should be fit to travel within a week, I would guess."

"We need to unite with our army before then," Osmond stated.

"And it's not wise for us to linger here much longer," Trevin added.

"Sorin is unaware of our whereabouts and is bewildered where to look," Amira said with such certainty that the entire table paused and stared at her. She flushed and avoided looking at anyone.

Caeden was getting ready to intervene when she visibly steadied herself and admitted, "The connection we share allows me to know what he's feeling and I can only assume it allows him to know what I am feeling as well. I don't get specific thoughts, only impressions of extreme emotions. Sorin wants me badly and is enraged we escaped. He is confused as to how we left the kingdom with his soldiers guarding the walls, but his arrogance won't allow him to consider the possibility we're still inside the kingdom. With this cottage being so secluded, it's unlikely his soldiers will happen upon our location." She paused before adding, "I've considered the danger this connection places you all in and want to assure you I am trying to guard my feelings as best I can while also monitoring him for any indication that we're unsafe. If at any time I feel as if my presence is compromising your safety, I'll—"

"Let us do our duty to defend you," Osmond finished for her, which was accompanied by grunts of agreement from the other Guard members.

"But—"

"But nothing, dearie. Finish your meal and relax. There will be plenty of time to worry later," Francine injected, siding with her husband.

Amira's posture relaxed, but Caeden could still feel her tension.

"The connection could be a useful tool for us right now, Princess. It'll give us time to relax and regroup,"

Dalek offered, then changed the subject by asking, "What's the plan, Captain?"

"Dalek is right," Caeden agreed, possessively tightening his arm around her waist before continuing, "This will buy us some time and we could all use the rest. Our priority before meeting up with our army needs to be getting as many of our people to safety as possible. The kingdom is soon to be our battleground. Today, we will all rest and try to find as many answers as possible from Marcelle's journals. Tomorrow we will get word to anyone still left within the kingdom and by cover of night, Murdock and Dalek, you will escort them outside the wall. With the damages and changes to the island, many people have come here seeking refuge. Luckily for us, Sorin has prevented them from entering the kingdom. We will unite and care for the people. In the meantime, our army approaches from the southeast. Alyx has been instructed to hold them half a day's ride from here at the southern crest, but they have been leaderless for too long. Trevin, brother, I'll need you to leave tonight."

At Trevin's nod, Caeden continued, "Our army will be divided between providing temporary aid for our people and preparing for war to reacquire our kingdom."

"The people must come first," Amira added anxiously.

"They will, but you will have your kingdom and your freedom from Sorin, as well," he vowed.

Their eyes locked and for a moment, the rest of the world melted away. It hurt to see her eyes so tired and sad. Caeden made a silent vow to destroy Sorin personally. If he could take Sorin out of the equation, it would prevent this whole situation from escalating. There would be no need for war; leaderless, his army would crumble.

Caeden's fierce determination must have shown on his face because Amira drew a shocked breath. He couldn't soften reality for her, so he said nothing as he watched her come to terms with it, and as he trusted it would, her expression quickly turned to one of acceptance. She nodded once; no words were needed. She broke their stare and turned back to the table. Yes, his woman was much stronger than they had given her credit for.

Their meal ended quickly with no more talk of plans, but once it was all cleared away, it was time to discuss what they had discovered from Marcelle.

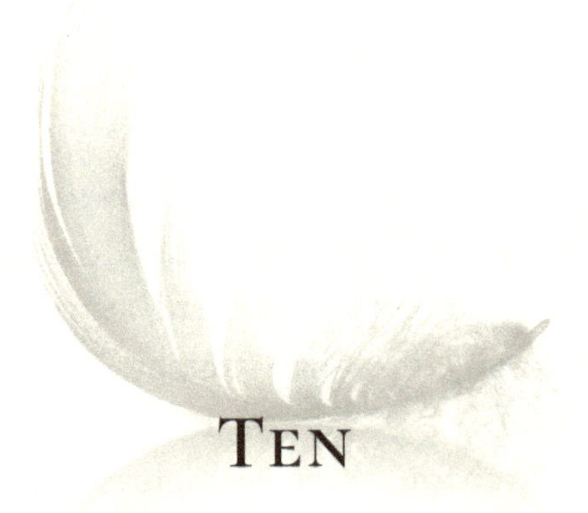

TEN

Amira could feel the tension in her Guard as they gathered in the sitting room, surrounded by Marcelle's journals. Amira didn't resist as Caeden pulled her onto his lap, which was becoming a habit of his. His arm circled her waist, his hand settling on her hip. Her blood raced through her veins, her breathing slightly irregular with excitement.

His nearness was wreaking havoc on her senses; every touch, sound, and smell became more vivid. She had to remind herself to focus on the matter at hand as she settled in and braced herself for what would come next, but after a couple minutes of silence, she actually had to prompt them to begin.

"I can tell this is going to be unpleasant," she began, and Caeden's arm tensed around her. She tried to put him more at ease by relaxing against him before continuing, "So, let's get it over quickly so we can move on to solutions." Trying to exude confidence, she turned to the one person she had learned she could depend on to give it to her straight. "Osmond, what have you found?"

If the room hadn't been so frighteningly tense, she would have laughed at the relief in Dalek's expression when she hadn't called upon him; as it was, she was too nervous for laughter.

"Princess, your aunt was a daft broad. She was obsessed with your father, played a part in the murder of both of your parents, was having a sordid affair with Sorin, and plotted to steal your kingdom," Osmond listed matter-of-factly.

Okay, that was a lot to take in. Her mind deflected by making a mental note not to ever ask Osmond to remove any bandages for her.

"What the hell is wrong with you? You could have handled that a lot more gently!" Murdock exploded, looking ready to strangle Osmond.

"If she had wanted to be coddled, she would have asked you, but she didn't. She asked me," he defended.

"But she's the princess for heaven's sake!" Dalek joined in, sounding offended on her behalf.

The three quickly digressed into a loud and heated argument. Trevin looked bored, as if this were usual behavior, while Caeden patiently gave her time to absorb the information, his fingers trailing gentle caresses at her hip and waist. Her mind, still looking to deflect the pain, focused on the outrageous interactions of her Royal Guard. She was absolutely fascinated with their behavior; they had never been so open and free in her presence before.

She couldn't contain the giggle that escaped when Dalek accused Osmond of being a "rat bastard in need of a hug," and Osmond's gruff return threat of "just try to touch me, boy" made her devolve into full-on laughter until her side began to ache. When she was finally able to control herself, she noticed silence had taken over the room. She looked around to find each man staring at her with a smile on his face; even Osmond was grinning at her. It occurred to her that maybe they weren't the only ones who had been stifling themselves. She wondered if she had ever truly been herself in their presence before; maybe it was her own fault that she'd always felt so separate and detached from everyone else. It was a sobering and painful realization, but it wasn't the time to dwell on it.

"All right," she said, reluctantly bringing them back on track, "anything else I need to know?"

"If there is, Trevin gets to share it," Osmond complained.

"Why me?" Trevin questioned in outrage, joining the conversation for the first time.

"Because if he decides to attack—" He paused to give Caeden a pointed look. "—at least you'd have a fighting chance."

Amira looked up to see an innocent expression plastered on Caeden's face. She wasn't fooled by it for a second; he wasn't handling this situation as well as he wanted her to believe. She grabbed his hand to give it a comforting squeeze, but instead he laced their fingers together and held on. His touch unknowingly centered her, giving her the strength and security she needed to continue.

"Well, Trevin, looks like you're up," she said, sending him a bright, encouraging smile.

Trevin shot Caeden a quick indistinguishable look before focusing his attention back on Amira. He cleared his throat and began. "As Osmond said, your aunt's mental state was far more deteriorated than any of us knew, and had been for a long while. Her journals suggest she was envious of her sister her entire life and it grew like a poison inside of her. She became fixated on your father the moment she realized your mother was in love with him. She believed it was her true birthright to rule Velius and, through your father, thought she had discovered her opportunity. But more than that, she thought if she could somehow win his affections from your mother, it would validate her as a person and be proof that she was indeed the rightful heir."

Murdock's solemn voice filled the momentary silence. "There is evidence that she used her knowledge as a healer to weaken Queen Maryam and prevent her from conceiving. You were indeed their miracle, as your father always claimed."

Tears pooled in her eyes and she looked down to hide them from the men. Caeden played with a lock of hair and his hand soothingly skimmed down her back. She tried focusing only on that feeling as she collected herself.

"Then the witch finally did our lovely queen in with a large dose of the poison she had been using to keep her as weak as a babe. Under all of our noses!" Osmond exploded in impotent frustration. Amira glanced up to see him pace angrily around the room.

"I've been reading her more recent journals," Dalek added, shaking his head in disgust. "It isn't easy to understand, but from what I gather, she finally let go of the dream King Vidar would ever love her and make her our new queen."

"I could have told her that!" Osmond interrupted.

Dalek threw him an irritated look before continuing. "It seems her last plan was to persuade you to make Sorin your consort. He convinced her they would rule together in your stead. When you didn't go for their plan, and with your maturity approaching, they decided to risk acting by force."

Dalek seemed hesitant to continue and Osmond jumped back in to fill the silence.

"They murdered King Vidar and tried to frame the Royal Guard," he added bluntly.

"Osmond, why don't you let us handle the sharing

from now on?" Trevin suggested with a shake of his head.

"Well, that plan actually worked pretty well," Dalek interjected with disbelief. "Even we were questioning Levi's guilt."

"Except Amira didn't fall for it. Against all of the evidence, she believed in Levi; she believed in all of us," Caeden reminded him. Nuzzling her neck, he placed a gentle kiss there. A tingle passed through her entire body, settling in her core.

"Aye, she did. Our princess is a smart girl," Osmond said, giving her a playful wink. She blushed at the attention.

It was a lot of information to take in and she struggled to find acceptance. Her aunt's betrayal of her had been rough, but her betrayal of Amira's parents was unforgivable. Thinking back, it all made sense: Marcelle's obsession with titles, her fascination with Vidar, her insistence at staying at the palace, and her bizarre relationship with Sorin. It was all plain to see, and yet they had all missed it.

Anger, disbelief, despair, hurt; they all warred for dominance within her. She knew her Guard was trying to give her a moment to come to terms with the information, but she wasn't sure if that was something she would ever be able to do. Her mind was chaotic and her thoughts raced; consequently, it took her a while to notice the strange sensations inside her. She felt tingly and butterflies fluttered in her stomach; she was excited... only she wasn't. Suddenly she understood what was happening; the excitement wasn't hers at all... it was Sorin's. She was terrified as his emotions overwhelmed her. Her breath hitched in her chest and her heart began to pound.

She feared he had found them. As much as she didn't want to have anything to do with Sorin, she needed to know. She closed her eyes and focused on the foreign feelings. It was like sorting through sludge; it was dirty and she felt tainted by mere proximity. Yes, he was definitely excited, but there was still an overwhelming sense of underlying frustration and confusion consuming him. She determined he still couldn't find them.

Then what had caused his sudden excitement? Abruptly it occurred to her: it hadn't been a coincidence he began to get excited at the exact moment her own emotions were in such turmoil. She must have let her defenses slip and projected her emotions to him. It sickened her to realize his excitement was in direct reflection of her pain. Bringing her focus back to herself, she withdrew from his mind and worked to quickly rebuild her walls against him.

She opened her eyes to find the world spinning. She was dizzy from lack of oxygen and was surprised to discover she had been holding her breath. Dragging in a big gulp of air, she glanced around to find five pairs of eyes all fixated on her.

She needed to calm herself, lock down her

emotions, so she did what she had been trained to do and stuffed it all down deep to deal with at a later time. She took a calming breath, let it out slowly, and put on her "princess face."

The tension in the room was thick, but before anyone could question what had happened, she quickly steered the conversation to a new topic. "I want to read through the journal about my mother, if you'll please put that one aside for me."

Caeden leaned forward and whispered in her ear, "You're not getting away that easy. I won't force you right now, but you will share with me what just happened."

She stiffened, but nodded her agreement, thankful for the slight reprieve.

"Dalek, did you find anything at all about the binding ceremony?" she continued.

"Not that I can decipher, Princess, but give us a little more time. We'll find it. I'm sure the answer is in there."

ELEVEN

A commotion in the hallway had the soldiers on instant alert, their weapons drawn. Amira found herself pressed against the wall with Caeden's broad shoulders blocking her view of the door before she'd even realized what was happening.

"We have company," Inaya announced as she burst into the room.

Peeking around Caeden, Amira saw Trevin gently shove Inaya further into the room as he, Murdock, and Dalek all rushed out. Amira held her breath; her heart was pounding so loudly she was afraid she wouldn't be able to hear anything that might indicate a struggle. Inaya crept closer and Amira automatically grabbed her and pulled her into a tight hug, vaguely noticing Caeden slightly shift so his muscular body now shielded them both.

"What's going on?" she whispered to her friend.

"There is a small group of riders approaching; that's all I saw before running to let you know. Maryse, Francine, and the baby are hiding in the back room with Levi. You don't think they found us, do you?" Inaya was visibly shaking and Amira rushed to reassure her.

"No; if it is Sorin's soldiers, they don't know we're here. Just a few moments ago, I felt him; my guard dropped and he slipped in," she confided. Remembering how it felt caused her to shiver, and she felt nauseated. Caeden's body tensed further at her words. She leaned into him and rested her cheek on his back; only then did he relax minutely.

The house was eerily quiet. They waited for what seemed like hours, but was probably only a few minutes, before a sharp whistle rang through the house. The tension in Caeden's body visibly eased, but still he did not put away his weapon or move from in front of them.

Trevin appeared in the doorway, silently motioning his head at Caeden, and then quickly exiting again. Caeden nodded to Osmond, who wordlessly took over his position shielding the females with his body. Amira took note that a lot was being said without a word spoken, until Caeden looked from Amira to Inaya and back before issuing a one-word command. "Stay." Then he was gone.

Amira's eyes narrowed. "Did you hear that? Did he

really instruct us to 'stay' as if we were pets?" she asked Inaya in outrage.

"Stay?" Inaya repeated, slamming her hands to her hips with attitude.

"Now, ladies," Osmond began, intending to placate them, until they turned their attention to him.

"Stay?" they questioned him in unison.

He raised his hands in surrender. Amira had never seen him so nervous; he almost looked scared as they advanced on him. She had to hide her grin.

"Now, ladies," he began again, swallowing roughly. "Captain meant no offense. There could be danger; that's all."

"There had better be danger," Inaya grumbled.

Amira nodded in agreement. Being irritated was much easier than being afraid; plus, it was amusing to watch grumpy old Osmond become flustered by a pair of tiny females.

"He just didn't want you two to run out there and do some foolish girl thing..." He trailed off, realizing by Inaya's indrawn breath and Amira's raised eyebrow that he had said the wrong thing. "Lord, put me up against ten fighting-mad males, but deliver me from two angry females!"

Caeden joined Trevin at the front door where he had detained their unexpected company. He realized their visitors were individuals both he and Trevin had known for practically their entire lives, but at that point they were reluctant to trust anyone and Trevin had allowed only one member of the group to approach: Jericho, Velius's long-time stable master. The other two members of the group, forced to remain standing at the front gate, were the stable hand, William, and Jericho's daughter, Sadie.

Caeden struggled to quell his frustration at seeing her. Sadie had been his persistent admirer for a while and he had neither time nor patience to deal with the drama that usually accompanied her. He turned his attention back to her father and brusquely demanded, "State your business."

"Captain," he bowed his head in respect, "forgive the intrusion, but there is word our princess is missing or possibly even deceased. We are one of the search parties on the lookout for her. We are hoping to locate her before Lord Sorin's soldiers find her." The tension in Jericho's body melted away. "We didn't expect to find you here, but I can tell by your lack of concern that our fears are for naught, thank the angels."

Neither soldier confirmed his suspicions, just silently waited.

"No one is sure exactly what is happening, but I'm relieved the princess is no longer under Lord Sorin's guardianship. He's bad news, that one. I won't bother you further, but if we can be of any assistance, we'd be honored to help."

Caeden looked to the others to find them nodding

in agreement. He made the decision and took a step back, inviting them into Murdock's home. "I think you may be able to provide us with some information that would be useful." He led them to the makeshift conference room.

After receiving the all clear, Amira and Inaya marched in from the adjoining sitting area. He arched his brow at Amira in silent question, only to watch her eyes flash silver and her eyebrow arch mockingly in return. He knew he should be concerned by her obvious anger, but he couldn't suppress his grin at her show of defiance. He loved it when she displayed her inner fire.

His grin seemed to irritate her more and she slammed her hands onto her hips and questioned, "Stay?"

Behind him, Trevin let out a weary sigh at the attitude being thrown out by both females. Caeden's grin turned into a full smile, but before he could respond, his name was squealed in a high-pitched voice. He turned to see Sadie running toward him and was barely able to brace as she launched herself at him. He was beginning to regret inviting them inside.

Sadie wrapped herself around him tightly and sobbed, "I'm so glad you're okay, I was so worried about you!"

He reminded himself to be patient with her as this was a difficult time for everyone and Sadie had always been an overemotional female; no doubt she was afraid and in need of comfort. He patted her back awkwardly, wishing Levi were available so he could push this duty off on him. Levi was much better at this sort of situation.

He struggled to disentangle himself without hurting her and was able to put enough distance between them to get a clear view of her face. There was no doubt Sadie was a beautiful female. She had big blue eyes, an angelic face, a sinfully curvy body, and she was always eager to please, but as usual, he felt no spark of interest in her. He noticed she bore dark circles under her eyes and looked worn-out.

"How are you holding up?" he asked in concern.

"Much better now that I'm with you," she purred, and leisurely rubbed her hand down his chest.

So much for concern; now he was just irritated. Grabbing her wrist to stop her caress, he heard a small gasp and his eyes snapped up to meet cloudy gray ones across the room. Amira bit her bottom lip and quickly looked away, but not before he recognized the hurt and confusion on her face.

Sadie brushed her body against his invitingly. He closed his eyes and searched deep inside himself for the strength he needed not to snap. His jaw clenched in frustration at the idea of Amira being hurt or feeling insecure. He had gently made his disinterest known to Sadie previously, but she had gone too far. He opened his eyes and made sure she could see his anger shining through.

"Sadie, I am glad you are uninjured, but you do not have permission to touch me. Ever. Are we clear on that?" he said in a low growl.

"I...I...," she stuttered.

"Yes or no?"

"Yes," she whispered.

"Good, now go have a seat by Francine," he dismissed her, pointing to the other side of the room where the females were making themselves comfortable. Amira smiled at something Inaya was saying, but her posture was rigid and the expression looked forced. She lifted her head as Sadie approached and something indistinguishable flashed in her eyes. They were immediately drawn to his; the compulsion to go to her was almost undeniable. He made himself look away before he gave in, as duty demanded his attention.

Jericho and William, who had already paid their respects to the princess and greeted the other females, now awaited him to join them at the table with the other Royal Guard members.

Caeden immediately began questioning them about the comings and the goings of Sorin and his soldiers. They were able to provide the Guard with information about the regular patrols Sorin had instituted since their escape, even knowing their rotation, schedules, and destinations. Working in the stables had given them quite the advantage when it came to obtaining information.

Caeden wasn't surprised to learn Sorin had

secluded himself within the palace, surrounding himself with his most trusted soldiers and allowing little access to him. It made it more difficult, if not impossible, to find him and end this quickly.

"They're planning something." Jericho's voice dropped and he shot a quick look across the room before continuing. "There is an excitement in the air, and the soldiers are buzzing about something, but I haven't been able to piece it together yet. Whatever it is, I have a gut feeling it isn't good."

"I've noticed it, too," William added. "The soldiers are being extra cautious about what they say in front of me lately. I thought I overheard something about a demonstration, but I can't be sure. When they noticed me, all talking abruptly stopped."

"Trevin and I will see what we can find out tonight," Caeden said, receiving a nod in confirmation from Trevin. He took a moment to consider his next course of action; he didn't like his choices, but decided to impose upon the men even further anyhow. "Your information has been invaluable to us, and I appreciate your service and loyalty, but I'm afraid I'm going to have to ask more of you. I'll understand if you deem the risk too great."

He paused to allow the two men to absorb what he had said so far. "You are both in a unique position to come into contact with a large number of our people without drawing attention or suspicion. We mean to evacuate as many as we can to get them out of harm's way. Will you help us?"

A calculating look entered Jericho's eyes as he thought it through. "There are very few of our people left inside the palace: a handful of chambermaids, the steward, and a couple of kitchen assistants. Most were dismissed when Sorin took up residence. Outside of the palace, there are quite a few families, field workers, and tradesmen. To these, it will be rather easy to spread the word, but the ones inside of the palace may prove to be more difficult."

"Do what you can. There is an emergency escape tunnel in the palace wall at the northeast corner; we will evacuate the kingdom through it tomorrow night. Get with Dalek and Murdock to set up the arrangements."

With his duty seen to, Caeden was eager to address personal matters. Thanking Jericho and William for their assistance, he quickly called the discussion to a close with a brief reminder for Trevin to get some rest.

Throughout the entire conversation, his eyes had repeatedly wandered across the room, but not once had she glanced his way. For years, he'd watched her eyes drift to him whenever they were in a room together, but that afternoon she had completely ignored him; it was unacceptable.

TWELVE

"Amira, honey, come here," Caeden demanded clearly from across the room.

She looked around, shocked, as all eyes swung between her and Caeden. Surely he wasn't speaking to her? But there he was, muscular arms crossed in front of his chest, looking straight at her with determination shining in his eyes. His behavior confused her.

By the way he had barely acknowledged her since their guests had arrived, she had assumed he wanted to keep their relationship hidden. It had hurt her feelings, but she trusted he had his reasons. The hardest part of the afternoon for her had been their physical distance; she had gotten used to his constant touch. Much to her displeasure, she felt bereft without it.

Now he was not only openly acknowledging her, but staking his claim as well.

She sent him a questioning look, but he only cocked an eyebrow in response. The next move was hers.

"Please excuse me," she said to the ladies.

Francine and Maryse had lost interest, having already accepted her relationship with Caeden, and were back to coddling Elijah. Inaya shot her a wink, and Sadie sat frozen with her mouth hanging wide. Amira knew it made her an awful person, yet she couldn't help but enjoy Sadie's reaction.

She slowly made her way over to him, taking her time to appreciate his magnificent form, his broad shoulders, thick-corded arms, and lean hips. Color rose in her cheeks, and heart pounding, she hesitated just a few feet in front of him.

"Yes, Caeden?" she asked softly, worrying her bottom lip between her teeth.

He reached out quickly, one arm coiling around her waist, the other at the side of her neck, pulling her body tightly to his.

"The princess needs some fresh air," he informed the room, dragging her behind him and out the back door.

He didn't stop until he had her safely in the protection of the trees, hidden from view but close enough to the cottage in case of danger. Placing her directly in front of him, he lifted her chin with his calloused fingers.

"She means nothing to me, nor does any other

female. You will cease being upset and will not allow another female to upset you again," he commanded firmly.

"Caeden, I..." She trailed off, unsure how to respond. She was having difficulty concentrating with his impressive form looming over her, and it was a bit unnerving being the sole focus of his attention. She took a step back, intent on putting distance between them in an effort to clear her mind, but Caeden was unwilling to accept that. His arms immediately snaked around her, bringing her body flush with his.

"And you will not shut me out. If you're mad, say you're mad. If you need to yell, you can do that too, but you will not close yourself off from me. You wanted to be mine, and you are. You. Are. Mine. You can't take it back," he said fiercely.

"I don't want to take it back," she answered quickly, and his shoulders relaxed slightly.

"Then talk to me, Amira," he said softly.

She sighed, then began, "I'm not mad at you. I'm mad at me." She tried to collect her thoughts. "I hated seeing Sadie touching you. It hurt," she admitted softly as his arms tightened around her. "It made me doubt myself, it made me jealous, and it made me so darn mad I wanted to pull her off you by her hair and put to use the moves you taught me in our lessons." Amira had to unclench her fists before her nails cut into her palms.

Caeden chuckled as he placed a kiss against her forehead.

"It's not funny, Caeden! It's shameful. I shouldn't have violent thoughts toward my people."

"Amira, you're always so hard on yourself. Your feelings are only natural, give yourself a break. If another male had his hands..." He didn't finish his sentence; instead, he shook his head, his eyes closing and jaw clenched. Amira ran her finger lightly down his tight jaw before seizing the opportunity to brush his hair from his face. His eyes popped open and his piercing gaze held her captive. "I'd kill him," he promised.

Amira sucked in a deep breath; she knew he wasn't lying.

"I don't want anyone else," she assured him honestly.

She found herself with her back pressed against a nearby tree, Caeden's lips pressed firmly to hers and his tongue caressing the seam of her lips, demanding entrance. She instantly complied and lost herself to his devastating kiss. It was unlike any they had shared before; it was fierce, urgent, and... hungry. Her fingers tangled in his hair; her body pressed tightly against his, and yet it still wasn't close enough. She needed more.

His hands urgently roamed her body, kneading and caressing, causing the desperation inside her to grow. His hands slid to her backside, grabbed tightly and pulled her hips more firmly to his hardness.

Instinctively, she hopped up, wrapping her legs around his waist and allowing him to support her weight; her only thoughts were of getting closer to him.

Their lips broke apart only to take in a much needed breath of air. He buried his face in her neck and nibbled and sucked a path to her shoulder. Her breath caught and a moan ripped from her throat as her body moved restlessly against his. A fierce growl met her ears, causing tingles throughout her body. His face was pressed into her shoulder, his breath panting against her sensitive skin, no longer kissing her.

"Caeden?" Her voice was breathless and husky. She wiggled her body against his, driven by a compulsion to ease her aching need.

"Shh...," he soothed, one hand petting her hair. He raised his head and met her eyes. "We have to stop now."

"I need...," she started, trying to explain what her body was screaming for, but was unable to find the words for these new foreign feelings.

Another growl tore from Caeden's throat and his lips slammed down to hers in a soul-stealing kiss, which promised so much more, but ended all too soon.

"I know what you need, Amira," he whispered roughly against her lips. "I will make you mine in every way, but not here. Not like this. You deserve better and I will make sure you get it," he vowed. Slowly, he let her legs fall back to the ground and held her steady until she could support her own weight.

Amira focused on steadying her breathing; her body was achy and her blood raced.

"Now that that's settled," he began after a few minutes of silence, suddenly looking serious. "How did I earn your anger before Sadie?"

Amira's mind still hadn't caught up and she must have given him a confused look because he explained further. "You were already furious when you entered the sitting room."

"You commanded me to 'stay' like a dog!" she remembered, indignant once again.

"Princess, it is still my duty to see to your protection. I will not always have the time to explain myself or state my orders into a polite request. Your safety and well-being will *always* be my top priority, and your feelings will have to come second. I need you to understand and trust me."

He looked so intense and sincere, she was forced to concede, giving him a nod in affirmation. Caeden shot her a grin.

"Good, because if you ever decide to disregard one of my orders, I'm going to spank that pretty little backside of yours."

She was too shocked to respond. She knew she should probably be worried because he sounded absolutely serious. If nothing else, she should be offended, but she couldn't deny what she was actually feeling was far different; it could only be described as excitement or anticipation. The memory of his hands grabbing and kneading her bottom only minutes earlier had her breath quickening and her cheeks flaming.

Caeden watched the different expressions dance across her face. With a satisfied grin, he bent down and kissed her possessively. "That's my girl," he whispered against her lips, and she shivered. "Time to get back," he said as he clasped her hand and led her back into the cottage.

Thirteen

Amira awoke with a start, instantly reaching for the comfort of Caeden's strong embrace. This was only their second night sleeping beside one another, but already she had begun to rely on his presence. Yet her hand met the cold empty space where he once slept. Heart pounding, she shot to a sitting position in a panic, her eyes scanning the room.

More awake, she remembered he had told her of his and Trevin's plan to scout the palace. His hopes were to find a way to end all the conflict quickly and quietly before anyone else was hurt. They'd lain together in bed, discussing their hopes and fears and planning for the rough days ahead. Caeden had said he knew it was a long shot for him to be able to get to Sorin and end it tonight, but he was determined to try. She sent a prayer for the angels to watch over him and bring him back safely.

She lay back down and thought over the evening. She was really enjoying her stay, helping to cook and clean, cuddling with the baby, and spending downtime with her Guard. For the first time, she felt like she belonged, but with that came overwhelming grief and guilt. Her father was gone; her kingdom taken over. The island had suffered a major natural disaster; her people had been hurt, killed, and left homeless, and the future of the entire island was uncertain. It felt wrong of her to find any contentment and peace at this time.

It was still early in the night, but there was no point in her trying to find sleep again. She knew her mind wouldn't be able to settle, and if it did, it would only lead to more nightmares. She had gotten pretty good at guarding herself and blocking Sorin when she was awake, but while asleep, her defenses were down and she was vulnerable. Thankfully, he had not come to her again in her sleep, but even in slumber she could feel his anger, his pain... his depravity seeping through the bond they shared.

Needing to do something productive, she climbed out of bed, pulled on a robe, and went in search of a cup of hot tea and her aunt's journals.

～

"Trouble sleeping?" A rough voice asked, startling her from her analysis of the journals in front of her. They toppled to the floor with a muted thud as she yelped, covered her racing heart with her hands, and stared at the man leaning in the doorway.

"Careful, or everyone else will have trouble sleeping as well with all of that noise," he said with his signature sexy grin.

Before she even gave her body the command to move, she found herself halfway across the room.

"Levi!"

His strong arms didn't hesitate to wrap around her and pull her into a tight hug. "Well hello, darling," he said in his flirty drawl, making her giggle.

She pulled back and looked him over from head to toe and back. "You look great."

"That's what I hear." He winked, causing her cheeks to flame, and she was unsure how to respond. "May I sit with you a while, Princess?"

"Should you even be out of bed?"

"Francine would have my as—behind, if she knew," he said, catching himself before swearing. "But luckily, that evil female has to sleep sometime. You won't tell on me, will you?"

Amira now understood how he had all of those females chasing after him, eager to do anything to please him. His sexy, pleading look was near irresistible.

"That look won't work on me, mister." She tried to be firm, but a twitch of his pouty lips had her giving in helplessly. "Fine, but you have to sit and rest; otherwise we'll both feel the wrath of Francine."

It was Levi's turn to laugh, which must have

caused him pain because he clutched his middle and winced. Amira wrapped her arms around him and tried to help him to the couch, but her tiny frame couldn't support much of his weight. They eventually made it over and collapsed together.

"Captain is a lucky man," he said sincerely. She blushed but couldn't help the grin spreading across her face. "Osmond caught me up to speed... I'm so sorry for your loss, Princess. I..." His voice cracked with emotion. Needing to comfort him, Amira placed her hand in his.

Levi had to clear his throat and take a deep breath before continuing. "Your family has always had my loyalty, but you, Princess, now have my love and eternal gratitude. Your faith and trust in me..." He shook his head, struggling to find the words. "I'm completely humbled." Her eyes filled with tears at his words, but remained locked on his beautiful green ones. "I need you to know there is nothing in this world I wouldn't do for you."

"Thank you," she whispered in return, processing the weight of his words.

He nodded and wiped the tears from her cheeks with his calloused thumb. "Now you better dry these tears before Caeden comes back and decides to murder me first and ask questions later." He smiled to lighten the mood, but was only half joking.

"Oh, he's not that bad," she defended. Levi cocked a questioning eyebrow in response, and she giggled.

Okay, so maybe he could be a little overprotective, she admitted to herself.

"So, what are you working on here?"

"Marcelle's journals," she answered, reaching down to snatch the two she'd been comparing from the floor. "I think I might have found something! You know how Marcelle hadn't accepted an apprentice and, in fact, had stopped training healers altogether? I've discovered why."

She opened the older-looking of the two and pointed to a specific passage. "Marcelle had a vision of a great healer, a 'natural healer' coming forth and taking her place as Supreme Healer, 'removing her from power' and taking her place within the kingdom. Marcelle was driven by ego and swore to prevent this from becoming reality. She took steps to suppress all other healers, but the vision continued to plague her. A lot of this doesn't make sense to me, but she often wrote about a great power capable of restoring 'natural balance.'"

"That's interesting, Princess, but—"

"Amira."

"What?"

Sighing, she explained, "Look around you, I have no kingdom—"

"You will have it back," he stated fiercely, making her smile briefly.

"Yes, I will, but my point is, here we are sitting on a couch together in the middle of the night talking... like regular people. There are no pretenses... just us. I don't have to be just the princess. I can be Amira," she finished softly.

Levi gently took her hand in his and gave it a squeeze. "I hear you," he said softly and by the look in his eyes, she knew he did. "So, Amira," he said after a brief silence, giving her his unintentionally sexy grin, "how will this help us now?"

Amira had to pull her attention from the distraction of Levi's handsome face and make herself concentrate on his question.

"Well," she began, pulling out the newer-looking of the two journals and searching for a certain passage to show him, "about a hundred years ago, Marcelle found her, this 'natural healer.' I haven't found the details, but Marcelle claimed to have successfully changed the female's fate by changing the course of her life."

"But she didn't kill her? The female lives?"

"Yes! And if we can get to her, she may have the power to undo this binding and find a different way to support the shield!" Amira said, unable to hold back her excitement.

"But who is she? How do we find her?"

"That's the best part, we've recently been introduced! It's the new scout, Kearney."

"THE ICE PRINCESS!"

The shock in Levi's voice startled her. "Shh! Lower your voice; you'll wake the entire house."

"Sorry." He shook his head as if trying to clear away

his stupor. "How can Kearney be this great and powerful healer?"

"Well...," she began hesitantly, unsure of the problem. "Marcelle mentions her again in her last journal. She says, 'Tonight we celebrate the departure of my greatest threat. Tomorrow she will begin her journey, only to discover her ending. The last piece of the plan will be completed and she will be a threat no longer.' Those words were written the night of the scout's launch."

"Hell, that doesn't sound good." He frowned.

"No, it doesn't. We need to get to her immediately, before it's too late." Helpless worry churned in her stomach. "Ummm... it sounds like you know her well. What did you call her? The ice princess?"

"Yeah, I knew her, or at least I thought I did," he answered on a sigh, "but that was a long time ago."

"Why do you call her that?"

Levi actually looked embarrassed as he mumbled, "She's untouchable and cold as ice."

"She turned you down, huh?" Amira asked with a knowing grin.

"It's complicated," he grumbled.

"I bet," she laughed.

"Look at you, being all brave and lippy." He grinned, then lunged for her. Before she could even yelp, he was on her, tickling her unmercifully. She squirmed and giggled helplessly, trying to keep quiet and not wake everyone.

They played until they found themselves in a tangle of limbs in a heap on the floor beside the couch, both grinning and out of breath.

"Francine will be so mad at us!" Amira chuckled.

"Let's not tell her." He winked.

"Deal."

"Come on, up you go," Levi said, hauling himself off the floor and bending to lift her up as well.

"Don't you hurt yourself more," she admonished sternly.

"Looks like you can be pretty mean yourself."

"Me? I'm never mean!" she indignantly replied.

"Don't worry, you can make it up to me." He pushed her to a sitting position at the end of the couch and proceeded to stretch out, lying with his head in her lap. "You can play with my hair while you read to me," he informed her.

"Females spoil you, don't they?"

"Naturally." He smirked.

She pinched him playfully on his muscular abs.

"Hey! Take pity, I'm a tired old man."

"Yeah, you are."

"See! I told you that you were mean."

"Hey, I was just agreeing with you."

"Well, now you can play with my hair for twice as long. Start reading, darling. We have a lot to figure out."

She was learning it might just be easier to give in to Levi.

Fourteen

S he has nightmares," Levi whispered, opening one eye to peek at Caeden, who was leaning against the door watching them.

"I know." He sighed heavily.

"Did you kill the sorry bastard?"

"Not yet, but I will."

The scouting expedition hadn't gone as well as he'd hoped. He hadn't been able to get near Sorin and the need to slowly and painfully destroy the man burned deep in his gut. He looked down at his bruised and bloody knuckles, taking satisfaction in the fact that the evening hadn't been a total waste. He and Trevin had been able to get their hands on one of Sorin's higher-ranking officers who, with a little persuasion, was more than willing to share every bit of information he knew. Jericho and William had been right; Sorin was planning something, and he had three days to figure out how he was going to prevent it without Amira finding out.

With heaviness settling in his chest, he looked at the tiny female sleeping curled up at the end of the couch. He couldn't lose her. There was no way to change what had already occurred, but he swore to himself right then that he'd spend the rest of his life making damn sure nothing happened to her again.

"Intel?" Levi asked, drawing his attention away from the sleeping Amira.

"We've got enough for Trevin to organize a strategy and get our forces prepared," he answered vaguely, then scowled at Levi. "You want to get off my female now?"

"Not yet, but I will," he said, throwing Caeden's words back at him.

Caeden watched Levi gently lift himself off and away from the princess. He still looked pale and he'd lost a little weight, but it was good to see his strength returning. Levi stopped next to him beside the door and turned to look at Amira.

"She's a lot different than I thought."

Caeden wasn't sure if Levi was talking to himself or not, but he answered with a "Yeah" anyway.

Levi turned his attention to Caeden, leveling him a serious look. "Don't screw this up, brother. If you do, I might be tempted to rethink my views on monogamy."

Caeden couldn't suppress the growl rumbling in his throat, the only warning Levi would get. Although Levi had a reputation for lax morals when it came to females, Caeden knew he could trust Levi around Amira. But that wouldn't stop him from teaching Levi a lesson if he weren't careful.

"Don't screw it up," he repeated, clapping his hand on Caeden's shoulder.

"I won't," Caeden promised between clenched teeth.

"See that you don't. She's..." He turned to look at her again, as if searching for the right word. "Special," he finished before making his way from the room.

"Yeah, she is," he agreed softly. It was time to take her back into his arms where she belonged. He gently lifted her off the couch; she was so small and fragile. He held her close and grinned as she instantly snuggled closer, wrapping her arms around him. Nothing in his life had ever felt so good; well, that wasn't true. Holding her in his arms while kissing and touching her gorgeous body felt really damn good, too.

Earlier, it had nearly been impossible for him to call a halt to their lovemaking. His body still ached with need of her. He remembered the way she tasted, her sexy moans as she rocked her sweet body against his, and the feel of her firm butt clutched in his grip as they had done their best to meld their bodies into one.

He had to stop these thoughts or he'd never be able to just lie beside her. His body was already responding fiercely, just from the memory.

"Caeden?" she whispered, her voice husky from sleep. His body tightened even more with need.

"Yeah?"

"How did it go?" she asked, nuzzling his neck.

"Could have gone better, but it was fine," he said, having a hard time concentrating.

"Okay. I'm glad you made it back safely."

That statement caught his attention as he carefully laid her on the bed and crawled in behind her, wrapping his front to her back and holding her close.

"Were you worried?" he asked, placing a soft kiss to her hair because there was no way he couldn't.

"A little," she admitted softly, causing his chest to tighten.

He hated that he had caused her any amount of distress, but it felt amazing to have the care and affection of this extraordinary female. "No need to worry, I'm right here," he reassured her.

She was quiet a minute before she softly whispered, "I think I found something helpful in Marcelle's journals." Her words were slightly slurred with exhaustion and he was sure she was at least half-asleep.

"That's great, but rest for now. We'll discuss everything in the morning." He pressed another kiss to her hair and closed his eyes. There was so much wrong in their world, but in that one moment, his world was perfect.

A soft moan from her own lips startled her into consciousness. She had been dreaming about being back in the woods with Caeden, wrapped in his embrace. The dream had felt so real; it left her body burning with need. Her breath came quickly, her skin tingled with excitement, and her core ached for fulfillment.

A warm hand squeezed her left breast as a calloused thumb slowly circled her nipple. Amira's eyes shot open and she barely caught the whimper of pleasure that threatened to escape her lips. She was immediately aware of her surroundings. She was in her borrowed bed at Murdock's home with a warm and delicious-smelling Caeden wrapped around her from behind. His strong arm was banded around her, securing her close to his body, and his hand cupped her breast, inciting a new and slightly frightening feeling inside of her.

Their legs were tangled together comfortably. She could tell by his even breathing that he was still sleeping soundly. Amira was warm and protected, lying there with Caeden. She should have felt blissfully content to lie like that forever, but she wasn't. She was restless and needy. Her body screamed for an unknown release.

She wiggled gently, not wanting to wake him, but needing to find ease for her discomfort. Her backside brushed against his front and his reaction was instantaneous. His hand tightened on her breast, drawing her body even closer to his as he pressed his hard manhood firmly against her bottom. There was no stopping her moan, and she was shocked to hear his echoing groan and feel his lips brush against her sensitive throat. His hips flexed against hers once more before his body tensed and his muscles locked. She knew he had awakened. He began to pull away.

"No. Stay, please," she begged, grabbing his arm.

He hesitated and she could tell he was waging an inner battle. Needing to convince him, she rubbed her bottom against his hardness purposefully; that seemed to help sway his decision. He surrendered with a deep growl.

He brought his mouth to her neck and wordlessly trailed gentle kisses down her throat. The kisses quickly turned more demanding as his hands roamed her body, finally settling on her hips, pushing and pulling, keeping rhythm as their bodies ground against one another.

Amira turned her head, craving his kiss; their lips met in an explosive clash of tongues, teeth, and desperation.

"Caeden," she whispered in a plea against his lips. She couldn't say more and wasn't sure what she needed to ask him for, but he seemed to understand.

He kissed her deeply as his hand slipped from her hip down to the front of her body, sliding beneath the edge of her sleeping pants, past her lower belly to her slick core. His growl of satisfaction rumbled through the room. She trembled in excitement. His touch was like electricity tingling through her, sparking exactly where she needed.

"Damn, you're perfect," he breathed in her ear. His finger slid lower, exploring where she had never been touched before and discovering the very heart of her. Slipping through her slick folds, he caressed her delicate nub, sending tremors of raw pleasure shooting through her entire body. The sweet torture built and became so intense it was frightening. She felt like she was coming apart inside. Her whimper was half pleasure, half fear.

"Shh, I've got you." His husky voice soothed her. "Let go for me. I've got you."

Fear fading, she relaxed and let the sensations consume her. Pleasure exploded inside her, stealing her control. Back arching, she clung to him as she cried out in ecstasy.

Breathless, she came back to herself to find Caeden watching her intently, softly stroking the sensitive skin of her lower belly. Embarrassment overwhelmed her. Rolling further into him, she hid her face in the crook of his neck.

"Look at me," his whispered softly, running his fingers through her hair.

Shaking her head, she denied him.

"Amira, look at me," his husky voice commanded.

Tentatively, she drew back and peeked at him through lowered lashes.

"That was the most beautiful thing I have ever seen," he praised her.

Love burst through her chest. Fearlessly, she arched forward, bringing her mouth to his in a fervent kiss. Her passion was quickly rekindled as he kissed her with the same urgency.

Abruptly, he pulled away, putting distance between their bodies. Craving his nearness, she tried to pull him back to her, but he held firm.

"We need to stop," he panted.

Pulling away from her took more discipline than he was aware he possessed, but he had to stop while he still could. Desire slipped from her eyes to be replaced with hurt. Chest aching, he pulled her into his arms and kissed her forehead. He had to make her understand.

"Amira, there is nothing in this world I want more than to be inside of you right now, but it has to be right for you. I won't dishonor you." His words and his eyes pleaded with her to understand.

"You want to be inside of me?" she questioned softly.

"Of course I do." His answer came out a little harsher than he had intended, but his body was still worked up and he was barely controlling the urge to take her and damn the consequences.

Instead of being upset by his tone, she smiled brightly up at him. His chest clenched and he had to kiss her. Between kisses, he answered her question once again, this time tenderly and reassuringly. "Of course I want you."

"I'm yours for the taking, Caeden," she whispered shyly. She must have seen him gearing up to deny her, because she quickly kissed him once again until he forgot his argument. Pulling away, she continued, "Being with you is right for me. It could never be dishonorable."

He could see the conviction in her eyes and knew she meant exactly what she said, but still, he needed to give her one last chance to change her mind. "We can wait until you're ready."

"I am ready," she assured him.

Boldly, she grabbed his hand and brought it back to her body. He could not resist as she rubbed his hand down her silky skin, pressing it intimately to her heated, liquid core. His control snapped at the sweetness she offered. Their mouths met in a frenzy and her fingers dug into his skin as her hand frantically roamed his body.

With the last of his willpower, he forced himself to leisurely stroke her wet folds, every move deliberate to prepare her for his invasion into her body. He watched her every response closely as his fingers explored further, finding her entrance with a tentative stroke. Her breath caught in her throat as she moaned irresistibly. Her hips rolled instinctively and he almost lost it.

"Your body is ready for mine," he said, his voice rough with desire.

"Yes." It hadn't been a question, but she answered anyway.

Their lower bodies were pressed firmly together, separated only by a thin layer of clothes. Caeden braced himself above her, looking down at the most beautiful creature in existence. It was unbelievable that she was his. Heart hammering, he grabbed a lock of her silky hair and watched as it passed through his fingers, taking a moment to collect himself.

Bringing his attention back to her, he asked solemnly, "Are you sure?"

She pressed her lower body against his in response, lifting her face to his for a hungry kiss. He gave in to her demand briefly before pulling away.

"Amira, you have to give me the words. I need to be sure this is what you want. You are mine, and this will happen, but it doesn't have to be now."

"I've waited years to be yours, and I don't want to wait a moment longer," she breathed; her voice was husky and low, but confident.

That was all he needed. Bringing his lips to hers, he resumed their desperate kisses and rebuilt their urgent need. Amira's restlessness increased, and suddenly it was crucial to be skin to skin. She must have understood his need because she immediately assisted him in removing their clothes.

He paused to stare down at her exquisite form, and he knew she was embarrassed, but she bravely stifled the urge to hide herself from him.

"You're incredible," he whispered as his intense eyes held hers.

She rewarded him with a shy smile that would have dropped him to his knees if he'd been standing. He gave her one last kiss before pulling back and watching his hand caress her inner thighs, easing them apart. She tensed slightly as he gently pressed his finger into her tight sheath. Needing to distract her, he kissed a trail from her neck down to her breasts. Latching on to the closest sexy, dusky-pink nipple, he sucked as he slowly dragged his finger in and out of her liquid heat. Her back arched and her fingers tangled in his hair, holding him to her chest. He bit down slightly and gave her nipple a soft tug as he added another finger inside her in preparation. Soon her hips were rising to meet his thrusts, demanding more, and he knew it was time.

Slowly, he lowered his body onto hers, careful to keep most of his weight off her. He rubbed his hard arousal through her slick folds, causing her to whimper in pleasure. Her mouth was on his neck, sucking and nipping at his skin. She was so passionate and enthusiastic. As much as he ached to be inside her, he hesitated. He wasn't ready to cause her any amount of pain.

She must have noticed his reluctance, because she whispered, "It's okay. Please don't stop."

"There will be no stopping now. I have to have you, my sweet Amira, but we're going to take this slowly," he assured her.

Gently, he tested her entrance with the tip of his manhood. She was so tight. He prayed his preparation would be enough. His hands shook as he slowly pushed himself inside her, little by little to allow her time to adjust. He could tell she was uncomfortable, and even though it was torture, he stopped his forward progress to take time to ease her by stroking her beautiful body and kissing every inch of her he could reach. He told her how lovely she was and how she drove him crazy, and then he whispered all of the naughty things he wanted to do to her.

Soon, it was she who was demanding he continue. She rocked her hips against him urgently, but he held her firmly in place. He wouldn't rush and risk any unnecessary pain. Completely in control, he slowly rocked in and out, reaching further every time. Coming to the barrier, he placed a gentle kiss to her lips.

"Wrap your arms around me," he commanded.

There was no fear in her silver eyes as she gave him an encouraging nod and wrapped herself around him.

Never breaking eye contact, he roughly whispered, "Deep breath, baby."

He pushed, gently but firmly, and breached her

innocence. Holding very still, he gave her time to adjust. She felt better than anything he'd ever experienced in his life, and he was dying to bury himself deep within her, but he silently vowed he would stay immobile for as long as she needed, even if it killed him. She took a deep shuddering breath and released it slowly, the tension leaving her body as her inner muscles adjusted to his intrusion.

He couldn't withhold his groan of pleasure as those muscles contracted around him. He tried to tell her how great she felt and how honored he was to be her first, her only, but he wasn't sure his words made sense. She must have understood, because she gifted him with a beautiful smile, making his heart hurt.

He buried his face in the hollow of her neck and placed tender kisses and tiny nibbles on her neck and shoulder. Her excitement returned and rose to new heights. She tangled her fingers in his thick hair and pulled until she brought his lips to hers.

Caeden withdrew an inch and slowly rocked back into her, a little deeper this time. Amira responded by arching her back and encouraging him to delve deeper into her aching need. She cried out in pleasure as he once again pulled back, and with a powerful thrust sheathed himself to the hilt. He worried he would lose his mind; she felt so good. They kissed urgently as they slowly rocked their bodies together.

Amira was drowning in intensity, never having known this kind of pleasure existed. Part of her wanted to stay like that forever, but a larger part was crying out for something more, something just out of reach.

As if reading her mind, Caeden broke their kiss. "I'm going to make this good for you," he swore roughly before shifting his weight and lifting her hips; she instinctively wrapped her legs around him.

"Good girl, keep them locked tight," he instructed. That was the only warning she received before she felt him pull out to the tip. His strength coiled, and he surged home firmly. This new angle and quick thrusts hit the perfect spot deep inside of her. Caeden reached between their bodies and once again stroked the delicate nub between her folds, causing that elusive something to explode.

There was no containing her screams of pleasure; she was uncaring of who could possibly hear as he continued the brutal pace. Never-ending explosions ignited, and just as she was positive it would blissfully kill her, Caeden surged forward one last time. Seating himself fully, he dropped his weight on her and, with a fierce growl of satisfaction, he found his own release, causing one final burst of pleasure so intense she lost all conscious thought. She had no idea how long they lay there together, but when she finally came back to herself, a beautifully naked Caeden was lying beside her, a gentle hand caressing the curve of her stomach. His breathing still wasn't quite normal. She turned to him, expecting to find a satiation in his eyes; instead she was met with stark intensity.

"Caeden?" She reached for him, slightly afraid.

"You're mine. I don't care whom you are bound to. You belong to me and no one else."

Her eyes filled with tears. She wanted to believe those words desperately, but deep down, she feared they weren't true. As long as she was bound to Sorin, she could never be fully Caeden's.

"That's all I want," she whispered.

"That's how it is," he returned firmly.

She refused to let Sorin ruin the moment for her. "And you're mine too." She smiled brightly.

"Every part of me. Always," he agreed with a grin.

Fifteen

aeden couldn't help but stare down with utter amazement at his female in his arms. *How could she be so absolutely perfect?* he wondered. Her hair was a tangled mess and there were dark circles under her eyes from lack of restful sleep, but he had never seen anything more beautiful than Amira curled up in bed beside him, her gray eyes satisfied and sleepy.

She breathed a contented sigh and cuddled closer. Pride filled him at the idea of putting that blissful look on her face; he had made her first time good for her. The smell of vanilla, which always seemed to linger on her skin, mixed with the scent of their lovemaking and tickled his senses. His body filled with desire again. He had never responded like that with any other female, but with Amira, every smell, every sound, every sensation was more vivid. He was fully alive... complete.

He now understood what King Vidar had meant about filling the unknown hole inside himself. He would not suffer the same fate as Vidar, he swore to himself, tightening his hold on her. He would not lose her. The sacred bonding words once again echoed in his mind, just as they had when they were making love. He suppressed the near overwhelming urge, knowing her age would prevent completion of the bond and unsure of the repercussions it would cause with her already being bound to Sorin. She let out a small groan as he instinctively pulled her closer.

Unfamiliar fear and desperation weighed heavy in his gut. How would he keep her from sacrificing herself once she learned of Sorin's plan? Her sense of duty would demand she trade herself for the lives of her people. He knew there was a chance she would despise him for it and he would never be able to gain her forgiveness, but he would use any means necessary to prevent her; he wouldn't give her a choice. Different ways to restrain her and hold her captive began flowing through his head.

"I'm going to the human world," she suddenly stated, drawing his attention. Her tone was confident, but her bottom lip trapped between her teeth gave away her nervousness and uncertainty.

His immediate instinct was to deny her, but he quickly realized this might be the solution he needed.

"And why would that be?" he asked curiously.

Hope mixed with distrust crossed her face, and he

had to work to suppress his grin. His female was beginning to really know him, and she had expected him to immediately shut her down.

"I have to retrieve the scout?" she stated, but it sounded more like a question. There was no hiding his grin now; she was just too sweet.

"Explain it to me, Amira."

The tension left her body as she rolled to lie propped halfway on his chest. He ran his fingers through her silky long hair, relieved he no longer had to deny himself such luxury. She distractedly traced shapes on his chest with her finger as she informed him that Kearney was a prophesied natural healer and possibly held the key to breaking Amira's bond with Sorin.

She looked him in the eyes, her expression pleading for him to understand. "It has to be me who goes; being royal blood, I'm bonded to all of our people. I should be able to locate her, wherever she is," she finished with determination, her argument sound.

He listened carefully, weighing her plan against the idea of restraining her to prevent her martyrdom, and accepted her way was the best possible solution. The human world was virtually unknown to them, but they had been sending scouts there for centuries. There would be very little threat involved, he decided. He'd vowed not to be separated from her again, and the idea of it tore his insides to pieces, but if the female could free Amira of her bond, then it was necessary she be retrieved. It would also give him the time he needed to prevent Sorin's plan from happening before Amira learned of his new threat.

"We'll make the arrangements and you'll leave today," he stated with a nod.

Deciding the shocked look on her face deserved a kiss, he brought his lips to hers. He had meant for it to be a gentle kiss, but as soon as their lips touched, need exploded inside him and the kiss quickly turned carnal. Her eager moan had him pulling her on top of him fully and grinding his hips to hers.

A harsh banging on the door had Amira scrambling off him and struggling to pull the covers around her.

"Don't go disturbing them, you insensitive oaf!" Francine's muffled admonishment came through the door.

Dalek's mirth could be heard clearly as his voice followed hers. "Aw, don't be like that, Mrs. Francine. I'm just trying to save your husband from being killed."

"That's what that meddling old boar deserves," Francine returned.

"I'm going to hurt them," Caeden grumbled.

The banging on the door started up again. "Captain, just thought you'd want to know, Murdock is probably going to kill Osmond. Then he'll probably go off and make an ass out of himself by getting between the two lovebirds. I don't imagine Trevin will take too kindly to that. But if two members of your Guard are an acceptable loss for undisturbed canoodling time, then I'm just gonna make a snack. Do you want anything while I'm up?" Dalek asked cheerfully.

Amira watched Caeden calmly get out of bed and begin dressing. The view almost distracted her from Dalek's next words.

"Oh, Mrs. Francine, I know you're not as callous as you pretend to be. Come, give us a hug! Hey, where are you going?"

Amira couldn't help giggling. Caeden only shook his head, whether from amusement or frustration, she couldn't tell. She thought she caught sight of a grin as he bent to give her a lingering kiss.

"Duty calls. Take your time and join us when you're ready."

With one last kiss, he headed for the door.

"You really do care!" Dalek greeted him. He tried to peek around Caeden, but Caeden blocked his view and pushed him away from the door. "Morning, Princess," Dalek called.

"Good morning, Dalek," she returned, smiling at his antics.

By the time Amira had cleaned up and dressed for the day, Caeden seemed to have gotten the situation under control. Murdock and Osmond were on opposite sides of the room, but both sported a few new bruises. Murdock was favoring his right side and Osmond had a bloody lip, but everyone was still breathing and it looked like the danger was over. Amira noticed that Murdock paced restlessly around the right side of the room. Her eyes were instantly drawn to Caeden; his back was to her, legs braced apart, and arms crossed over his chest. He was separating Murdock from the rest of the group.

Two steps into the room, a hand reached out and pulled her back to a table beside the door. "Hop up here and watch the show with me, darling," Levi's smooth voice requested.

Amira eyed him carefully where he sat perched on the table. "You want me to sit on top of the table?" she asked incredulously.

"Live recklessly, Princess," he teased, giving her a wink and causing her to blush brightly. He was too charming for his own good. He jumped down and smoothly lifted her onto the table before climbing back up beside her.

"What's going on?"

Caeden was now holding Murdock in place with a hand on his shoulder, telling him something quietly. Murdock seemed to reluctantly agree. Amira wished she could hear what was being said.

"What do you know?" Levi asked.

"Only that Murdock was going to kill Osmond,

Trevin wasn't going to be happy, Francine doesn't like hugs, and Dalek needed a snack."

"Well, that covers most of it," he said with a chuckle. His face turned serious as he told her, "Your girl decided to run off last night."

"My girl?"

"Inaya. Seems she's convinced we have traitors in our army. She didn't like Trevin going out on his own, so she decided to become his backup."

"Inaya left with Trevin?" Amira was shocked; those two barely got along on a good day.

"Oh, fuc—heck no." Amira rolled her eyes at Levi's near profanity. "Trevin would never willingly allow Inaya to possibly place herself in a dangerous situation. In fact, he forbade her from accompanying him, but she followed him."

Amira groaned. "No wonder she ran off! Does he not know her at all? He should know never to try to forbid her from doing anything."

"Apparently, he's pretty dumb when it comes to females."

"Unlike you, right?" she teased him.

"Absolutely," he agreed, completely unrepentant.

She smiled, then asked her next question. "Then why did Murdock go after Osmond? I don't understand."

"Well, I'm not sure if you noticed, but Osmond can be kind of blunt. Murdock was all set to tear off after her, and Osmond stopped him."

"But what did he say to get Murdock so upset?"

"He mentioned that Trevin has incentive to keep her safe and he didn't take into account that he was speaking to her brother when he spoke of them being together."

"Together?" Amira wasn't following.

"Yeah, you know... together," he repeated.

When the meaning dawned on her, she all but shouted, "But they barely get along!"

"Seriously, Princess?" Levi asked in his smooth drawl, giving her his full attention and shooting her another wink. "That's just foreplay for them, darling."

Amira was sure she'd never blushed so deeply in her life and quickly turned her attention back to Caeden. Her mouth instantly dried and her heart raced; he was so incredibly handsome and his attention was completely centered on her. Desire flashed intensely in his ice-blue eyes and her breath quickened in response.

"You all right there, Amira?" Levi asked with a knowing smirk.

"Sure. Wait, what did you ask?" she questioned, giving her head a shake in an effort to clear it.

"I asked if you were all right," he repeated once he stopped laughing.

"Yes, I'm fine, thank you," she said in her princess voice, but ruined the effect by smiling. "So, what will we do about Inaya?" She was trying not to worry about her friend, but she knew Inaya's impulsiveness often led her to trouble.

"There isn't much we can do right now; but don't worry, she's a smart girl. She'll catch up with Trevin and he won't let anything happen to her," he reassured her, giving her hand a comforting squeeze.

Amira knew he was right. Inaya was impulsive, but she was far from stupid. Plus, growing up surrounded by soldiers, she had picked up a thing or two.

"What about Murdock? He's so angry," she whispered. Unaccustomed to her Guard being so candid and at ease in her presence, she was unsure of how to respond.

"Captain will talk him down. Besides, he knows Alyx is at the soldiers' camp. Their brother will guard her... virtue."

"Hands," a low voice growled.

Startled, Amira looked up to see Caeden standing in front of them, staring at their joined hands.

"Aye, Captain," Levi answered with a crooked smile, and released her hand.

SIXTEEN

All right, now that's settled, we need to discuss a different matter," Caeden addressed the room. While the other Guard members pulled chairs closer and settled, Caeden made himself comfortable next to her. Jolts of electricity tingled through her from where his body pressed against hers. Being the princess, she was not used to being touched casually, but even innocent touches from Caeden were having an extreme effect on her.

Caeden quickly informed the Guard of the information about the scout, concluding with an order. "Osmond, you will escort the princess to the human world to locate this female and bring her home."

"No way!" Murdock exploded. "First my sister runs off to join the damn army, and now you're asking me to watch Amira, who is practically my other sister, run off to the human world? No, this is not going to happen. I cannot believe you of all people are suggesting it."

Caeden's body was tense and a muscle ticked in his jaw. *This is not good*, Amira thought. She could tell he was barely controlling his anger. She placed her hand on his arm and let it trail down until she could intertwine their fingers.

"It was my idea, and it's my decision to make," she stated firmly.

"Just as it was Inaya's fool idea to run off after Trevin. That doesn't make it right, but if that is your decision, then I'm coming with you," he returned.

"No, you're needed here," Caeden countermanded.

Amira could see Murdock gearing up to argue more, so she added, "Caeden is right. You have a wife and a new baby. Plus, you and Dalek are needed here to escort the people out of the kingdom tonight."

Murdock let out a frustrated breath before saying, "I don't like it." He looked at Caeden, and it was as if an entire silent conversation took place in a matter of seconds. Amira was unsure of exactly what had passed between the two, but felt she needed to say more. She reached out with the hand that wasn't holding Caeden's and touched Murdock's arm in gratitude and reassurance.

"Murdock, I appreciate your concern, really, but I can do this. I need to do this," she told him softly.

He nodded in understanding.

"There is little to no risk involved with this journey," Caeden informed them. "In fact, the human world might even be safer for her right now."

Amira noticed Levi's rigid posture right before he opened his mouth to question, "What about the threa — Did you just pinch me?" he asked Amira incredulously, covering the sensitive area on his side.

All eyes swung to her. She pasted an innocent look on her face, her hands folded neatly in her lap. "I'm sorry. I'm not sure what you're talking about," she said sweetly.

Everyone seemed to be confused, so she put on a bright smile. She hadn't told Caeden about the threat to the scout, and she couldn't allow Levi to tell him either. Guilt gnawed away at her insides for not disclosing the complete truth, but there was no way he'd let her go if he knew the scout was in danger and, therefore, she would be as well.

"It might not be— Ouch!" Levi had begun again, and she had been forced to interfere once more. That time when she discreetly pinched him, he didn't call her out on it, but instead glared at her. She pleaded with her eyes, praying he would understand. His look promised he would be seeking answers, and they had better be darn good.

"What's your problem?" Osmond questioned gruffly.

"I have a stitch in my side." He didn't sound very convincing; apparently, Levi was a terrible liar.

"Maybe you should go rest?" Dalek suggested, but he shot Amira a suspicious look.

"Don't turn into some wet nurse on me; I'm fine. In fact, I was going to suggest that I accompany the princess as well."

"I don't know, are you sure you're up to it?" Caeden asked hesitantly. Being on Amira's opposite side, he was unaware of their silent communication.

"Like you said, there is very little danger involved," Levi said, meeting Amira's eyes as he kept up her lie of omission.

"Okay, pack up; you leave within the hour," Caeden instructed, before turning to Amira and gently lifting her off the table. "Come," he invited softly, leading her from the room to the bedroom they shared.

As soon as the door closed behind them, Caeden pulled her into his arms.

"How are you feeling?" he asked softly.

Amira was mesmerized by his tender expression. He wasn't even trying to hide his affection. Her heart was heavy, and she suddenly felt like crying. For years she had imagined him looking at her like this and now she could barely believe it was real.

When she realized what he was really asking, her face flamed with embarrassment and she had to look away.

"I am well," she answered shyly.

His fingers at her chin brought her face back to his.

He leaned down, briefly bringing his lips to hers before pulling away.

"Good." His voice was rich and smooth.

Suddenly, he was all business. "Your trip should take no more than seven days; two days of travel each way, and three days of rest and to prepare her to return. We know her itinerary, therefore it should be a rather simple journey. If you have not returned by the seventh day, I will come for you myself," he vowed.

"Caeden—" she began, not sure if she meant to protest or reassure him, but he didn't give her the chance to do either.

"Don't make me come for you."

He grabbed her arms firmly, not hurting her, but clearly illustrating the gravity of his words. "You will come back to me safely," he commanded.

"Always," she answered. Although it hadn't been a question, he seemed to require her agreement, so she gave him the same promise he had made to her.

He took a deep breath and nodded once before releasing her.

"Let's get you ready then."

Caeden waged an internal battle with himself. The closer it came to time for Amira's departure, the less confident he felt about this plan. Logically, he knew it was necessary and most likely the safest course, but his instincts demanded he keep her by his side.

He hated the idea of her going without him and only two guards to accompany her. He knew it might attract unwanted attention if he sent more soldiers with her; that was why the scout only traveled with one guard. But Amira wasn't the scout; she was the princess, the last surviving member of the royal family, and more than that, she was his everything.

He couldn't let himself think about the dangers she might encounter; otherwise, he might give in to the temptation to snatch her and run, forgetting about the kingdom and their people. He would gladly spend the rest of his long life just the two of them, dedicating his life to her happiness and protection. But his honor wouldn't allow him to do that, nor would the princess ever consent or be able to find contentment at the expense of others.

He ran his fingers through his hair in frustration as he paced the small confines of the bedroom, trying to get himself under control. It was almost time to go.

Amira had gone to say her farewells to Francine, Maryse, and the sweet baby, but found herself cornered at the end of the hallway by an agitated Levi.

"When I said I would do anything for you, I didn't mean I would help you recklessly put your life at risk by withholding important information. You better have a damn good reason for me to lie to my captain; otherwise, I'm ending this now."

He was so frustrated that he didn't even bother trying to refrain from swearing at her. Maybe she had asked too much from him. But the course was set, and she was positive it was the right path. An urgent panic was building inside of her; she needed to get to Kearney as soon as possible, and to do so she had to get Levi on her side.

"Please, lower your voice, Levi," she begged, looking around nervously to ensure they were still alone. He took a deep breath and let it out slowly.

"Explain," he snapped, but in a lower voice this time.

"I don't like lying either, especially to Caeden, but you know if he thinks there is any danger, he won't let me go," she tried reasoning.

"Maybe it's best if you didn't," he argued.

"It has to be me, you know that. If Caeden knew, he wouldn't let me go, or he would insist on coming along. He is needed here. Our army, your brothers, need him here." Amira could tell her reasoning was swaying him, but he wasn't quite ready to give in yet. "Besides, the danger isn't even directed at me. Kearney is the one in trouble, and if we don't get to her, there is a good chance she won't survive." *If she isn't dead already.* But Amira wouldn't say that part aloud. "I don't know what history the two of you have, but please, Levi, please help me save her."

Levi stood silently, head down, fingers pinching the bridge of his nose. Amira waited patiently for him to decide. She wouldn't force him to go along with her deception. She held her breath as he lifted his head and stared at her a long moment.

"We tell Osmond as soon as we are on our way so he will be prepared," he finally said.

"Yes, of course," she said with a sigh of relief.

"Okay," he said with determination as he turned to walk away.

"Levi?" She waited for him to turn back to her before continuing. "Thank you for volunteering to come along to protect me."

"Anytime, Princess." His flirty nature returning, he smiled wickedly and winked, causing her heart to flutter in her chest. She stared fixedly as he left. *Levi is devastating to the senses and he knows it,* she thought with an amused grin. Prompting herself back into action, she went in search of her new friends to say her good-byes.

SEVENTEEN

The trip to the dock, which would give them transport to the human world, was distressing for Amira. Twice they'd had to adjust their path to avoid detection from Sorin's patrolling soldiers. She could tell her Guard was eager to engage the soldiers and take back control of their land, but now wasn't the time. They couldn't risk exposure.

The journey took longer than normal and the detour caused them to pass through the Meadow of Spirits. At their approach, something snapped inside her and she was engulfed in a pain so great she wasn't sure how she would survive. She instantly found herself pulled from her mount and sitting in front of Caeden on his, wrapped in his strong arms, her face buried in his neck. He offered her no words of comfort, only held her tight, caressing her back and hair as the grief consumed her.

Images of her father's body being devoured by flames flashed through her mind. She cried until her eyes were swollen and her voice hoarse from her sobs. She vaguely realized it was the first time she'd allowed herself to grieve her father's passing. When her tears were spent, she was left feeling slightly numb, but strangely at peace.

Caeden had taken her to a quiet, secluded area where her Guard had stood watch, allowing her to safely grieve. She looked around at the strong, fearless males who had shown her such kindness and consideration, males who risked their very lives for her and asked for nothing in return. She was completely humbled by each and every one of them. She knew she was undeserving of such loyalty, but was incredibly grateful to have them.

It occurred to her that a month ago, she never would have allowed them to see her so distraught, but in a short amount of time they had become close. Although her father and her aunt were gone, she was no longer alone. Her Guard was now her family.

She wiped her face on her sleeve and searched for the words to express what she was feeling.

"All done then, darling?" Levi asked in his sexy drawl, letting her know words were not needed; they understood.

"Yes, thank you." She smiled timidly.

He winked and led the procession out of the clearing. As each Guard member passed, he paused briefly in front of Caeden and Amira and bowed his head in respect. By the time only she and Caeden remained, tears were once again threatening to fall.

He tilted her chin up and stared into her eyes for a silent moment. He lowered his head slowly and, just before their lips touched, whispered, "I love you."

There was no restraining the tears then as Caeden kissed her tenderly. Her emotions had gone from one extreme to the other. She was so happy, she worried she would burst. He pulled away and wiped her tears.

"No more crying," he insisted.

She nodded in agreement, gathered her courage, and breathed, "I love you, too."

"I know," he said with a sexy smile. "Now, are you ready to continue?"

She nodded again and he spurred his mount forward. She was relieved when he made no move to return her to her own horse. She cuddled into him, savoring the feel of his strong arms around her. She realized how much she was going to miss him, but refused to allow it to depreciate their time together.

Over the last couple of days, the princess had become skilled at blocking herself from him. Sorin had repeatedly tried to gain access to her through their bond, but remained unsuccessful.

Having had a taste of the power flowing through her, and feeling her essence inside of him, it was unacceptable for her to deny him now. He craved that feeling again and was becoming desperate. Nothing else mattered anymore. He had never known that type of energy and beauty existed; now he was driven by the need to possess it, control it.

His hands shook with need and his mind constantly raced. The only time he found any peace at all was when she was asleep; that was the only time she allowed herself to become vulnerable. After the first night, he'd learned to be cautious and refrained from joining their consciousnesses completely and pulling her into a dream state with him. When he had done it before, it had been purely by accident, unaware he had the ability.

But he too had been spending his time wisely, learning and perfecting his skills at controlling their bond. He could always feel the exact moment she lowered her guard. He had learned to use a gentle touch and stay just outside of her consciousness.

She would eventually sense him, but with each try he seemed to be able to stay a little bit longer without detection. Of course, her unconscious mind was full of abstract thoughts and feelings, and was nowhere near as good as her real self, but it was enough to get him by until they could be rejoined.

For days he had struggled to feel anything at all from her; leaving himself wide open to her just in case something slipped through. Then today, the world shifted and was thrown completely off its axis. While in a meeting with his commanding officer, a wave of euphoria crashed into him so hard it brought him to his knees.

Foreign feelings of completeness, love, and serenity, mixed with lust and excitement overpowered him. Lust and excitement he was quite familiar with, but the others, until that moment, he never truly believed were real. It wasn't hard to guess what the princess was up to. Apparently, she had more in common with her aunt than he had first suspected. He wanted to rage, to find a way to punish her for her betrayal, but he was helpless to do anything but feel.

He quickly dismissed his concerned officer before collapsing to the floor and allowing the feelings to overtake him. His mind was at war with the feelings coming through the bond. Different visions and scenarios ran through his mind of what *his* princess must be doing with other males. He imagined her passing herself around to each and every member of the Royal Guard. Letting them defile her in every possible way while she enjoyed every minute of it, possibly begging for more.

Sorin had hungered for her to expose herself to him, but he had never dreamed this would be what was revealed. He had no idea how long he lay helpless on the floor, but it was enough time for him to formulate a detailed and fitting punishment for her treachery and unfaithfulness.

~

Caeden watched the transport carry her further and further from the island. As the distance stretched, so did the hollow, empty feeling inside of him. The urge to go after her and bring her back rode him hard. He forced himself to look away from the vessel, and turned his attention to the two men at his side.

"I trusted you to have a reason for allowing this; now would be the time to explain," Murdock said through his clenched jaw.

Caeden bristled at his tone, but reminded himself it was only out of concern for Amira. Both men were staring at him expectantly. The fact they hadn't cornered him earlier to demand answers was a true testament of their faith and trust in him as their leader. He had hated keeping a secret from his brothers, but he couldn't risk Amira finding out.

"Sorin has hostages," he informed them bluntly. "Trevin and I learned of his plan last night while questioning a member of his inner circle. He plans to spread word of a public execution in two days' time. He has eight hostages: men, women, and children. He will execute them all unless the princess returns to him or someone turns her in."

Both men exploded with curses and threats. Caeden gave them time to vent and come to terms with their situation.

"So you sent her away to protect her?" Dalek guessed when he was able to control his anger enough to converse.

"Yes," he answered simply, giving them time to process his actions.

"That foolish female would have rushed back to the palace to save them without a thought to herself," Murdock thought out loud.

"Okay, let's begin phase two of your plan," Dalek said as he turned to ready his mount.

"Phase two?" Caeden questioned.

"Yeah, the part where we extract the hostages and, hopefully, kill Sorin in the process," Murdock informed him, giving him a slap on the back.

Complete faith and trust, Caeden thought again with a content smile.

EIGHTEEN

Are you out of your ever-loving mind?" Osmond exploded, his voice echoing through the small transport. He wasn't accepting their little deceit well. "I can understand her part in this." Amira winced as he threw his arm out in her direction. "She's female and doesn't know any better!"

Hey! Amira thought, taking offense. She opened her mouth to set him straight, but caught Levi's subtle headshake and the serious look in his eyes. Wisely, she concluded it might not be the appropriate time to try to sway Osmond's views on the gentler sex.

Osmond was so caught up in his rant he had missed their silent interaction and continued, "But you, Levi, are Royal Guard and understand the necessity of complete honesty and the consequences of hiding information from the captain and your brothers, especially regarding our princess. Are you daft? That must be it. Sorin's soldiers must have given you a brain injury that we have been unaware of. Yes, that's what we'll tell him." Osmond grasped on to that idea and seemed to be muttering more to himself at that point. Amira decided it was best to follow Levi's lead and allow Osmond to have this conversation by himself. "That might be enough to save your raggedy hide when Caeden finds out you knowingly put his female in a dangerous situation. I'll stand by you this once, since your brain has been idled, but next time you're on your own. You hear me, boy?"

"I appreciate you graciously understanding," Levi answered, struggling to hide his wicked grin.

"Well, I'm an understanding person," Osmond said seriously.

Amira couldn't help the snicker that escaped her. She realized her mistake when Osmond turned his attention to her.

"And you, young lady, get the excuse of ignorance one time only. If you knowingly put yourself in danger again, I'll bend you over my knee and tan your backside."

The threat shocked her momentarily, but she was learning Osmond wasn't nearly as hard and uncaring as he appeared. His gruffness was actually quite endearing.

"Yes, sir," she answered, bowing her head and doing her best to look contrite.

"Now, Princess, I'm not angry at you," he said, his voice gentling as he crouched in front of her. Her head snapped up in surprise when she realized Osmond was actually trying to console her. Her eyes met Levi's over Osmond's shoulder and he winked, his smile devious. She struggled to hide her own smile and brought her attention back to Osmond. *The big softy*, she thought. "I don't want you to worry; you're not in any immediate danger. I'll take care of you, and Levi, even with his severe brain injury, will do his duty," he tried to reassure her.

"I know you will." And she did. She had complete faith in her Guard.

Nodding, he stood; discussion over.

"Now, where is the food packed? I'm wasting away here," he grumbled.

"Let me get it for you," Amira offered as she stood and walked over to their supplies. Something snapped painfully deep inside of her, and the world suddenly went black.

Sorin had already worked himself into a frenzy by the time Amira remembered to block their bond that morning. His body was in desperate need of a release. He'd grabbed the nearest chambermaid and locked them together in his room for the entire day. With a clear mind and a sated body, he now lay comfortably in the king's bed; his bed, he reminded himself.

His skin tingled and burned deliciously from dozens of bloody scratches across his body. He loved it when they put up a good fight. Yes, today had turned out to be rather satisfying indeed, he decided.

Suddenly, he felt a painful snap deep inside of him, and the world went dark.

The return trip to Murdock's cottage was completely uneventful. A large part of Caeden had hoped they would run into Sorin's patrols again and be forced to engage. He was ready to end the conflict, and if that required them to singlehandedly take out Sorin's army one soldier at a time, he was eager to begin.

They had finished settling their mounts when the sky suddenly turned black, the wind howled, and large pieces of ice began falling from the heavens. Rushing inside for cover, they found Francine and Maryse staring out the window, wearing stunned expressions.

"What's happened?" Maryse asked, rushing into her husband's arms.

"I don't know," he whispered, pulling her to him tightly. They watched in silence as the ice furiously rained down, only to stop completely minutes later. The wind died and the sky cleared. Caeden would have thought he'd imagined it, save for the large clumps of ice littering the grounds and the soft drizzling rain serving as evidence of the strange phenomena.

"Do you think Amira is okay?" Maryse asked in a shaky whisper.

"She better be," Caeden growled and stomped away.

Nineteen

Her head was pounding and she prayed for the bed to stop shaking so the queasiness in her stomach would settle.

"Amira, open your eyes and look at me," a disembodied voice demanded.

Don't they know my head will explode if I open my eyes?

"Come on, girl. Wake up," another gruff voice demanded of her. Why wouldn't they leave her alone?

"Go away, and stop shaking the bed, I don't feel well," she tried commanding, but the words sounded confusing even to her own ears.

"There she is. Come on, beautiful girl, look at me. Let me see those gorgeous gray eyes."

Through her pounding head and her confusion, she recognized that sexy drawl. What was Levi doing inside her bedchamber? Her eyes flew open and instant regret slammed into her as the world spun around her.

"I'm going to be sick," she whispered urgently, covering her mouth.

"Here, girl, do what you need to do," Osmond said, shoving a bucket in front of her face.

Amira didn't have time to feel embarrassed as her stomach evacuated all its contents. When all that was left were dry heaves, Amira found herself propped up against a very concerned-looking Levi. He was rubbing her back soothingly and cooing nonsense in her ear, which actually made her feel better. A terrified-looking Osmond crouched in front of her.

"What happened? Did we crash?" She began to panic.

"No, darling, we're fine and still en route. You passed out when we passed through the shield. How are you feeling? Any better?" Levi asked, his tone low and troubled.

Amira closed her eyes, doing her best to ignore the pounding in her head, and searched deeply inside herself for the connection that bound her to the shield and the island of Cashile. She immediately felt the dark ties that bound her to Sorin. Instinct had her shying away from it, afraid of exposing herself to him. Unlike the sick, malevolent, unnatural bond she had with him, the bond with Cashile was fresh and serene. She searched herself to find that familiar feeling, but to her devastation, it wasn't there.

Fear stole her breath and the pounding of her heart magnified the pounding in her head. What happened? Did passing through the shield negate the blood bond? Her thoughts raced as panic set in. What had she done? A sob tore through her chest and tears began to fall. She found herself pulled into Levi's muscular arms.

"What is it, Amira? Where are you hurt?" He pulled back far enough to frantically scan her face for some clue.

"Th-the b-b-bond, it's gone," she sobbed brokenly.

"What? Darling, calm down. Take a deep breath and tell me again."

She took a deep breath and repeated, "The bond is gone. I can't feel it anymore."

"You're no longer bound to Sorin?" Levi asked in confusion.

She shook her head desperately. "No, that bond is there, but the bond tying me to Cashile, I can't feel it anymore."

"What does that mean?"

"I don't know." Hopelessness began to take over. She had failed her people, her father, and all of the royal family who had carried the bond before her.

"Try again," Osmond's rough voice demanded.

"What?" She was startled out of her inner turmoil.

"Check again, Princess. Why would only Sorin's bond remain? It doesn't make sense."

"I—"

"Please, check again," Levi interrupted.

"Okay." She took a deep breath and focused inside herself. Once again, she immediately felt Sorin's tainted bond, but nothing else. But Osmond was right, it didn't make sense. Instead of shying away from it, she gathered her courage and examined her connection to Sorin.

She felt his darkness, his emptiness that demanded to be filled with the pain and suffering of others. The amount of rage and self-loathing he carried was terrifying and heartbreaking at the same time. Just when she had decided she couldn't handle any more, a familiar sensation stirred within her.

Her hope blossomed. She began to filter through the darkness, disregarding anything that came from him, and... there it was. Her bond with Cashile had become intertwined with her bond to Sorin.

The only explanation she could come up with was by leaving the island and passing through the shield, she had somehow transferred the bond fully to him. She could still access it through him, but he was now responsible for keeping the shield functioning and strong. Why had she not considered the consequences of her departure? For the first time, she was actually grateful for Sorin and their corrupt union.

~

Sorin awoke feeling like he had been trampled by a herd of large animals. His entire body ached and he felt as if the weight of the world rested on his shoulders. Something was different, wrong. He closed his eyes and searched for the peaceful, beautiful, euphoric feeling he had come to associate with the princess, only to find strain, burden, and responsibility. His eyes popped open as fury consumed him. What had she done?

Word of Sorin's plan to force Amira out of hiding with the execution of innocent lives had spread like wildfire, causing fear and panic. The official story from the palace was that the individuals were being punished for the murder of Princess Amira, but, of course, if anyone could provide proof that she still lived, it would prove their innocence and save their lives.

The people were unsure of what to believe, what with the king's recent passing and having not seen the princess in a while. Jericho, William, and Sadie had done their best to reassure the people who remained within the palace walls of the princess's safety, but as they gathered for extraction, the only thing that was clear was the need to be far from Lord Sorin and his soldiers. His depravity and cruelty was apparent to all.

"Where is the princess?"

"Will she surrender herself?"

"Why have you not prevented this from happening?"

"Is Sorin our new ruler?"

"Is this weather indication our shield is failing?"

The questions were being shouted from the crowd, and only served the purpose of instigating more anger, fear, and anxiety.

"Quiet," Caeden raised his voice above the crowd. "Panic will not aid us here. Princess Amira is safe and well. A plan is already in motion to save our people and regain our kingdom, but in order for it to progress, we must first get you all to safety. I regret the need for you to abandon your homes, especially in this abnormal and unpleasant weather, but I assure you it is only temporary."

The turbulent storm from earlier in the day had died down to a continuous drizzle, but the wind brought forth an uncomfortable chill, to which the people of Cashile were unaccustomed.

"Now, we must stay together and move quickly and silently. Once we are outside the walls, you will be escorted north to the temporary shelters that have been constructed. There you will safely await word from a member of the Royal Guard that it is secure to return to your homes. Is that clear?" Caeden paused until he had their agreement. With a final nod he commanded, "Let us move out, and remember to stay together."

The hidden passage was only about a mile from

their starting point, but traveling with civilians by light of the full moon through the woods in the falling rain was difficult and slow. Less than half an hour into the journey, a female fell, shrieking as she twisted her ankle, alerting nearby patrols. Thumping footsteps could be heard thundering toward the group.

Caeden drew his weapon and waited for his enemy's approach. He knew it would take time for the other guards to arrive, with only him leading the group, Dalek bringing up the rear, and Murdock scouting ahead. He prepared to defend his people alone. Only, the enemy never arrived, and the footsteps ceased. Listening closely, he heard muted sounds of a struggle in the near distance: a few grunts and groans, and then complete silence.

Tensing, he eased his breathing and waited to see what would happen next. Everyone stood frozen in anticipation as a lone silhouette emerged from the trees. Caeden immediately relaxed as Alyx's muscular form became clear to him. Excellent, the second part of their plan was already in progress.

Alyx paused briefly to place his right fist over his heart and bow his head in a sign of respect usually reserved for the royal family, before he disappeared once again into the trees. His actions prompted a few shocked murmurs from the crowd, but Caeden motioned for them to continue. The rest of the trip was slow going, but without incident.

Caeden watched as the last of the civilians passed

through the hidden exit to safety. Eagerly, he turned to his men and read the anticipation on their faces. It was time to begin taking back their kingdom.

TWENTY

The first stop on the scout's itinerary was the small human island called Iceland, where she would spend the first several months of her trip acclimating and integrating herself into human society. Their people retained dwellings all over the world for the scout's personal use to make the transition easy and the trip as productive as possible. The Iceland location was the most secluded, located near a dormant volcano miles from civilization.

Amira's head had continued to pound nonstop for the entire two days it had taken them to reach their destination. Along with lack of sleep, she felt ready to drop from sheer exhaustion. By the worried looks Osmond and Levi kept sending her way, she knew she didn't look much better than she felt.

"Not much further, Princess, and we'll find you a

nice comfortable bed to rest in," Levi tried reassuring her.

They had been forced to make camp outside the previous night, and she had allowed them to believe their lack of proper accommodations was responsible for her lack of sleep. She refused to admit she was terrified, not only of making herself vulnerable to Sorin, but also that she would somehow lose her connection to Cashile completely if she didn't remain vigilant.

The guards had taken turns standing watch throughout the night, but she knew neither of them had gotten much rest either. They were all in serious need of a nap and some downtime, but as they approached their destination, instead of finding relief, her sense of unease increased. What had started as slight apprehension was now painful cramps in her stomach, and as the house came into view, she understood why. Something was very wrong. The front door was ajar. The drapes in the windows were torn, giving an unobstructed view of tipped-over and broken furniture. Strange music with a heavy thumping beat could be heard from a hundred yards away. Both Guards dropped their packs and pulled out their weapons.

"Wait here," Osmond ordered, starting toward the house as Levi planted himself in front of her.

"No," Amira argued, catching both males off guard. They turned to stare at her in confusion. "You're not going in there by yourself."

"Princess, you cannot remain out here by yourself," Levi reasoned.

"No, but we can all go in together." She continued quickly before they could argue, "There is no telling what you will find inside and I can help. I'm not as defenseless as I appear. I've been training with Caeden for over a year; I can handle myself."

They stared at her incredulously before turning to look at each other in question. *Fine*, she thought with a sigh, *I'll prove it*. Without giving herself time to think it through, she struck quickly, applying pressure to the sensitive nerve point in Levi's sword arm while grabbing the weapon with her other hand and striking out with her left foot to the back of his knee. As he dropped to his knees, she pressed herself firmly to his back and gently brought the sword to the vicinity of his throat.

"We're wasting time," she complained as Osmond stared silently in shock. She was unsure of Levi's reaction, as she was unable to see his face. Both males remained completely silent. Only then did she question the wisdom of performing her demonstration on the proud male. She lowered the weapon and took a careful step back, watching him warily.

Osmond's bark of laughter drew her attention.

"Holy hell! She did that better than you could've," he scoffed between large belly laughs. "Maybe I should take her inside and leave you out here for your own protection!"

She glanced down to see how Levi was receiving Osmond's playful ribbing. He was still on his knees, but he had turned to face her. The look of awe on his face astonished her.

"Sweet deity in heaven! I adore you, woman," he declared with his hand clutched to his chest for emphasis. "Forget about Caeden and run away with me. I'll build you a cabana on a secluded beach and we can spend the rest of our lives sparring and making beautiful babies together."

He looked so earnest and sounded so hopeful, Amira couldn't help but giggle over his silliness. The pounding in her head and the cramping in her stomach eased as some of the tension left her body. She placed her hand to his cheek and tried to look serious.

"That's a beautiful dream, Levi, but it could never work out between us. Sure, you're gorgeous, but a pretty face will only take you so far. Eventually I'd get tired of always kicking your butt," she teased with a wink, renewing Osmond's hearty laughter.

"I think my heart is broken," he pouted.

"Get your ass up off the ground before some other fool thing pops out of that mouth and the captain ends up breaking something else of yours," Osmond growled playfully.

"I'm not sure I'll ever recover." Levi shot her another pouty look before hopping up.

Retrieving his sword, he turned his attention to

Osmond and was once again serious. "Give the girl a blade and let's do this."

They had all needed that moment of fun, but playtime was over as they crept silently up to the house. Osmond entered through the open door first, checking for danger before signaling them to follow. Garbage covered nearly every surface and the smell of rot permeated the air. Amira gagged before bringing her hand up to cover her nose and mouth.

Typically, they would have split up in order to search the area, but with Amira accompanying them they stayed together. Osmond led the way and Levi guarded her back. The entryway opened up to the spacious living room. Osmond immediately led them over to the large stereo on the wall to the left. He switched the power off and the thumping beat blessedly stopped, the resulting silence ringing in their ears.

"Hey, I liked that song!" came from a slurred male voice from the only piece left standing of the large sectional sofa.

Osmond quickly shifted his body to completely block Amira's as Levi made his way over to the disembodied voice.

"Hey, I know you!" the voice slurred cheerfully. "Did you come to play with our toy?"

"What is the meaning of this? Why are you here?" Levi questioned in return.

Levi's unyielding tone must have clued the male in that something was not right. Amira peeked around

Osmond's back to see the male struggle to sit up and rub his hand over his bloodshot eyes. She recognized at once that he was Nephilim. She knew most all of her people, but it took her a second to realize who he was. His name was Marcus and he was a soldier in Sorin's territory.

"Wait, why the hell are you here? Are you the female's owner?" When Levi didn't answer immediately, Marcus rushed on, "Look, man, we didn't expect you for another couple days. We were informed you'd been delayed, and King Sorin said we could have our fun with the female. If you are unsatisfied with her physical state, you should have kept to the goddamned schedule. We made certain to leave no lasting marks and she'll be fully healed within a few days."

Amira wasn't sure exactly what that meant, but it terrified her nonetheless. Worry for Kearney's well-being warred with anger at Sorin being referred to as king.

"Where is she?" Levi's voice quivered with fury.

"No worries, there is enough to go around," Marcus tried placating, still not understanding his precarious position. Amira couldn't prevent her indrawn breath, and Marcus's head snapped in her direction. "What the hell is she doing here?" he asked, shocked.

"I'd like to hear the answer to that, too," a new voice called from the doorway.

She recognized him as well; his name was Peter. He

had often accompanied Sorin on his visits to the palace. She made note of his unruly appearance. His clothes were filthy and torn in several places, his hair was a black tangled mess, and his eyes were bloodshot as well. The gun in his right hand was pointed directly at her. It seemed he had adjusted quickly to this world's weapons.

Osmond moved to block her, knowing the gun most likely wouldn't hurt him but could easily kill her. The gun fell harmlessly to the floor as a knife fully embedded itself into Peter's wrist. Levi suddenly appeared at his side, ripping his knife out of Peter, wiping it off, and replacing it in his belt.

"Have a seat with your friend," he invited smoothly.

The two males shared a look before Peter complied, clutching his bloody wrist to his chest. Marcus was now sitting up, looking more aware, but their glazed eyes made her question if they were under the influence of some kind of narcotic.

"I will not ask nicely once more, where is the female?"

"Sh-she is downstairs. L-look, we were just doing what we were told." Marcus had to raise his voice, as Levi was already making his way to the hallway leading to the stairs.

Osmond had wordlessly stepped forward to take Levi's place. Amira met Levi at the top step.

"You may want to stay up here," he warned.

"I'm going," she answered firmly, placing her hands on her hips and preparing to argue. She was slightly surprised when he only nodded and proceeded down the stairs, leaving her to follow.

Levi slowly opened the door at the bottom of the stairs. The room was completely dark. As the light from the doorway spilled inside, Amira saw the room was bare except for a small, torn-up, empty mattress on the floor in the far corner. Confused, Amira scanned the room again. This time, her eyes locked on the female silhouette curled up in the corner opposite the mattress. The body was completely naked and covered in purple, red, and green bruises; she was utterly still.

Without thought, Amira pushed past Levi and rushed to her. The female startled awake, jumped to her feet, and began blindly swinging her clenched fists. If it hadn't been for Levi's strong arm circling Amira's waist and dragging her backward, one of those fists would have connected directly with the side of her head.

Heart racing and fear riding her hard, Amira cooed, "Shh... it's okay. It's okay now. Calm down. I'm Princess Amira, remember me? My Guard and I are here to help you." She held up her hands in an innocent gesture and continued to talk soothingly to the frightened female. As Levi reluctantly released her, she slowly inched forward. "We're going to take you home," she promised.

Kearney let out a heartbreaking sob and launched

herself at Amira, taking them both to the ground before Levi had a chance to steady or catch them. She wrapped her arms around Amira's waist and buried her face in her chest. Kearney's entire body was shaking with the force of her tears. Levi moved as if to pull her off Amira, but she quickly halted him.

"I'm fine. Please find her a blanket."

He grabbed one off the mattress and quickly brought it over. Kearney's body tensed and she sobbed harder at his approach. At her distress, he halted and tossed it into Amira's outstretched hand. He stood back and watched as Amira soothed Kearney with soft words and tender caresses. When it seemed he couldn't wait a moment longer, through clenched teeth and balled-up fists he asked, "Princess?"

Amira's silver eyes flashed up to his. She knew exactly what he wanted—no, needed.

"Justice, Levi. Get me justice," she commanded.

With a nod, he was gone.

TWENTY-ONE

Excitement coursed through his veins. Today she would return, Sorin assured himself. Three days! She had been missing for three days, but today she would return to where she belonged. He knew her weakness, and today he was going to use that weakness to bring her to her knees.

He grinned at his reflection in the mirror. He knew he always looked good, but today he looked exceptional. He was dressed in his finest clothes, because after all, he was making his grand debut as ruler of Cashile.

For three days, he had been forced to stay sequestered inside the palace, but now he was the one who held all of the power. For some reason unknown to him, the bond had shifted more firmly to him. Not that he was surprised, because after all, there was no one more worthy or deserving than he was. It had taken him a little time to understand and come to terms with this new responsibility, but he quickly realized the advantage it gave him.

Soon Princess Amira would realize the tables had turned, and that she was the one who needed him. But he knew she was proud and would need an extra little push; he would be glad to provide it. Today's demonstration would surely bring her crawling back to him. And if she showed the appropriate amount of contrition, he would show her how generous he could be and only execute two or three of his hostages. He would even allow her to plead for the lives of the children; then he would graciously grant her request. He couldn't help but grin at himself again in the mirror as he imagined how the scene would play out.

Confirming the hour of his debut had arrived, and relieved to finally vacate the chamber, he headed for the door with growing excitement to greet his awaiting audience. Once the princess was once again in his keeping, there would be no more reason to hide away. He would eliminate the Royal Guard and have the army of Velius under his command once again.

The leader of his army eagerly awaited him just outside the chamber door. Upon his exit, the soldier dropped to his knee. Sorin knew the soldier should have anticipated his arrival and already been on his knees in proper respect, but he was in too fine a mood to let that little slip bother him now. He could always punish him later, he reminded himself. For now, he would force the soldier to give his report from his knees instead of signaling for him to rise.

"Has the podium been erected to my specifications?" he asked.

"Yes, my lord."

"My what!" Sorin barked, his good mood slipping a notch.

"My apologies, my king," the soldier corrected himself.

Slightly mollified, he continued, "And the hostages?"

"Awaiting your arrival at the front entrance, my king."

"Excellent. Arise and let us begin," Sorin said cheerfully.

"My king?" The soldier sounded nervous, causing Sorin to hesitate.

"Speak," he commanded.

"The villagers..."

"What of them?" Sorin prompted.

"They have yet to arrive."

"What!"

"Two days ago, they were informed their presence was required, but today when we opened the gates, not one passed through," the soldier rushed to explain. "When we went to collect them... they weren't there to be found."

"How can that be?" Sorin demanded.

"I-I do not know, my king."

"This is her doing! Fine, she will receive no generosity from me. Today they will all die, and she will learn her place well." His chest heaved with pent-up fury. He turned to leave, but was halted once again.

"My king?" came the soldier's soft voice.

"There is more?" Sorin asked incredulously.

"Just... just a small matter with the patrols, my king."

"Speak quickly," Sorin barked, out of patience.

The soldier seemed to be choosing his words carefully as he stated, "Some of the patrols have failed to, umm... check in in a timely manner, my king."

Sorin relaxed a little at this news. This was a problem easily solved.

"At the next check-in, execute anyone who is tardy for dereliction of duty. Make an example out of them," he instructed flippantly. After that day, he would have plenty of soldiers to spare. That thought cheered him considerably and returned the pep to his step.

It was time to retrieve his princess.

Twenty-Two

Caeden felt no uncertainty or apprehension as he watched Sorin exit the palace, making himself vulnerable for the first time in days. His mind was clear and focused. He was determined to end the conflict.

In the last eighteen hours, he and the army of Velius had systematically taken out each and every one of Sorin's patrol units and exterior guards, replacing them with their own. Now in disguise, they stood ready for the opportune moment to make their move.

Being easily recognized, he and the rest of the Royal Guard were stationed toward the rear of the platform that would serve as Sorin's stage. He watched in disgust as Sorin made his way toward the platform, surrounded by the bound hostages and even carrying one of the crying children in his arms. The last of Sorin's remaining soldiers circled the group, keeping guard. Their eyes stayed focused on the open gate, expecting an attack from that vulnerable location, yet not thinking to check within the walls or even look at the waiting soldiers gathered around the platform.

Caeden took a moment to scan his brothers. Trevin stood focused, his eyes never leaving his target. Dalek looked tense as he scanned the courtyard. Murdock was staring at the child in Sorin's arms, his eyes blazing with fury. Each Guard member had their designated task. He and Trevin would focus on the main objective: reaching Sorin. Dalek would lead the soldiers stationed around the courtyard against Sorin's remaining soldiers, while Murdock and a few of the soldiers closest to the platform secured the hostages.

As Sorin reached the center of the stage, Velius's soldiers drew closer, circling the platform as would be expected of a regular crowd, but also placing themselves in a better position to attack. Caeden watched as Sorin scanned the crowd in front of him, too excited by the attention and too self-absorbed to notice anything amiss. Caeden hadn't thought it possible, but his aversion toward Sorin grew.

With a hateful smirk, Sorin addressed his audience, "It looks like our invited guests have declined our offer to witness justice this day. No matter, I will honor my duty as newly appointed ruler of the kingdom of Velius. These criminals will be executed for the abduction and murder of Princess Amira of Velius." Sorin's raised voice rang out over the courtyard. He probably believed the princess was somewhere nearby and would reveal herself when she understood he was not bluffing. Caeden knew the show was only for her benefit.

Many of the hostages were openly weeping and a few even cried out at Sorin's announcement, but Caeden couldn't allow himself to become distracted. He needed to be alert for the prime moment to sound the attack.

"But I am a just and fair ruler," Sorin continued. "I will allow anyone to bring forth evidence of their innocence before I carry out their punishment."

As he paused, several of the hostages exclaimed their innocence and some even pleaded for their lives or the lives of the children, but their words were ignored as Sorin scanned the courtyard for evidence of Amira.

"Very well, let us begin," he said on a sigh as he released the child in his arms and motioned for one of the soldiers to position the hostages. He made a production of having them placed on their knees at the far side of the stage so he could bring them forth one at a time to make their execution as dramatic as possible. When the last of the hostages was situated and the soldier returned to his post, Caeden knew it was the moment he had been waiting for. Circling his hand in the air, he gave the signal to attack.

~

Sorin's smile slid from his face and was quickly replaced by utter confusion. A roar had arisen from the back of the podium, and suddenly his soldiers were charging the stage. To his shock, his army drew arms against one another and began brawling in the court-yard. The sound of steel against steel and groans of pain as injuries were inflicted overwhelmed his senses, leaving him frozen in shock.

Suddenly his feet were swept out from under him and he found himself on his knees. The rest of the world faded away so the only things that now existed were the harsh floor beneath him, the strong hands holding him in place, and the displeased Captain of the Royal Guard of Velius demanding his full attention with the sharp blade he held pressed against his throat.

"You were correct, there will be justice today," the captain said in a terrifying growl.

Fear tasted like acid in the back of his throat, making it difficult to swallow.

"You... you can't kill me," he choked out.

"Oh, but I can. Sorin of Ammon, I charge you with treason. And as you were prepared to demon-strate today, that crime carries the punishment of execution."

Sorin's hands shook and his heart raced, but he knew he had one more move he could make, and if he did it just right, it would buy him the time he needed to get himself out of this mess. He forced a cocky grin and hoped he appeared more confident than he felt.

"Kill me and you kill your princess as well," he informed them with relish, and was gratified to see hesitation and concern mar the captain's expression.

"That's right, you—"

"Bind him," the captain instructed the soldier behind him, rudely interrupting his chance to brag.

"You can't do anything to me!" He raised his voice to continue. He held the power, and soon they would realize they hadn't won.

"Gag him, too," Caeden instructed as he carelessly walked away.

How dare he dismiss him and leave him on the ground like a piece of garbage, Sorin fumed to himself as his wrists were shackled together. Sorin knew Caeden's weakness.

He yelled at Caeden's retreating form, "When I get my hands on Amira again, I'm going—" He was unable to finish his threat as a cloth was rudely shoved into his mouth. He turned his head to glare over his shoulder and found Trevin staring down at him impassively. He tried to put the soldier in his place and demand his release, but to his annoyance, it only came out as muffled nonsense. The impertinent soldier had the nerve to cock his eyebrow and then turn his attention to the chaos around them, completely disregarding Sorin altogether.

Caeden forced himself to walk away. The calm determination he had felt earlier, now completely abandoned him and was replaced with a burning anger so great he feared it would consume him. He had failed her, and worse, he could have thoughtlessly killed her. He had been so tempted to slice Sorin's throat and be done with it all. His hands shook at the thought of what he'd almost done. How had he not considered the consequences of their bond? He berated himself harshly.

In order to release the extreme emotions coursing through him, he threw himself into the fray. Needing a challenge, he fought weaponless against Sorin's armed soldiers and still he found himself almost effortlessly defeating one soldier after another. All too soon he was alone, and looked around for a new enemy to engage. To his disappointment, everyone who had not been defeated had surrendered.

"Clear the courtyard, imprison all survivors, care for the injured, and search for stragglers," he commanded quickly.

Turning to Trevin, refusing to even glance in Sorin's direction, he gave his last order, "You know where to take him."

Trevin nodded in acknowledgement and Caeden turned to leave; with the situation under control, he needed to get away.

Twenty-Three

Caeden stared out across the water, watching the waves smoothly make their way to the shore. The calming environment did little to soothe the storm inside him.

"When was the last time you slept?"

He wasn't surprised when it turned out to be Trevin he'd heard approach.

"The night before she left," he answered, not bothering to take his eyes off the water, which also happened to be the path and direction Amira would return from.

With a heavy sigh, Trevin sat beside him, staring at the ocean.

"I don't know how to fix this," Caeden finally admitted, breaking the silence.

"Some things are not for us to change."

"That's bullshit!" Caeden exploded. "This was not

meant to be and you know it. She was never meant to be his, she has always been mine. I will not accept this!"

"What choice do you have? You can accept the situation for what it is and hope the solution presents itself with the scout, or you can turn away from her."

"Never. I will never give her up," Caeden stated adamantly.

"Then you will deal with what is, and face what may be together. We'll all face it together, brother," Trevin said, reminding him he wasn't alone.

Caeden took a minute to reflect on his words, and as much as it bothered him to admit it, he was powerless to change what was. He had no choice but to accept it for now.

"How did you get so wise?" Caeden asked on a sigh.

"He's only wise until it comes to his own love life; then he's a complete moron," Murdock said from behind them, startling Caeden. He turned to find Murdock and Dalek a few feet away.

"Your sister is a difficult, headstrong, impulsive female," Trevin grumbled.

"Aye, she is," Murdock agreed with glee, "and now she is your headache."

"If I can just convince her of that," Trevin said under his breath, making the other guards grin at one another and dissolving the tension.

"Status report?" Caeden requested, once again ready to deal with the situation.

"Zero losses on our side and only minor injury. Sixteen deceased from the army of Ammon, many injured, all in custody," Trevin reported.

"Civilians?" Caeden asked.

"Returning to their homes," Murdock announced.

"And our guest of honor?" was Caeden's final inquiry.

"Not appreciating his new accommodations. For someone who takes pleasure in locking others in a dark cellar, he really has a problem with it himself." Caeden arched his eyebrow in silent question and Dalek explained, "He's terrified of the dark."

Caeden couldn't help his laugh of surprise. He knew it was wrong to take pleasure in another's fear and misery, but it was such a strange and unexpected twist. It did make sense though; someone who carried such an amount of demons and darkness inside of them would fear what could be waiting for them in the dark.

"Poetic justice," Murdock remarked. Caeden didn't disagree.

"Come, let us finish this day; I'm in need of some rest," Caeden suggested, clapping Trevin on the back and starting back to the palace.

Twenty-Four

Amira was unsure how long she had sat on the cold hard floor holding Kearney as she cried, but she would have gladly sat there all night to provide any amount of comfort to this hurt and abused female. She hadn't noticed when Osmond and Levi joined them, but they now sat quietly at the foot of the stairs. Each was lost in their own thoughts as Kearney released all of her pent-up pain and emotion, and worked to collect herself. The heartbreak and rage Amira felt escalated with every look at the bruises marring Kearney's body, every sob escaping her lips, and every shudder wracking her slender body. Peeking up at her guards, she knew they were feeling the same. The need to do something burned inside of her; the feeling of helplessness fueled her anger more. She'd had considerable experience containing her emotions, but right then, it took all of her experience and energy to do so.

"Kearney, honey, can we get you cleaned up? Would you like to shower?" Amira asked softly when she noticed the tears were subsiding. At her nod, Amira untangled herself, stood, and bent down to help lift Kearney.

Kearney stood on shaky legs, head down and blanket clutched to her chest, refusing to make eye contact with anyone. As they approached, Osmond quickly made his way upstairs to ensure their safety before their ascent. Levi waited patiently a few feet from the door until Kearney passed before grabbing hold of Amira and pulling her to a stop. Kearney paused at the foot of the stairs, face still turned away.

"You'll need to assess her injuries," he said quietly as he gently brushed the tears off Amira's cheeks, only then did she become aware that she too had been crying. "We'll ready some food and a place for you both to rest."

"Thank you." She hated to ask, but she needed to hear it. "Sorin's soldiers?"

A slight sob escaped Kearney, drawing their attention to her rigid form.

"Justice," he answered firmly.

"Both of them?" Kearney's shaky voice questioned.

"Absolutely," he vowed.

"Thank you," she whispered softly, her body relaxing slightly as she started up the stairs.

"Get her to talk about it," he advised Amira as they followed her up. Amira nodded her agreement, knowing the pain and damage of such an experience could spread like poison and eat away at a person's soul without release.

At the top of the stairs, Osmond acknowledged them with a silent nod before leading them down the hallway, through the master bedroom to a large bathroom. Closing the door behind them, Amira started the shower to allow the water to warm. She took a deep breath, and then turned to face the abused and frightened female.

"How badly are you injured?" she asked, unsure how to begin, but deciding the direct approach was best.

Kearney closed her eyes; a thoughtful look appeared on her face, as if she were taking a mental inventory.

"The concussion has healed. Contusions to the face, neck, torso, back, arms, and thighs. Bone fracture to the left ribcage. Mild abrasions to the knees and palms. Minimum internal trauma. All damage will repair itself within days." Her eyes opened again to study the floor when she finished. The detached way she had listed her injuries was eerie and concerned Amira.

"You sound very knowledgeable and confident in your assessment."

Kearney shrugged in response.

"Would you permit me to examine you?"

Kearney's head jerked up and her body became rigid. "That's not necessary, Princess."

"Very well, would you like me to stay or do you require privacy?"

Kearney hesitated, looking a bit embarrassed. "Would... would you please stay?"

Amira jumped up to perch on the counter in response. Kearney seemed a little taken aback by Amira's unprincess-like action.

"My Guard has been a terrible influence on me," she explained with a shrug.

"I bet," Kearney responded vaguely.

Amira could see the first hint of a smile as Kearney passed her, dropping the blanket only seconds before entering the shower stall and pulling the curtain closed.

"I guess you need to know what happened." Kearney sighed.

"Whenever you're ready to tell me."

"I'd like to get it over with."

Amira realized that being concealed by the curtain gave Kearney the security and anonymity she needed to find the courage to share what had happened.

"My guard, Fredrick, and I began our journey as planned. The trip here went smoothly. Fredrick, he"— her voice wobbled before she continued—"he was so very excited. He talked nonstop. He said it was an honor to be chosen for this duty and wanted to discuss every possibility. I-I mainly pretended to ignore him, like I do everyone else. I treated him badly, like he was a burden to be endured."

"Why?" Amira couldn't help but ask.

"Because he was so happy and friendly... so nice."

"I don't understand."

"He was so easy to like and I couldn't risk that, so I tried to make it impossible for him to like me."

"Why?" Amira still didn't understand.

"It's safer that way."

"Safer for whom?"

After a moment of silence, Kearney continued her story, making it clear she wasn't going to answer. "On the third night of the trip, there was a huge storm. We still hadn't yet reached the house and were camping in a clearing south of here. The rain and hail beat down on us. Fredrick did his best to protect us by building a shelter under some trees. The wind howled and the ground shook. It seemed as if the Earth was screaming out in discomfort. I had never heard of or experienced anything like it. Neither of us slept that night; we just tried to get dry and stay warm."

Amira realized that storm must have been the results of the destabilization of the shield. She never thought to consider the domino effect it could have on the human world.

"The storm passed quickly and the next day, we made our way here. We became concerned when we recognized signs of occupation, but decided to approach cautiously. They had been waiting for us and attacked immediately. Fredrick wanted me to run, but he was outnumbered two to one. I wanted to help, but I was more in the way than anything..." Her voice trailed off as she relived the events.

"You did what you thought best. That was truly brave of you," Amira tried to reassure her. "What happened next?"

Kearney took a deep breath. "They killed him. They got him on the ground and stabbed him repeatedly... drawing it out before finally beheading him." Her voice quivered as she continued, "I'm sorry, Princess. I couldn't help him."

Amira could hear the tears in her voice and had to swallow down her own grief before responding.

"Kearney—"

But Kearney cut her off before she could continue. "They locked me in the basement. I heard voices coming and going, but I never saw anyone except Marcus and Peter."

"Did you know them from before?"

"No."

Amira didn't want to ask, but she needed to know. "What happened after they put you in the basement?"

"I didn't see anyone for several days. I'm not sure how many; without windows it was hard to tell. When they finally came down—" Her voice cracked, and when she began speaking again, it was in the same detached tone she had used while listing her injuries.

"There was something not right about them. They were nervous and sweaty. Their eyes were bloodshot, and when they spoke, they didn't make sense."

Amira's heart raced and her breath quickened in useless fear. "Did they tell you why they were here?"

"They were here for me. They said someone was coming for me... they never said who, but I heard them refer to them as my 'owners.' They joked that they were going to get me 'ready and break me in.' I'm not that easy to break," she finished fiercely, finally showing emotion again.

"No, I don't think you would be," Amira agreed. "Do you want to tell me what they did to you?" she questioned softly.

"No," came the whispered response.

"Okay, but when you're ready, I'm here for you. Anytime." When it became clear Kearney wasn't going to respond, she asked, "Do you know who else has been here, or anything else about whom they were expecting?"

"No, they never said any names, but I think they were like us."

Amira sucked in a sharp breath. "Like us? Nephilim?"

"I think so. They seemed to know all of the visitors well, and when they did speak of my 'new owners,' they spoke of them coming from the human world, but it was someone they all seemed to know and respect, if not fear. I know it doesn't make sense, because no one from Cashile, except the scout and guard, are supposed to be here."

"Marcus and Peter weren't supposed to be here either, but they were, so anything is possible." Amira didn't know what to think or how any of it was even happening, so there was no way she could deny any possibility. "You've been in there a while, why don't I go check for your clothes while you get out?"

"Sure, I just need to wash one more time," she answered, sounding a little panicked.

"Okay." Amira understood the need to be clean after being touched by something so foul and dirty.

The first thing Amira noticed when she entered the room was it was now completely clean. All of the garbage had been removed, the furniture set to rights, and the bed had even been made. It warmed her heart to see the thoughtfulness of her Guard.

Folded on the bed were Kearney's clothes, and on the bedside table were two plates of food.

Amira took the clothes to the bathroom, but stepped out to give Kearney some privacy.

Twenty-Five

"How did you know to come?" Kearney immediately asked as she exited the bathroom.

"Come have some food and rest, and I'll tell you." Amira motioned to the bed. She waited until Kearney began to eat before telling her about the king's death and the plot to steal the kingdom. Kearney listened silently until she came to the part of Marcelle's journals.

"I'm sorry, Princess, but I'm not this natural healer you were searching for. It's true Marcelle hated me, and she had good reason, but it's not because I was a threat to her." She hesitated, and just as Amira was sure she would have to prompt her to continue, Kearney boldly met her eyes and shared a secret she would never have expected. "I killed my brother."

"What?"

"It was unintentional, yet I'm responsible just the same." Finally looking away, she finished, "So you see, I can't be the person you're looking for."

"There's got to be more to it," Amira questioned.

"It doesn't matter; there are some things you just can't undo."

"But—"

"I'm sorry, Princess, I'm not whom you need me to be." A single a tear trailed down her cheek before she angrily brushed it away. "Look, I am really sorry about the king's passing and all you've been through. I will help you in any way I can, but I can't be something I'm not."

"I'm sorry," Amira whispered, reaching out to hold her hand. She felt horrible for causing her more distress. "You've been through so much. I didn't mean to lay all of this on you now. Please forgive me."

"There is nothing to forgive. You saved me. I will be eternally grateful to you. I just wish—"

"It doesn't matter right now. It'll all work out." Amira gave her an encouraging smile, which didn't quite meet her eyes. "Right now you need to heal."

"Okay, but... will you stay with me for a while?"

"Of course."

Amira helped her settle in the bed, before making herself comfortable in the chair to sit vigil.

Her eyes were blurring and kept threatening to

close and refuse to reopen. Kearney was finally resting peacefully, so she felt no guilt at seeking her own bed. Exiting the room, she closed the door softly behind her. She turned and stumbled, yelping as two strong hands grabbed her waist to steady her. She looked down to discover she had tripped over Levi, who was sitting on the floor, back to the wall and legs stretched out in front of him.

"Well, that's an interesting guarding technique," she said when she was able to catch her breath. "If you don't scare the intruder to death, maybe he'll trip and break his neck in the fall."

Levi shot her a crooked grin but said nothing in return.

"May I sit with you?"

"You'd have to sit on the floor," he teased.

"Me? I live recklessly; I sit on tabletops and everything."

"Princess Amira the rebel." He smirked.

His grin turned into a full-out smile as she settled beside him.

"Princess Amira the tired rebel," she returned with a groan.

"Go rest," he said, soberly now.

"I will soon, but first tell me what has you here waiting to trip unsuspecting innocent females?"

His lips quirked only slightly. "How is she?" he asked.

"I don't know," Amira answered honestly. "She's been through so much, but she seems like a strong person."

"Yeah, she is," he agreed.

"Do you know her well?"

"I knew her a long time ago," he answered vaguely.

"What happened?"

"She changed. We both did," he said in such a way she knew he wasn't going to explain further.

"Would you like to go in and sit with her?" Amira wondered.

"No, she wouldn't appreciate that," he said regretfully.

Amira let out a heavy sigh. It was too confusing for her tired brain to figure out. Knowing no more answers on that topic would be coming, she asked the question weighing on her mind.

"Do you think some of our people are living here in the human world?"

Levi's head snapped in her direction. "What do you mean?"

Amira recapped the conversation she'd had with Kearney.

"What do you think?" she asked when she finished.

"I don't know, but there's a way to find out."

He sounded distracted and she could tell he was already making plans.

"How?"

"We set a trap."

If she weren't so tired, the excited gleam in his eyes might have frightened her, but right then, it was a struggle to hold her head up.

"Okay," she mumbled as she finally lost the battle to keep her eyes open.

Twenty-Six

Dozens of invisible arms wrapped around her body, tightening and slowly squeezing the life out of her. The more she struggled, the tighter they became. Her throat hurt and her voice was hoarse from her unanswered cries for help.

"No one will come for you," Sorin's voice came through the darkness in a bored tone, "and if they did, there is nothing they could do for you. I am your only salvation, just as you are mine."

"You're a monster," she croaked.

"And what would you know of monsters?" he sneered. "You know nothing!"

"Let me go," she commanded.

"I can't. I'm your other half, we belong together. If I'm trapped, you should be trapped with me. It's only right." Frustration now stained his voice. "Why do you deny me? You feel me inside of you, just as you are in me. There is no denying that." His voice suddenly softened and he pleaded, "Come to me. I can ease your suffering. I can protect you and give you the world. Just come to me and we will be as one, as we were meant to be."

"We are not meant to be! You took something beautiful and sacred and perverted it into something dirty and wrong. You forced this upon me, and before my dying breath, I will see you pay for your sins!"

"Very well," he screamed, becoming visible beside the altar she was once again strapped to. He slammed his fist against it in anger. "Continue to suffer. I offered you a place by my side, now you'll only have a place at my heels! You will have nothing. Nothing! No home, no family, no palace, no people, no bond, and no power! Already it has shifted to me, soon I will have it all, and you will come crawling to me, begging—"

"Princess! Princess!" A frantic female voice interrupted and the altar began to shake.

Sorin's lips were still moving as he continued to rant and make threats, but a different, distant conversation had captured Amira's attention.

"What has happened?" She recognized Osmond's harsh bark.

"I-I don't know. I heard her cry out and she won't awaken," the panicked female explained.

"She has nightmares. Let me through." She recognized Levi's voice, but she still couldn't see him. Sorin had somehow faded away as she had concentrated on the disembodied conversation around her. The arms that had held her were now gone as well. She was left with nothing but darkness. She felt the altar dip at her side and realized she was lying on a comfortable bed. Levi's husky drawl came from close by.

"Now come back to us, darling. You're scaring our poor little scout here." He paused for a moment before continuing, "You're being a terrible host and displaying despicable manners."

"I have impeccable manners, and you darn well know it!" Her eyes snapped open so she could give him an icy glare.

"Oh, there she is. Welcome back," he said with a wicked grin and a wink.

"One of these days, some female is going to see through your pretty face and bring you to your knees," she threatened.

"You already have, darling," he said, to Osmond's great amusement.

"This isn't funny. Why are you all laughing?" Kearney asked in frustration.

"I'm sorry you were frightened," Amira said sincerely and tried to explain. "I've learned that if you can't laugh about your problems, sometimes they become overwhelming and insurmountable. I can't let my problems become powerful enough to break me."

Kearney looked like she was processing that lesson. "But what happened? You sounded like you were in pain and I couldn't wake you."

Amira quickly met her guards' eyes before answering vaguely, "Just a really bad dream." She was unwilling to reveal the complete extent of her situation.

Kearney must have realized they were hiding something, but she respected their privacy because she said, "We all have our demons to face, I guess."

"Breakfast, then decision time," Osmond barked before exiting.

Amira readied herself quickly and met her companions in the kitchen. Breakfast consisted of burned toast, runny eggs, and an unpeeled orange.

"Osmond's turn to cook?" she guessed.

He gave her a sheepish grin and a shrug. *I'm really beginning to know my Guard,* she thought with a grin.

"I've caught Osmond up on the situation and your suspicions, Princess," Levi began, getting straight to business. "This mysterious 'owner' is expected to arrive within the next few days. I believe you're right; if it is one of our people, it doesn't make sense to have the scout come all this way only to follow her and take her back to Cashile. He must be living here in the human world, and if there is one, there might be many. We need to find out."

"How do we do that?" Amira questioned after forcing herself not to make a funny face while swallowing a spoonful of slimy eggs.

The males shared a look before Osmond answered, "I'll take you and the female"—he paused to nod his head in Kearney's direction—"back to the transport and Levi will stay behind to ask a couple questions."

"You'll ask a couple questions?" Amira asked in disbelief. Levi nodded his affirmation, so she continued, "And what if he decides not to answer?"

"I'll persuade him," Levi said as if it should have been obvious.

"And can you trust any information you 'persuade' from him?" At his answering shrug, Amira felt her frustration reaching a critical point. "And what if he's not alone? What then?"

"I'll improvise."

He sounded unconcerned. Amira watched him carelessly shrug once again, and she lost it. "Levi, you cannot take on an unknown number of possibly trained soldiers by yourself!"

"Sure I can," he returned.

"You arrogant—" she started to shout, but Osmond interrupted.

"We don't have many choices here, Princess. It's imperative we find out what is going on here in the human world, but we cannot risk you being discovered here. One of us must secure your safety and the other will stay behind."

"There has got to be another way," Amira implored, starting to feel desperate. She knew this wasn't a good idea.

"There isn't," Levi assured her.

"You're wrong, there is," Kearney spoke for the first

time, drawing everyone's attention. She took a nervous breath before continuing, "You can let them take me."

Amira was too shocked to speak, but Levi wasn't. "Absolutely not," he all but exploded.

"Just hear me out—"

"No." Levi cut her off.

"Listen to me," Kearney shouted at him. His jaw clenched, but he remained silent. "I've been thinking there is a reason they targeted me personally, and I don't believe it was for the reason Marcus and Peter thought. I think they believe I am this 'natural healer' Marcelle claimed I was, or maybe they just need my expertise as scout, but it doesn't matter. They must need me for something; that means I have some value to them. I can let them take me, and then find a way to get the answers back to you." She gave a pleading look to Amira, knowing the ultimate decision was hers.

"I don't know...," Amira said, unsure.

"Princess, you saved me believing I'm something that I'm not. I can't help you with whatever you're going through, but I can help you with this. Please let me," she implored.

"I'll go with her," Levi announced.

"What?" Kearney questioned in shock.

"I go with you; that's the only way this is happening," he stated firmly.

"How do you propose to do that?" Amira questioned, trying to push emotions away and think diplomatically, considering the entire situation.

"Won't be hard to convince them I turned traitor, most believe I murdered the king anyway." Kearney's sharp indrawn breath distracted them for a second before he continued, "I'll be able to guard her and be in a position to obtain firsthand knowledge of the information we need."

"Osmond, what do you think?" Amira questioned.

"If the female is willing and able, I think it's a fine plan. With Levi present, there is a better chance of success and her safety. Plus, it'll give him a little more time before Caeden kills him."

Amira shot him an aggravated look before considering the plan again. "Are you sure you're able to do this?" she asked Kearney.

"I can do this," she said confidently, but bit her bottom lip nervously.

"What about you, Levi? You're just barely healed."

"You've been injured?" Kearney asked, but immediately looked like she wished she could take it back.

Levi ignored her, but gave Amira a crooked grin and said in his sexy drawl, "You're just worried you'll miss me, huh, darling?"

"Terribly," she answered with a very unprincess-like eye roll.

"I do believe she's considering exchanging Caeden for me," he bragged jokingly to Osmond, earning him a sound slap to the back of his head.

"There is that brain damage surfacing again," Osmond muttered to himself.

Hearing Caeden's name brought heaviness to Amira's chest and made her homesick. She pushed the feelings away, knowing the quicker they had things settled, the sooner she could be on her way back to him.

"Okay, if you are both determined on this course of action, I will allow it. Levi, you have complete authority to make any decisions you deem necessary." Levi nodded in acknowledgement of her faith and trust in him.

She turned to Kearney and continued, "Kearney, thank you for your service. This is more than I would have ever asked of you. You are truly brave. Your safety is important to me. Levi will protect you." She briefly paused, noticing some silent communication between Kearney and Levi. Unable to understand, she continued, "If at any time you feel it is too much or your safety is at risk, Levi will immediately remove you from the situation." Levi nodded in agreement. "You have to trust him and do as he says," she warned, remembering Kearney admitting she purposely tried not to get along with others.

"I'll try," Kearney said, looking aggravated but sounding sincere.

"Thank you; that's all I ask."

"Great, now that's settled, let's get this planned out and us packed up," Osmond ordered impatiently.

TWENTY-SEVEN

The view from the cliff near the scout's Icelandic residence was breathtaking. Amira stared out over the black sandy beach to the wild icy ocean. A chill swept through her body as the frigid wind picked up, but she wasn't ready to tear herself away from the beautiful sight she would never be able to see again.

"It's a lot colder than it normally is this time of year," Kearney remarked thoughtfully, coming to stand beside Amira and handing her a quilt to wrap around herself.

"Thank you." Amira smiled and waited patiently for Kearney to find the courage to say whatever had brought her out here.

"When I was younger, everything was so beautiful," Kearney said, staring across the ocean. "Our world had so much possibility. Growing up in a scout family,

I'd hear countless stories of all the changes and the mysteries left to solve, but that wasn't my path. I wasn't supposed to be the next scout. That was supposed to be my brother's fate. Back then, everything was clear to me. I was naïve."

Her voice faded, but Amira knew she wasn't finished and patiently waited.

After a moment of silence, she continued, "Everything changed so quickly. The world became harsh and scary. I-I didn't know what to do." The pain in her voice brought tears to Amira's eyes. "Everything I was so sure of, everything I depended on, was gone. I lost myself and became someone even I didn't like." She sighed heavily. "And now it seems as if everything is changing again; coming full circle. The past I fought against and struggled to bury deep has returned. Now here I am once again, lost without an anchor; questioning everything I thought I knew. What do I do? I can't be that girl I used to be, and I'm tired of trying to be someone I'm not."

Amira watched a tear slide down Kearney's cheek and felt her chest tighten in compassion.

"Our fate is not for us to decide or control. We can only adjust ourselves to what is and try to make the best decision from the choices we are presented with. It's pointless to try to change the past. We can only look to the future. I have faith we are right where we are meant to be; life has a way of challenging us to mold us into whom we are meant to be." Amira couldn't help reflecting on all the changes that had taken place inside of her in the last few weeks.

"It isn't a decision you need to make. All you need to do is learn to appreciate the beautiful person life has molded you to be and take each day, each challenge, as they come and decide what is the best choice to make at that moment."

Both females remained quiet for a while, lost in thought while staring at the indomitable force of the ocean.

"How did you get so wise at such a young age, Princess?" Kearney asked, finally breaking the silence.

"I'm not. The future terrifies me just as much as it does you," she admitted with a sad smile.

Not sure how it happened, she found herself wrapped in Kearney's embrace, the weight in her chest easing slightly.

"We'll be okay," Kearney pulled away slightly to look her in the eyes, "and if you ever need me..." She trailed off.

"And I will be here for you, as well."

In silent agreement, they made themselves comfortable as they awaited the guards to finish their preparations. Neither female wanted to spend any more time than necessary in that house.

There were so many questions Amira was dying to ask, but she refused to intrude on the peaceful moment and the opportunity slipped away.

"Time to go," Osmond announced after they had been sitting quietly for some time.

Standing up and wiping herself off, Amira turned to appraise her Guard. Osmond stood, bags in hand, ready to leave immediately. Levi stood a few feet away, head down, hands in his back pockets, looking unsure. Going to him, she put her hand on his arm.

"Are you okay?"

His head shot up and he gave her a wicked grin, which she could tell he'd forced.

"Sure, just wondering who will protect me when you leave," he teased.

"I'm sure you won't have any trouble finding some other female to meet your needs," Kearney snapped, shocking Amira.

"No, I probably won't," Levi responded, shocking her even more. She'd never heard him use such a harsh tone with a female before; usually he was overly charming.

Amira looked between the two of them in confusion as they stared at one another in a silent standoff. She had a feeling she had missed something. She knew they had history and up until then, they had barely spoken to one another, but at least they had been civil. Her tired brain couldn't catch up.

"Maybe Osmond should stay behind instead," she suggested.

Levi's "No" and Kearney's "Yes" were instantaneous. Amira looked to Osmond, but he only gave a useless shrug.

Levi scowled at Kearney until she dropped her eyes and conceded, "No, we'll be fine."

"Is there something I need to be aware of?" Amira questioned in concern. They both shook their heads, but neither met her eyes.

"Let us be on our way then, Princess," Osmond said, turning away and starting down the path, not bothering to say farewell to the others. Not having much of a choice, she rushed to Kearney and wrapped her in a hug. Kearney tensed up before relaxing and returning the embrace.

"I'm sorry," Kearney whispered in her ear. Amira pulled back to look into her eyes.

"You'll find your way. We both will," she reassured her before turning to Levi.

She wrapped him in a tight hug, too.

"Come back to us soon," she told him and pressed a chaste kiss to his cheek.

He gave her a distracted nod as he scanned her face in concern. "I wish we'd had more time to allow you to rest."

"I'll rest on the transport," she assured him.

"Safe journey, Princess," he returned solemnly.

With one more hesitant look between them, she reluctantly rushed to catch up to Osmond where he awaited her down the hill by the edge of the tree line.

Tiring easily, she was slightly winded by the time she reached him.

"Do you think they'll be okay together?" she panted.

"Sure, as long as one doesn't smother the other in their sleep," he answered with a shrug. "Come along, I want to be as far from here as possible before we make camp tonight."

By the time they settled in, Amira didn't have the energy to even attempt to fight sleep. Her body and her mind were both exhausted. She joined with Sorin immediately as sleep claimed her. Instantly, she knew something had changed. There was still an ominous feeling, except it no longer emanated from Sorin. He sat silently on the floor with his back against the wall. He stared at her intently, but said nothing. The room was entirely dark, save for one flickering candle sitting on a lone table in the middle of the room. Amira circled the room slowly, waiting for him to begin his usual cajoling and threats, but it never came. Instead, he followed her with his eyes. She opened her mouth to ask what was going on, but he quickly shook his head, eyes darting around the room in fear. She approached him cautiously and knelt in front of him. His frantic eyes returned to hers as he placed his finger to his lips.

"Quiet, he'll hear you," he whispered.

"Who will?" she asked quietly.

"You need to leave before he finds you."

"Sorin, no one else is here."

"He reveals himself in the dark." Sorin's eyes darted around the room again.

This male had destroyed her life and killed her father; she wanted to be happy for his fear and distress, but she wasn't. She cursed herself for feeling any compassion for him. Her anger had her pacing the room, raising her voice.

"And what will he do when he comes?" she yelled at him.

"Please, Princess, lower your voice," he whispered desperately.

"Will you finally be punished for your crimes?" she asked harshly.

"I am already being punished," he whispered fiercely, anger shining through his eyes.

"Good."

She lifted her chin and stared into his eyes before leaning forward slowly, so there was no question of her intent.

"No!"

His scream echoed through the room as she blew out the single candle, leaving them in complete darkness.

She awoke with Sorin's wretched sobs ringing in her ears. What had she done? How had she become so cruel? Hot tears streamed down her face and she felt sick inside.

"You know, I recruited into the army at the same time as your father," Osmond said from where he sat with his back resting against a tree, looking out into the night, startling Amira.

"No, I didn't know that," she answered, quickly wiping her tears away.

"Vidar and I were friends practically our whole lives. I was even there the day he met your mother."

"Oh." She hadn't even considered their relationship.

"She was a beautiful person. She loved your father and she loved Cashile. She would have done anything for our people, just as you have by coming on this trip. They both would be proud of you."

"But I was wrong, and I failed," she denied.

"You didn't fail. You saved that girl by coming here. Sometimes doing one right thing, saving even one person, can make everything else worthwhile."

"I don't know..."

"I do," he said in a manner that invited no argument. "You planning on sleeping anymore?"

"No, why?"

Osmond nodded in the direction he had been staring and said, "Because I've lived a long time, but I've never seen that before."

Amira turned to see the large full moon was shining a bright ruby red. Her breath caught in her throat as dread washed through her. That couldn't be good.

"Seeing as neither one of us is sleeping, mind if we pack it up and keep moving?"

Amira could only shake her head as she untangled herself from her multitude of blankets to begin helping, more eager than ever to be home. Weather permitting, it would only take one more day's travel in the transport; that thought made her move even more quickly.

TWENTY-EIGHT

Caeden, Murdock, and Dalek had each spent countless hours questioning Sorin, but if he knew of a way to reverse the bonding, he wasn't sharing. In fact, it seemed as if he'd completely withdrawn inside of himself. After his capture and imprisonment, he had been more than willing to express his displeasure and had been extremely vocal, but something had changed during the night and he had become completely unresponsive. Caeden had returned before sunrise that morning to discover the dim lights in the cellar had somehow disengaged and Sorin had unintentionally been left in complete darkness with only his thoughts to keep him company. Now, almost half a day later, he sat stone still, not moving and barely blinking.

"I think I like him better this way," Dalek

announced, earning him a slap to the back of the head from Murdock.

"Hey, why did you do that?"

"Because Osmond isn't here to take care of it," he answered with a shrug, relieving some of the tension and causing Caeden to grin. To his frustration, they weren't making any progress and far too many things required his attention. Last night's bloodred moon had been replaced with signs of a massive storm brewing. The temperature had once again shifted, with a biting wind coming from the northwest, and angry gray clouds were on the horizon. Getting everyone back into their homes and providing food and shelter to all who had lost their homes in the previous storms was a huge undertaking, and now they had to prepare for whatever was to come.

Making each task more difficult than necessary was the constant interruption from concerned individuals needing reassurance or seeking information about the princess's well-being. He had soldiers stationed as lookouts awaiting her return and he was to be notified as soon as she was spotted, but still he fought the urge to go after her. *Just a couple more days*, he reminded himself. Until then, there was plenty to keep him busy.

"We're wasting our time here. Continue to search through the journals, there has to be an answer somewhere." He dismissed them, heading for the cellar stairs.

"Don't forget about the meeting with the females," Murdock reminded him.

"Heading there now," Caeden answered with a nod. Several females had come to him requesting an audience; without a member of the royal family available and with the loss of the leaders of the other territories, the people were looking to him and the Royal Guard for direction.

"Do you think they just need more reassurance?" Dalek wondered.

"I'm not sure. They requested a formal meeting in the conference chamber. I'll meet you in the study when it's over," he informed them before heading off.

Caeden paused outside the conference room. The overwhelming chaos of several different conversations all taking place at the same time made his head begin to pound before even entering the room. Wanting to get it over with, he pushed through the doors, but hesitated at the sight that greeted him. There were a lot more females present than he had expected, and they all stopped midsentence to stare at him. The ridiculous urge to flee crossed his mind and he had to remind himself that he was a deadly soldier and Captain of the Royal Guard. He was not intimidated by a group of females... a very large group of females.

Francine stood at the front of the room and motioned for him to take the empty chair at the head of the table.

"Captain, thank you for taking the time to meet

with us. We understand you are busy," she began as soon as he was settled. Francine seemed to be the elected leader, so he nodded in response. "It is our understanding Princess Amira will be returning in a few days." She seemed to say that for the benefit of the females present, so he once again nodded in agreement. She gave him an approving smile and continued, "There is much to do before her return in preparation to make it official."

"To make what official?" he asked in confusion.

"Her coronation, of course. She needs to be crowned queen."

Of course she would become queen. With everything else that had occurred, Caeden hadn't given it any thought, but hearing the words made it a reality. The consequences of their relationship began flashing through his head. She would be queen, and if she chose, that would make him her consort and king. It was a staggering thought. They hadn't discussed that part of their relationship as of yet, and he wasn't going to presume to know her thoughts on the subject. The only thing he was sure of was she was his and would remain his. He realized Francine was still speaking and he made himself concentrate on her words.

"The Supreme Healer presides over such ceremonies, but we are without a Supreme Healer and no apprentices or anyone else in line to replace her. What are we to do?"

Murmurs of concern rang out amongst the

females. Caeden raised his hand to get their attention, afraid to let them get out of control.

"Each territory and village has their own healer, correct? I assume you females gathered today are they?" At their nods of agreement he continued, "You all have different degrees of skills and knowledge. I suggest you form a council and begin sharing your knowledge and training with one another. I expect it will be necessary for the tough times ahead. Once the council is formed, we will release the former Supreme Healer's journals to you so that our information, traditions, and way of life do not perish with Marcelle."

Shocked and excited words of agreement sounded throughout the chamber. Caeden was once again forced to wait for the females to calm themselves before he was able to continue.

"The princess will return soon, and having a coronation ceremony will be helpful in settling some of the fear and uncertainty within our people. Once you have your council formed, decide who will preside over the ceremony. Speak with Lady Inaya; she will assist you in the preparation and will have final authority. When the princess has returned, we will address the lack of a Supreme Healer. Thank you for taking the initiative and if there is anything you need, please come to me or any member of the Royal Guard. Now, if you'll excuse me," he said, ready to be finished with the meeting.

"Captain, wait." A soft voice halted his escape. Turning toward the voice, he waited and tried to hold on to the last of his patience. "I was wondering... are the rumors true?"

"Vivi," Francine said sternly.

Caeden cocked his eyebrow in question.

Vivi ignored Francine with a smirk and continued, "Are you really having an affair with Princess Amira?"

Shocked gasps could be heard around the room.

"You meddlesome little—" Francine didn't get a chance to finish.

"You will use respect when you speak of your future queen," Caeden growled. His shoulders were tense and he didn't bother trying to disguise his displeasure. He didn't give a damn what anyone said about him, but he would not abide anyone speaking adversely about Amira. "Is that clear?"

"I-I am sorry for my impertinence, sir. I won't repeat or even listen to any more rumors," she stammered through her apology.

He exited without giving further acknowledgement, but heard Francine tearing into the female as the door closed behind him. He took a deep breath to try to release some of his anger. There was no way he was letting Amira go, but he would need to do a better job of protecting her privacy and reputation.

TWENTY-NINE

One day turned into two as a massive storm built and the ocean churned with unrest, but for Amira, the time passed quickly. The entire first day was spent in a deep sleep, only waking at Osmond's insistence when he deemed it time to eat. He began to tell her stories to keep her awake, which was completely out of character for him. Amira appreciated his effort and tried to remain conscious.

"I've been a member of the Royal Guard for a long time now. In fact, I've been Royal Guard for longer than some of the other members have been alive," Osmond told her the morning of the second day.

"Just how old are you, Osmond?"

"Now don't you go being cheeky. I'll tell you what I want you to know," he answered gruffly.

"That old, huh?" she couldn't help but tease, surprising herself with her boldness.

He gave her an irritated look before responding. "I was about to tell you a story about Caeden, but if you don't want to hear—"

"No, please, I'm sorry. Please continue," she interrupted quickly.

"I thought that'd get your attention," he said with a playful wink, which made her giggle. "As I was saying, I've been around a while."

"A long while," she couldn't stop herself from saying, actually earning her a grin before he quickly hid it. Other than that, he chose to ignore her as he continued his story.

"And I've served under some really good soldiers, but none like Caeden. You were still pretty young at the last recruitment. Do you remember it at all?"

She could only shake her head, not wanting to interrupt now that the story had caught her full attention.

"I didn't think so. Every other century, the Royal Guard has recruitment, and at that time, any soldier who wishes can challenge to join. The existing members have the option to step down or accept the challenges to keep their position. The last one, almost ten years ago, was the first time Caeden challenged. Trevin, Levi, and I were already members and took up the challenge. Asher, the former captain, decided to step down. All of the other former members were defeated."

The mention of Asher brought a smile to

Amira's face. He had been a constant in her life growing up. She had been devastated when he stepped down and moved to Kimi to start a family with his new bride.

"I'd never seen anyone fight as Caeden did during the challenge." Amira could hear the admiration in his voice as he reminisced. "It shouldn't have been such a surprise; after all, Caeden had already made a reputation for himself with how quickly he had risen up the ranks, and at such a young age."

Osmond paused and she looked at him questioningly.

"What, you're not going to badger me about Caeden's age?" he asked, disgruntled.

"I'm a princess. I do not badger," she answered in a haughty tone, but ruined the effect when she giggled and admitted, "Besides, I already know Caeden's age."

He shook his head in what she assumed was amusement and continued. "Challenges lasted a fortnight, and word of Caeden's skill spread throughout the island. It was the largest crowd in our history. I have to admit, it was a mite unsettling to be on the other side of his blade." Osmond made a coughing noise to clear his throat, as if that last part had been difficult to confess.

"I wasn't the only one troubled by his skill. He'd fought like the world depended upon his success. He was so focused and driven; rumors began to spread of his ulterior motives. There were even murmurs of his intention to seize control of the kingdom," Osmond said ruefully with a shake of his head.

"What?" Amira was outraged. "How could they even dream of such a thing?"

"It's not unheard of. Sorin is a prime example of such corruption," he answered, shrugging.

"Sorin and Caeden are nothing alike!"

"The captain doesn't let many close; he never has. No one could be sure of his agenda at the time. We only knew that winning was imperative to him. And he did. He won every round against every opponent he faced."

Osmond might have been worried ten years ago, but he seemed fairly proud of that fact now, Amira noted.

"Why do you think it was so important to him?" she questioned.

Osmond shrugged again. "Maybe he felt he had something to prove, or maybe he just thrives on the competition and the victory. Who knows? Does it matter?"

"I guess not," she admitted. It was just another intriguing aspect of her warrior that she was eager to uncover.

Exhaustion was once again threatening to take over and Amira was having a difficult time keeping her eyes open.

"Rest now, girl. We'll be home before you know it," Osmond encouraged.

"I couldn't possibly rest without knowing..." She had to pause to yawn and he waited expectantly. "Just how old are you?"

"Cheeky female." She heard him mumble as he walked away, leaving her to fall asleep with a smile.

On the first day of the trip home, she had rarely found herself back in the dark room with Sorin again while asleep. When she did, she would always find him the same, sitting on the floor, staring into a single burning candle. He said nothing and neither would she. Instead, she would sit opposite him and watch him until the dream faded.

By the second day, she found herself in his company more and more, and was no longer content to sit and watch. She began pacing the room until her agitation built to a point where she could no longer contain it.

"Why? Why did you do this to me? To my family? To our people?" she demanded, and was surprised when he actually answered.

"Because I had to. I had to take what was mine," he said without malice, only as if stating a fact.

"I was never yours. The kingdom of Velius was never yours!" She couldn't prevent her voice from rising.

His head turned and his eyes bored into hers for

the first time in days as he questioned, "And what made it yours?"

The question threw her for a second before she finally responded with, "My family was deemed worthy to be the royal family."

"So does that mean I was deemed unworthy? Not good enough? Lacking? Why? Why was I born so undeserving?" These questions threw her off guard, but the pain in his voice completely unnerved her. "I did nothing wrong! I tried to be a good boy." His voice cracked and tears came to Amira's eyes. "But the demon came anyway."

Sorin turned to stare into the light once again. "He always knew where to find me," his voice turned eerily remote, "and he'd show me how vile and bad I really was. I had to stop him. I had to show him I was worthy; that I didn't deserve this. And when I took my rightful place as king, everyone would know, and he could never hurt me again."

Sorin began to sob and Amira's heart broke for him. Someone or something had turned him into the wretched person he had become. She felt torn and broken inside and wished to be anywhere but there. She let her back slide down the cold wall until she once again found herself sitting opposite of him; only this time she couldn't look at him, so she too stared into the candle as her feelings overwhelmed her. Neither one was capable of saying anything else.

"Princess?" A gruff voice startled her awake. She sat

up quickly and was grateful to find herself back in the transport. "Are you all right?" Osmond asked, giving her a funny look.

She had to think about it and do a mental inventory before she could answer honestly. "Yes," she said hesitantly. "Why?"

"Besides the obvious fact that you have slept for two days, we just crossed through the shield."

Amira rushed to the window. Seeing the island made her feel whole and secure once again. "We're almost there!" She smiled brightly at Osmond.

"What about the bond?"

She took a moment to check. "Same," she answered, her excitement dimming a little. She had hoped the bond would shift back upon her return.

With a nod, he turned to ready their gear. Not wanting to be idle with her thoughts, she joined him and tried to shake off the lingering sadness from her exchange with Sorin.

The transport doors were thrown open just minutes after they docked and Caeden sauntered in wearing a wicked grin. He easily caught her as she threw herself into his arms, tangling his fingers into her long hair and kissing her breathless.

"You're here," she whispered against his lips when they finally broke apart.

"Always," he promised. He scanned her face intently, "Are you okay?"

She tried to smile, but failed. "It didn't turn out like I had hoped," she admitted.

Osmond made himself scarce, unloading the transport while Caeden and Amira cuddled together, and she explained to him about their trip. He remained silent until she questioned, "Are you angry I withheld information?"

"No, because you were right, I wouldn't have allowed you to go, and it sounds like that was where you were needed. I'm proud of you, just don't do it again," he finished firmly.

"It didn't help our situation."

"No, but you helped Kearney's, and you discovered another possible threat to our people. As for our situation, it has changed a little." He told her about Sorin's plot and capture.

"I knew something was different with him," she murmured aloud as she thought of how their interactions had drastically changed.

Caeden tensed as he asked, "What do you mean? Does he still come to you?"

"Yes, but it's different now. He is no longer threatening. Something is wrong with him. He seems... broken."

"A couple nights ago, the lights in his holding cell failed, leaving him in complete darkness for hours." Amira sucked in a sharp breath; had she been responsible for that? Caeden arched his eyebrow in question, but continued when she didn't respond. "He has a severe phobia of the dark and has been unresponsive since."

Guilt and shame weighed heavy inside of her.

"But if he is still responsive with you, maybe we can use that to gain the information we need," Caeden finished hopefully.

Thoughts raced so quickly through her head, she could barely get out a soft, "I'll try."

Misunderstanding her hesitation, he rushed to reassure her. "I know he scares you, and I don't want you to have to do it either, but we're running out of options. It doesn't have to be today or even tomorrow. Let's get you home and rested first. Your people are anxious for your return, and you need to prepare for your coronation," he said with a grin, trying to distract her and relieve some of her tension.

"M-my coronation?"

"Yes, you will be queen, remember?" he teased with a wink. "The females have been running themselves ragged to make it special for you, especially Inaya."

"Oh my..." She knew she must look silly sitting there with a dazed look on her face, but at his announcement, all the chaos in her brain came to a halt. She'd always known she'd be queen someday, but she still felt taken by surprise and completely unprepared.

Caeden lifted her up and with a gentle kiss whispered, "Let's get you home."

The change in Caeden came so swiftly, it left

Amira confused and bereft. He had been smiling and holding her hand up until the moment they exited the transport. At the door, he dropped her hand, and as he stepped on land, his face became impassive. He took his place at her right and two steps behind, in perfect Guard formation. She tried to catch his eye, but he was intently focused on their surroundings. A loud cheer erupted and her attention was drawn to the crowd of soldiers who had come to escort her home. At least a dozen males had come to ensure her safe return to the palace.

She greeted them kindly and when they were prepared to depart, it was Osmond who approached to assist her to her mount her horse. Again, she looked toward Caeden, but he seemed completely oblivious to her presence. She tried not to feel the sting of rejection, reminding herself he was just doing his duty, but her chest still hurt and she had to fight back tears. She distracted herself by taking notice of all the changes around her. The temperature was much colder than it had ever been before, and the sky was gray and threatening. A chill ran up her spine and she pulled her blanket tightly around herself.

As they came to the palace entry, the soldiers held back the crowd, allowing them to dismount. The Royal Guard immediately converged and began escorting the princess inside, but at the top of the stairs she stopped them with a whispered, "Wait."

Caeden looked at her in question. She gave him a shaky smile and with big gray eyes full of fear, she turned to address her people. She clutched her shaking hands behind her back, but her expression was serene. Those conflicting details made his chest ache for her. A hush came over the crowd; all were eager to hear what she had to say.

Her voice shook as she began.

"In this time of suffering and grief, it is more important than ever for us to stand together and support one another. I am sorry for my absence in your time of need, but I am so very proud of the strength and compassion you have given to one another."

An angry boom of thunder interrupted her and shook the ground, causing more than one person from the crowd to gasp in fright. Amira tried to smile reassuringly, but didn't quite succeed.

"As you can see, the difficulties we have faced are not over yet, but together we are strong and will overcome any challenges that lie before us."

A deafening cheer rang out. Having a leader with such a beautiful spirit would help to heal and strengthen their people. Caeden could feel the hope and peace she brought to their people; his own heart felt lighter at her speech. He had to shake himself from his awe of her as she turned to enter and reclaim her home.

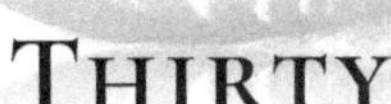

Thirty

ddressing her people had been terrifying. Knowing she was responsible for their tribulation weighed heavily on her. Seeing them gathered and hopeful, but looking to her to lead them and make things right, almost brought her to her knees. She sent a quick prayer for guidance and the strength she would need to bring them atonement.

As she turned, she caught Caeden's eye; there was something indecipherable shining in their warm depths. For a moment, his detachment was missing. Her heart skipped a beat and her breath caught, but all too soon, the look faded, the ice returned, and he was once again the vigilant guard there to protect her from hidden danger. She didn't understand what was going on with him, but now was not the moment to ask.

The large doors of her home loomed before her.

Returning was bittersweet; she was returning to the same building, but not the home she had once known. The security it used to provide had been stolen from her; fear and grief threatened to paralyze her. She was surrounded by people but felt small and alone.

The moment she walked through the doors, she was almost tackled to the ground. An overly excited Inaya slammed into her by way of greeting and suddenly she was no longer alone. Luckily, they were both saved from meeting the hard floor by Trevin's quick reflexes. After steadying them both, he surprised her by giving her a quick squeeze and whispering, "You did good." She realized she was surrounded by her Guard, not for protection, but to be officially welcomed home.

Inaya held her tightly, regaining her attention. "I'm so sorry I abandoned you when you needed me. I've been so worried," Inaya said.

"I've been worried about you, too. We're supposed to go on our adventures together," she said, making Inaya chuckle.

It became apparent her Guard wasn't going to wait patiently for them to catch up when Murdock pushed his sister out of the way.

"My turn; you two can girl talk later," he grumbled. Giving Amira a tight hug and a kiss on the cheek, he whispered, "Glad you're home."

She didn't have time to process that before she found herself in Dalek's arms and lifted off the ground.

"I forgot how tiny you are," he teased with a hearty laugh, earning him a swift kick in the shin. "And feisty, too!" He winked and set her back on her feet.

She was shocked at her own behavior, but they were all looking at her with a mixture of pride and joy. They had won. They'd defeated their enemy and regained the palace. She smiled brightly, and tears threatened to spill over. "Thank you," she told them. The words were inefficient to express the love and gratitude she felt, but their smiles and nods seemed to say they understood.

As her Guard backed away, she noticed all of the people in the room, waiting for her attention. It was a bit overwhelming, but she caught herself before she let it show on her face or in her body language. It was her responsibility, and she would face it.

"They can all wait," Caeden whispered, suddenly standing by her side. "You can go upstairs and rest first," he suggested.

"No, I'll do my duty first," she said, a small sigh slipping out before she could catch it.

"As you wish, Princess," he said, stepping back. "Would you prefer your meetings to be conducted within your father— your office," he corrected himself quickly, "or in the study?"

She gave him an understanding smile; she still had a hard time believing her father was gone. There was a lingering pain in her chest at the thought of going on without him. It would be an adjustment for everyone.

"The study, I believe. Thank you," she replied formally in return, still perplexed by his distance.

It was nearly dark outside by the time she finally emerged from the study. She had spent the entire day in meetings, catching up on current events, making decisions, addressing concerns, and generally reassuring everyone who had come to meet with her. Their island was still in chaos and the different territories no longer had leaders for the people to turn to, so they were all looking to her. They had not been prepared for the climate shift or the storms, which the shield had always protected them from. Even after an entire day, there was still so much left to do.

Her last meeting of the day had been with Inaya and the committee, led by Francine, which was responsible for the coronation ceremony that would take place the following evening. She had tried to convince them to put it off, but everyone agreed it would be good for morale, so she had finally given in.

Feeling more exhausted than she had in her entire life, she climbed up the stairs to the comfort and security of her room and fell into bed, not even bothering to undress, and was instantly asleep.

What felt like only minutes later, she jerked awake as the bodice of her dress loosened and was pulled away. Fear held her silent until panic took over, demanding she struggle and fight. She twisted, trying to claw her way from the bed, kicking and swinging at anything touching her. Before she could make it to the edge, a heavy body pressed the length of hers, pinning her to the bed. A deep voice finally penetrated her fear.

"Amira, it's okay. It's me."

"Caeden? What are you doing?" she asked as she pushed against him. He allowed her to dislodge him, only to sit up and pull her in his lap.

"I was trying to make you more comfortable. Have a long day?" He studied her face in the dim light, looking concerned.

She ignored his question and concern, remembering she needed answers from him.

"No, I meant, what are you doing here?"

"Where else would I be?" he asked as he nuzzled the sensitive skin of her throat. She shivered, and moaned at the feeling of his lips, tongue, and teeth nibbling at her. He was distracting her; she needed to focus.

"I don't know, standing guard outside my door and ignoring me?" she suggested irritably. He chuckled against her skin and it felt so good, it was hard to stay mad.

He lifted his head to search her eyes and was completely serious when he admitted, "I hurt you today. I'm sorry." He placed a gentle kiss to her lips.

"Why did you do it? Why did you pull away from me?" She hoped she sounded only mildly curious, not wanting him to see how badly it had hurt her.

"What's between us is no one else's business. You

are constantly the focus of attention; therefore, around others I will maintain a proper formality."

"So, you're saying you want to hide what is between us?" she asked in disbelief, her voice rising slightly.

"It's for your own good." His voice was a soft growl.

"My own good, or are you trying to avoid all of the burden that comes with being with me?" she questioned, trying to pull away from him. She was hurt all over again and suddenly very afraid of his answer.

He swiftly sat her on the bed and stood beside it, looking down at her. "Is that really what you believe?" he asked, running his fingers through his hair.

Looking up at him, she immediately felt guilty for letting her emotions color her words. Caeden was a good and honorable male. To insult and question his character was wrong. The anger drained out of her and she admitted softly, "No, I was wrong to say that. I'm sorry."

He knelt down beside the bed, putting them at eye level. He toyed with a lock of her hair as he considered his next words.

"I gave you reason to doubt me today," he said softly. "I'm sorry for that, but for now, it's better if we continue on this way." He didn't give her time to argue. "I love you. You are mine. Your 'burdens' are mine. Any responsibility you carry, I'll share the weight if I cannot carry it for you. Always."

His fingers were tangled in her hair, and he used it to tug her forward. Their lips met in a kiss, which wasn't gentle and loving, but fierce and consuming. Their lovemaking was different from before. It was desperate and rough, each needing to possess and reaffirm their claim on the other.

In the midst, Caeden stared intently in her eyes and her breath caught. The need to solidify that claim and bind them together was nearly irresistible, but something in his eyes changed and he buried his face in her throat. The moment passed, words unspoken. She was deeply disappointed, but he didn't give her much time to dwell on it as he satisfied her again and again. By the time he was finished, her mind and body were once again too exhausted to do anything but fall back into a deep sleep, except this time, she did it with a sated smile on her face while wrapped safe and secure in Caeden's arms.

She awoke as the sun kissed the horizon, and she wasn't completely surprised to find the bed beside her empty. They really hadn't resolved anything. Her sigh filled the empty room; she would have to try to change his mind again. In the meantime, it was time to start her day. She would start with the most unpleasant part first, she decided. It was time to visit Sorin.

Her hands shook the entire time she readied for the

day and continued to do so while she descended the stairs to the cellar. When she had questioned why he was being held down there, Caeden had explained the remaining soldiers loyal to Sorin were still occupying the regular holding cells and it was important to keep him secured in seclusion. Looking around at the cellar now, she agreed it was both secure and secluded, and looked nothing like the cellar it used to be.

Fear locked her in place as she reached the bottom step. The posted guard had come to attention the moment he had noticed her arrival, and was waiting expectantly for her to address him, but she found it difficult to push the words out. She had come to terms with seeing Sorin in her dreams and felt relatively safe that he wouldn't be able to harm her in his current state, but in reality he could easily hurt her. Just as she was about to talk herself out of this plan, the guard spoke up.

"Princess Amira, is there something you needed?"

"I-I had thought to visit the prisoner," she stammered her explanation.

"Alone?" He looked around as if he had somehow missed one of her guards trailing behind her, as if that were possible. Finding no one, he suggested, "Why don't you wait for a member of the Royal Guard to accompany you?"

She realized he saw her as weak and incapable of doing this on her own. She couldn't blame him. She had stood there acting like a scared rabbit ready to flee at the first hint of a threat, instead of the future Queen of Velius and ruler of Cashile. She straightened her shoulders and lifted her chin. That night, she would be crowned queen. And queens were not ruled by fear.

"No, I will see him now," she declared as she walked past him.

Looking uncomfortable, he started to protest. "But—"

She gave him what she hoped was a sweet smile and interrupted, "Besides, I'm not alone. You'll be here to protect me, right?"

His posture shifted instantly, his spine straightened, and his voice even deepened as he very seriously said, "Yes, of course, Princess. It is my honor."

She felt a twinge of guilt for manipulating him, but reminded herself it was something she needed to do by herself.

"Please escort me to his confinement area."

"Right this way, Princess."

He led her down the left walkway to a heavy door with a barred window.

And there he was. Just like in the dream, he sat with his back to the wall, staring blankly ahead.

"He hasn't moved or spoken in days," the guard informed her.

She nodded and requested for him to open the door, her eyes never leaving Sorin's motionless form.

"His chains allow him access to the bunk and anywhere along the far side of the room, so please stay within this area." He motioned to the front half of the room. She nodded her understanding. "Would you permit me to escort you inside?"

"No, thank you. Please wait outside the door." She smiled confidently, although she was feeling far from it. She kept her shaking hands clutched behind her back and tried to slow her racing heart with a deep breath.

She paused at the threshold, certain her presence would snap him out of his catatonic state, but minutes passed without a glimmer of acknowledgement or coherence. Her fear of him began to morph into concern, which was a feeling she wished to not have on his behalf, but was unable to prevent. She knelt down to his level and tried to catch his eye from across the room, only to find them lifeless and void.

"Are you all right?" she asked softly, breaking the oppressive silence. When no answer came, she wondered aloud, "Can you even hear me?" Still nothing.

Needing clarity, needing to understand, and driven by the instinct to help him, she opened herself up to their bond. Fear and desperation invaded her senses. She suddenly found herself sitting on the floor breathless; the hopelessness and despair were too much for her. She severed the link and struggled to breathe through the lingering feelings as they slowly faded.

"Princess, are you all right?" the guard asked nervously from the other side of the door.

"Yes, I'm fine. Please remain out there," she croaked out when he made a move to join her. He looked unsure, but followed her orders.

She picked herself off the floor and slowly made her way over to the broken shell of a person who used to be Sorin. Cautious, as if approaching a dangerous animal, she extended her arm slowly so he would know her intent, and rested her hand gently on his shoulder. She knelt in front of him and tried again to reach him.

"I know you're in there. There is nothing to fear here." She indicated the brightly lit room. "It's safe to talk with me. I can help you. We can help each other."

It seemed as if nothing she said made a difference. She thought back to their last conversation, searching for anything that might reach him. A thought occurred to her; hesitantly she said, "Sorin, you know the demon can't get you here, right?"

Instantly, she knew that had been the wrong thing to say. Three things happened simultaneously; outside, thunder boomed so loudly the building shook, Sorin made a noise that sounded similar to a dying animal, and her inner shields crumbled, consuming her in darkness.

Her first realization was that her entire body was throbbing. *How strange,* she thought as she opened her eyes to find worried brown ones staring down at her. She was too disoriented to feel any real fear or shock, but was a little disconcerted when she couldn't immediately recognize who the eyes belonged to. She did know that she was lying on her back and her head was propped in his lap. Even though he was looking down at her, she knew she didn't have his attention because he was murmuring to himself about torture and disembowelment. *What an odd topic choice.*

Her mind began to clear and she realized he was the guard posted at Sorin's door. She also realized she had no idea what his name was. She had been so caught up in her own task that she hadn't even thought to ask. Shocked by her own rudeness, she interrupted his muttered ramblings. "Excuse me, I don't mean to intrude, but what is your name?"

As if just realizing she had awakened, he fairly shouted, "Thank the angels, Princess! Are you all right? It's all my fault. I'm very sorry. I stepped away for only a few seconds. I'm so sorry! Captain is going to kill me!"

He was rambling again, but her mind was finally clear. She sat up and looked around her, seeing she had been lying on the bench at the guard's post in the cellar. How she got there was a mystery.

"What is your name?" she asked again, interrupting the soldier's detailed description of how Caeden would murder him and dispose of his dead corpse.

"It's Hershel, Princess."

"Hershel, I need you to focus and tell me what

happened." She could tell he was struggling to concentrate through his panic. "I'm all right. Everything will be fine, but please tell me what happened."

He nodded and began. "You were in the cell speaking with the prisoner when suddenly there was a loud blast outside and the world began to shake. I ran upstairs to find out what had happened. It sounded like the building above us had collapsed. When I reached the top, Felton, the guard stationed at the outside door, informed me it was only mighty thunder and lightning occurring very near. I rushed right back down and found you on the floor. I'm sorry, Princess, I'm not sure what he did to you. He didn't even look as if he had moved. I should have—"

Amira stopped him there. She had a feeling he could continue on for an indefinite amount of time. "I'm fine. He didn't touch me," she assured him. Her mind was still piecing together exactly what had happened, but she did know Sorin hadn't been trying to hurt her. "I need to finish my conversation with the prisoner," she informed him as she rose.

"No, no, no." He was suddenly blocking her way.

"What do you mean, 'no'?"

"I mean, umm... Captain will be here any minute. Please, wait for him to escort you in any further interaction with the prisoner."

"Caeden? Caeden is on his way here?"

There were little butterflies in her stomach at the

thought of seeing him; unfortunately, the little guys were warring with the giant butterflies that were in a panic about him finding her there.

"Yes, I sent Felton to retrieve him as soon as we knew you had been hurt."

"I'm not hurt!"

Great, just great. The little butterflies lost the battle and she was overcome by the fight or flight instinct. She eyed the stairs wistfully, but knew she wouldn't be able to leave Hershel alone to face Caeden. She brushed the dirt off her gown, took a deep breath to steady herself, and waited.

She didn't have to wait long before she heard what sounded like the cellar door being ripped off its hinges, followed by thunderous stomping rushing down the stairs. She noticed Hershel had moved closer to her side and was briefly amused by the thought that he hadn't done so in an effort to protect her, but himself. She quickly hid her amusement as Caeden, followed by what looked to be her entire Royal Guard and a quarter of her army, appeared before her.

"What happened?" he growled as his hands roamed her body, checking for injury.

"Uh-oh, Caeden, you're breaking the rules. What will people think?" she asked, trying to break the tension.

"Now is not the time to play with me," he warned, and held her from pulling away. "Where are you injured?"

She realized she was still a little hurt and resentful about waking up alone, and decided to push him. "But how will I keep you as my dirty secret if anyone sees we care for one another?"

A snicker came from behind Caeden. She thought it might have been Dalek, but she couldn't see around Caeden to check.

"Where. Are. You. Injured?" he demanded.

With a heavy sigh, she gave in. "I'm not hurt, nothing is wrong. I'm sorry you were bothered."

He stared at her for a moment; she thought he might be trying to detect if she was being honest. When satisfied, he nodded.

"What happened?" he barked.

"Noth—" she began, but he interrupted her.

"Not you," he said in a softer tone, before commanding, "Hershel, report."

His eyes stayed locked on hers during Hershel's entire recount, and to Amira's frustration, he was thorough. When he was finished, Caeden nodded and Hershel was escorted away along with the rest of the soldiers. She was entirely surrounded by the Royal Guard, making her feel very small and weak in comparison. They each stood at least a foot taller than her and a minimum of a hundred pounds heavier. Their size alone was intimidating, but displeasure on each of their faces was frightening. She reminded herself they weren't mad at her; they were upset because she had given them a scare.

"Now, fill in the blanks, starting with why you came here without one of us and why you thought it was okay to walk right up to a dangerous murderer all alone!" Caeden's voice had started soft, but ended in a rough growl.

The way he had to work so hard not to yell at her was a good indication she needed to reconsider her previous thought. Maybe they were mad at her.

Caeden was extremely sexy when he was angry, but she couldn't let that distract her or he'd walk all over her. Slamming her hands on her hips, she asked, "Should I have informed you of my plans before or after you snuck out of my bed this morning without even a kiss good-bye?"

"Either would have been fine," he answered, unimpressed by her show of attitude. His lips twitched and she realized he was fighting a smile.

"Am I amusing you?"

He ignored her question and asked, "What happened in that room?"

With a sigh she gave in.

"I tried to reach him, but I said the wrong thing and his emotions overwhelmed me. That's all. I'm sorry to have wasted your time."

"Seeing you is never a waste of my time." Caeden's husky voice sent a quiver deep inside of her. He toyed with a lock of her hair absentmindedly while he spoke. "Next time you are determined to do something foolish, bring a guard with you."

She was so enthralled by his tone that she almost missed his insult. Foolish? Before she could work up the appropriate indignation, he continued, "What are your next plans, baby?"

Her heart leaped at his use of an endearment and she decided she could forgive his insult.

"Just a meeting," she answered.

With a nod, he declared, "That should be safe enough."

"Of course it's safe. Inaya and I—"

"Your meeting is with Inaya?" he cut her off to ask.

"Yes," she answered hesitantly.

He looked over her shoulder to where the other Guard members had withdrawn. She had forgotten they were still present.

"Trevin, you want this one?"

Trevin answered with a shake of his head. "Not a good idea right now." He looked to Murdock. "Can you handle them?"

"When you two finally stepped up, I thought I was finished chasing after those two," he grumbled, but nodded.

That settled, Caeden brought his attention back to her.

"Don't be too difficult for him," he told her, grinning.

"We don't need a babysitter, Caeden," she informed him.

He stole her breath and frustration as he pulled her

close, nuzzled her throat, and whispered, "The next time I sneak out of your bed, I'll give you more than a kiss good-bye."

Before she could respond, he was already making his way up the stairs.

"Close your mouth, Princess." Dalek smirked as he passed her to follow Caeden out. Osmond left with only a nod in her direction, but Trevin stopped in front of her to have his say.

"Drink tea, talk fashion, do... female stuff." He made an aggravated motion with his hand. "Just stay out of trouble." Then he too was gone.

"Your mouth is hanging open again, Princess," Murdock informed her with a deep chuckle.

"Did he really say that?"

"Yeah," Murdock answered, snickering.

"No wonder he's having so much trouble with your sister!"

Murdock laughed so hard at that, he was left clutching his stomach and wiping tears from his eyes. "Come on, Princess, let's go see if I can keep you two ladies occupied."

She began to follow him out, but as she passed Hershel, she remembered to have a word with him.

"Sorin's cell is never to become dark. Make sure he is cleaned up and as comfortable as you can make him."

He was her enemy, but he was also one of her people. She felt responsible for him. She had felt his fear and pain, knew he was locked inside of himself in unbearable agony, and she would do everything thing in her power not to add to it, if she couldn't find a way to ease it.

THIRTY-ONE

You're sure about this?" Francine asked, pulling Amira's attention away from the window where she was captivated by the storm cloud threatening Cashile.

"Absolutely," she answered, giving Francine a bright smile.

Francine let out a very un-Francine-like squeal and jumped from her seat. "I'm so happy for you both! The council and I will have everything ready to take place directly after your coronation."

"Thank you," she said, and dismissed her so she could begin preparation for the evening's events.

"It's your big, *big* day, but you don't seem very excited," Inaya remarked, joining her at the window, where she was once again staring at the sky.

"I am, but... something happened today. I've been

trying to work it out in my head. The conclusion I'm coming up with isn't good... but I'm afraid I'm right."

"Run it by me, let me see if I can help," Inaya encouraged.

"When I upset Sorin today, there were physical manifestations of his emotions in the weather. I think... I think he may be responsible for this storm and everything else that's going on."

"You're referring to the massive thunder today, right? But couldn't that have just been a coincidence?" Inaya asked.

"It could, but I don't think so. After my father's death, the shield began to weaken, allowing the cold climate of the northern hemisphere to penetrate. The island's climate shifted so quickly that it set off a series of storms and other natural disasters, but after the bonding ceremony, the shield became stable and it has remained stable." She turned to make sure Inaya was following. "The only thing that has changed is that Sorin is now responsible for the bond. As his mental status has deteriorated, so has our weather. The moon even became red the night of his capture, the night I..." She swallowed hard, and changed what she was about to say, unable to admit her cruelty. "The night he withdrew inside of himself."

"Wow." Inaya fell against the wall, as if the news left her too weighed down to support herself. "What does this mean? What are we going to do?"

"I don't know. I'm not sure how much more the

island can take... and it looks like this is going to get bad." Her attention was once more drawn to the window.

"Have you told anyone else?"

"Not yet, there are a couple details I need to work out first."

"Whatever you need, I'm here," Inaya reminded her.

"I know." She smiled.

"If you had said your meeting included Francine, Caeden wouldn't have assigned you a babysitter," Murdock interrupted as he made his way into the chamber.

"But where is the fun in that?" Amira questioned, and both females burst into laughter.

"You're both brats," he returned with an amused grin and a shake of his head. "So, is all of your business concluded for the afternoon?" he asked when they had finally gotten themselves under control.

"For now," Amira answered.

"Then what's next?" He clapped his hands in a 'bring it on, I'm ready for anything' fashion.

"When is the storm predicted to hit?" Amira asked, obviously confusing him with the change in topic.

"It's still out a ways over the ocean, so we're esti-mating early tomorrow evening."

"The rest of the Guard is out there preparing?" She motioned to the window.

"Yes," he answered hesitantly. "Why?" He sounded a little afraid.

Amira barely contained her grin. "The tea is gone and we're out of female stuff to do." She shrugged and turned to Inaya. "Feel like playing with the big boys?"

"Of course, just let me change," Inaya answered excitedly.

"Wait, wait, wait!" Murdock shouted quickly, jumping to block his sister's path. "You females want to help weatherproof buildings, stockpile supplies and food, herd and pen animals, and get dirty and sweaty and... Don't you need to be getting ready for tonight?" he asked, grasping at the question as if it were a lifeline.

"It's barely midmorning, we have plenty of time for that." Inaya waved him off. "Plus, it sounds like fun."

"Fun!" He looked to Amira in question, and Inaya took advantage of his distraction to skirt around him.

Amira gave him a mischievous smile. "I need to change as well. Shall we meet you outside?"

"Meet me in the front hall," he commanded. Amira almost felt sorry for him as he stood there looking resigned and full of dread.

Caeden wiped the sweat from his brow as he watched Trevin's angry approach. Trevin rarely became angry, so he had a pretty good guess as to what had set him off —or who, to be more specific.

"Why are you allowing this?" Trevin demanded.

"What did she do now?" Caeden asked with an amused grin.

"She? Try *them*."

That knocked the grin off his face quickly. "What did they do?"

"You mean you haven't seen them yet?" Trevin had a wicked gleam in his eyes.

It was going to be bad. Caeden prepared himself. He took a deep breath before saying, "Take me to them."

Trevin led him through the palace gates toward the small village outside the walls.

"What are they doing way out here?"

"The last I saw, those two stubborn females were dragging a crate of food reserves, which weighed twice as much as they do combined."

"What do they think they're doing?"

"Helping to prepare," Trevin quoted them.

"Couldn't they find a way to help from inside the palace walls?" Caeden asked, exasperated.

"I tried that logic, but your princess declared this was where they could be of the maximum service."

"And just where is Murdock in all of this? He's supposed to be keeping them safe and out of trouble," Caeden growled.

"Can you believe they put him to work, too? He was doing his best to follow orders and trail behind the little imps."

Under different circumstances, Caeden might have found the situation hilarious, but it was too soon after Amira had been in danger for her mischief to amuse him. Right on the heels of that thought, he spotted Murdock about fifty feet in the distance, standing next to a two-story home waving his arms in the air like a madman, yelling and cursing the sky. *Maybe this is amusing,* he thought with a grin, until he spotted a brunette with an angel's face peering over the top of the roof. His blood turned to ice in his veins and he was sure his heart stopped completely.

"Really, Murdock, you're making quite the scene," Amira tried to reason with him.

"Princess, this has gone too far! You will come down immediately!"

"Murdock, all of this yelling really is distracting. We probably should be focusing; we are on a roof, after all," she answered in a patient tone usually reserved for small children.

"You're on a... I know you're on a roof!" He began waving his arms again and yelling phrases she had never heard before. She looked over to where Inaya was working a few feet away and asked, "What's a bollocks?"

Inaya grinned, and then poked her head over the side to look down at her brother. "You know, if you're going to use that kind of language in front of Amira, then you can be the one to explain the meanings to her," she chided.

He looked shameful for a moment before going on the offense. "As for you, young lady, do you realize you are responsible for risking the life of your future queen?"

"Me? How am I responsible? It was her idea to volunteer for this job," Inaya defended.

While the siblings argued back and forth, Amira tried to continue working, but a particularly colorful comment from Murdock caught her attention and she couldn't help but join back in.

"Hey, I understood that one! But I don't believe that is even physically possible," Amira said cheerfully.

"Don't make me come up there and show you," he threatened.

"Can you bring that extra tarp on your way up?" she returned, but as she turned her attention in the direction of the tarp, movement caught her eye. Caeden and Trevin were quickly approaching and neither looked very pleased; in fact, they looked down-right furious. "Uh-oh."

"What?" Inaya asked, turning to see the males approaching. "I think it's time to go," she announced, heading to the ladder propped against the rear of the building.

"Don't leave me!" Amira squealed.

But Inaya was already making her descent. She

reached the ground moments before the males rounded the building. Trevin gave chase as Caeden stomped up the ladder. Amira straightened and prepared to plead her case. Before his name fully passed her lips, he bent, his shoulder pressed against her midsection, and she was lifted off the roof. Caeden turned swiftly back to the ladder.

"Caeden, you'll drop me!" she shrieked.

A growled, "Be still," was his only response. She thought that was good advice. From her position, she had a perfect view of the unforgiving ground as Caeden steadily made his way down. She clutched his shirt and squeezed her eyes tightly closed. When they reached the bottom, she was too grateful for their safe arrival to demand to be put down immediately. She vaguely noticed Trevin disappearing around the building, but her attention was drawn to Murdock, who looked in danger of injuring himself with his great big belly laughs.

"You think this is funny?" she demanded, awkwardly crossing her arms over her chest. He was still nodding and laughing as Caeden toted her out of sight.

"Umm... Caeden?" she asked hesitantly as he silently carried her down a path between buildings and around corners. She had no idea where he was taking her, but he seemed intent on carrying her the entire way.

"Be quiet."

It sounded like a warning. She decided it was probably best to acquiesce, at least until he put her on her feet.

He entered a building and closed the door firmly before setting her down and walking away. She looked around to see he had brought her to an empty stable. She brought her attention back to him. He paced a couple feet away from her, mumbling to himself as he ran his fingers through his hair in agitation. Her first instinct was to try to sneak away while he was distracted, but she had a feeling that wouldn't work out to her benefit.

When she couldn't take the silence a moment longer, she tried again. "Caeden?"

He paused to stare up at her; head bowed, fingers still tangled in his hair. She was sure he had never looked so angry, and possibly never as sexy, either.

"What were you thinking?" His voice was eerily calm.

"What? You mean just now?" Her cheeks flamed with embarrassment. Had she been that obvious?

"When you decided to climb up on that roof!" His voice was no longer calm.

Relieved that she hadn't been caught, she tried to reason with him. "The roof was damaged in the last storm; it needed to be covered with a tarp to protect it until it can be repaired."

She was wrong, he could look angrier.

"So you, who have no experience doing physical

labor, decided to climb up on a damaged, possibly unstable roof to do the job? Is that what you're telling me?"

"It wasn't a difficult task, Caeden," she defended.

"It was a dangerous and foolish task!"

"It needed to be done," she argued in frustration.

"But not by YOU."

"I was trying to help!" she yelled. "I was trying to be useful and productive for once."

"There are other ways to be useful."

"If there is a job that needs to be completed, why shouldn't I be the one to do it?"

"Because you are the ruler of Cashile, our future queen!"

"I'm just a person! What makes me different? What makes me worthy to be queen if not my actions?" Sorin's accusations swirled through her head.

Her uncertainty was clear and seemed to calm his anger. In a much softer and more reasonable voice he answered, "Amira, I can understand and appreciate your motivations, but you don't have to prove yourself. Your bloodline was chosen for a reason. You have a greater purpose, a greater responsibility, and you cannot risk yourself in such a needless fashion."

"What is my purpose?" she asked in a small voice, tears gathering in her eyes.

He pulled her into his arms and ran his fingers through her hair. "I'm sorry, I can't answer that for you. Each person must discover their own purpose."

He held her quietly and she was grateful he didn't try to offer her excuses or empty promises. She tilted her lips and kissed him gently.

"Will you accompany me to the ceremony tonight, not as my guard, but as my escort?" When it looked like he might deny her, she added, "Please?"

He searched her face carefully, looking for any trace of doubt. "Are you sure?"

"Absolutely," she answered without hesitation.

"And will you be climbing up on any more roofs or conducting any other foolish activities today?" His eyebrows rose in question.

She had to think that through before she could answer honestly. His lips twitched in a surprised grin at her need to pause and consider her answer.

"No, I don't believe I will," she finally answered.

"Thank the heavens," he said, not bothering to hide his grin, and she found herself grinning back. He grew serious and stated formally, "Princess, it would be my honor to escort you tonight."

She flung herself back into his arms and kissed him with all of the excitement and love exploding inside of her. The kiss quickly turned carnal, but Caeden ended it before either one of them was satisfied.

"Love you, Princess," he whispered against her lips.

"I love you, too."

"Good." He nibbled gently on her bottom lip. "Now let me walk you home, where you can get ready and stay out of trouble."

"Are you sure you don't want to carry me back?" she teased as he pulled away.

In return, he playfully lunged for her. She yelped and darted away, rounding a support beam to put between them. When she turned to watch his next move, her breath caught in her throat at the intensity of his stare. Eyes locked on his prey, he took a step toward her. Her warrior was excited by the chase. Heart pounding, she stepped back.

"Now that I think about it, I'm not ready to return to the palace just yet." The huskiness of her tone surprised her.

"Is that right?" He stalked forward, matching her retreat step for step.

"Yes. I believe there is one more foolish action I need to take first."

His eyes narrowed. "Which is?"

Instead of answering, she made her move. Turning, she darted toward the back of the stable. If the purpose were to escape, it would have been a bad decision, but escape was not what she had in mind at all. A rough growl rumbled behind her and she knew he had taken the bait. She only made it as far as he allowed.

A strong arm wrapped around her waist, hauling her up against his hard body. His heavy breath brushed her neck, sending a shiver down her spine.

"Indeed, it is foolish to try to run from me. I will never let you get away."

Before she could formulate a response, his mouth

latched on to her neck, teeth scraping the sensitive skin, tongue soothing the pain but creating a deeper ache. Instinctively, her body arched against his as she blindly reached for him, needing to touch him, needing to hold him close.

His hand slid from her waist, up her ribs to cup her breast, squeezing firmly, rolling and pinching her nipple between his fingers. His rough touch thrilled her and all logical thought escaped her. She no longer cared they were in a stable or that she was not behaving as a princess should. She needed him.

Her hand snaked between their bodies, cupping him through his pants. With a groan, he pressed himself into her palm more firmly, biting down on her neck as he did so.

"Is that what you need, Princess? Will it sate this need you have to do something foolish?"

"Y-yes."

It was a breathless whisper, but he must have heard her because he reacted instantly. His hand to her chin, he tilted her head, giving him access to her mouth, taking it in a savage kiss. She was so caught up that she didn't realize he'd begun to undress her until the cool air hit her naked chest. Breaking the kiss, she tried to turn in his arms, but hands latched on to her hips, tugging her backside firmly against his rigid erection.

"No, just like this," he growled in her ear, sending a jolt of excitement through her. Grabbing her hands, he placed them on the shoulder-high stall wall in front of them, bending her forward slightly. "Keep them there," he commanded.

She did as she was told as he quickly divested her of the rest of her clothing. She'd never felt so vulnerable and exposed in her life, but as his hand caressed the length of her spine down to her butt and squeezed possessively, she'd never felt as sexy either.

When his lips replaced the warmth of his hand on her flesh, she jumped and tried to turn, but his strong arms held her in place.

"No, stay just as you are. I need this." His desire was clear in his tone, and she wanted nothing more than to please him.

Glancing over her shoulder, she realized he was kneeling behind her, giving him an intimate view of her body. Part of her acknowledged she should be embarrassed, but that thought was quickly lost as his tongue made its first pass across the very core of her. It was a feeling like no other she had ever experienced, and she instantly craved more, which Caeden seemed more than happy to oblige. Unconsciously, she found herself arching her back and widening her stance to give him better access. He devoured her like a starving man, and when his tongue pierced her opening, she thrust back eagerly, her body exploding against his mouth.

He seemed to know when she could take no more. With one final swipe of his tongue, he pulled away. She had never felt more content or more alive than she did at that moment. Once again, she tried to turn to face him, but was halted by his one-word command.

"Stay."

She didn't have to wait long before the heat of his warm, naked body surrounded hers. His hands were in motion—one squeezing her breast as the other slid down her body to reignite her need for him. His fingers zeroed in on her pleasure spot, caressing it with just the right amount of pressure. Unexpectedly, her body coiled for another release. He must have felt it too, because he chose that moment to surge forward, fully impaling her. The mixture of the pleasure and pain, and the overall rightness of their connection, sent her spiraling into an ecstasy that she never dreamed existed.

Caeden was relentless in his passion as he took her from behind. Thrusting over and over, he fed her every desire and fulfilled her every need, using his hands and his mouth to heighten the pleasure. And when his climax finally came, Amira found she received as much satisfaction in it as she had her own.

THIRTY-TWO

Pacing at the foot of the stairs, Caeden waited to escort Amira to her coronation ceremony. His mind was swirling with doubts. He needed to protect her honor, but she was determined to oppose his efforts. He should have been firm and denied her request, but he had seen the insecurity in her beautiful gray eyes, and with the sweet way she had begged, it had been impossible to say no.

He couldn't help worrying over what this would do to her reputation and her credibility. Their people were afraid and in a state of unrest. Amira couldn't afford a scandal or to be the cause of any more doubts. How was he going to fulfill her request and safeguard her against any possible fallout at the same time?

"You could try to trust her judgment."

Trevin's voice startled him from what he thought had been his inner dialogue, but must have been muttered ranting. He stopped midstride and looked up to find Trevin leaning against the wall, legs crossed in front of him. He looked too relaxed to have just arrived.

"She's not the naïve, starry-eyed female we once thought her to be," Trevin continued. "Hasn't she proven herself to be a strong, competent ruler who values the needs of her people?"

"I have no doubts on her competence—"

"Then trust her judgment on this." Trevin straightened away from the wall and took a few steps closer. "Don't let what others think come between you. You belong together, that's plain for anyone to see." Trevin slapped him on the shoulder and turned him to face the stairs. "Now claim your princess."

And there she was at the top of the stairs. Their eyes locked and everything else faded away. She was the most beautiful sight he had ever seen. As she descended, he allowed his eyes to travel down to take in the rest of her glory. The soft, silky skin of her throat and shoulders was left bare, inviting his soft kisses and teasing love bites. Her breasts were encased in a tight corset-style bodice, which bared an enticing amount of cleavage without being indecent. The gown cinched tightly around her small waist before flowing gracefully to the floor.

He hadn't commanded his feet to move, but suddenly found himself standing at her side in the middle of the staircase. Her eyes were shining mercurial silver. Without thought, he pulled her body firmly against his and captured her lips with his own.

Reluctantly ending the kiss, he whispered against her lips, "You look incredible." He watched as her eyes brightened even more and her cheeks pinkened bashfully.

She thanked him softly, then allowed her eyes to trail down the length of him, taking in his formal attire. When she remained frozen in place, he had to ask, "Am I suitable?"

"You're magnificent," she answered in a daze, before turning bright red with embarrassment.

Caeden's laughter echoed on the stairs. He couldn't help it; she was delightfully charming and unintentionally entertaining. As she softly giggled beside him, his tension slid away. He loved her. She was his everything and he needed her to know that. He bent, kissed her gently, met her eyes, and told her in no uncertain terms exactly what she meant to him.

"No one has ever loved another as much as I love you. It just couldn't be possible."

Her eyes filled with tears, but her smile brightened the room. She bit her bottom lip nervously and he waited patiently for her to share whatever thought had come into her mind. It came soft and sweet, and almost brought him to his knees.

"That's great," she whispered, "because I've had your coronation prepared to take place after mine."

"Excuse me?" His brain had difficulty making sense of her words.

"I adore you," she said, almost shyly. "I want you as my consort; as our king."

"Amira..." It ripped him apart to have to remind her. "We can't join in the sacred blood bond, not while you are still bound to Sorin. If we tried, most likely it wouldn't be successful, but it could also be dangerous for you." The hurt shining in her eyes made his gut clench. "I'm sorry."

"I know this," she answered with a sad smile, "but I still want you to take your place at my side through the marriage ceremony. And maybe... someday..." She trailed off.

"We'll find a way," he promised.

"And tonight?" she asked, looking hopeful.

For the second time that day, he found himself asking, "Are you sure?" His voice was husky with the emotions he was struggling to contain.

A silent tear fell to her cheek as she smiled beautifully and nodded.

Trevin's advice echoed in his head as he watched that single tear slide down her cheek and fall to the floor. He was going to trust her judgment.

"Okay." He offered her his arm. "Let's do this."

He knew his acceptance hadn't been eloquent or romantic, but she didn't seem to mind as she latched on to his elbow and allowed him to lead her down the stairs and out into the courtyard where the ceremonies would take place.

Walking out with Caeden at her side, seeing her people gathered together, illuminated by the enchanting candlelight, she felt a sense of rightness that had been missing since the death of her father. They made their way down the candlelit path to the stage, where Francine and the newly appointed council of healers would preside over the ceremonies. At the top of the stairs, Caeden pulled her to a stop, his eyes holding her captive as he brought her hand to his lips. A soft kiss, conveying his feelings for all to witness, stole her breath.

"I love you," she whispered.

"Always," he promised in return. "Now go accept your rightful place as queen. I'll be right here."

His words gave her the confidence and reassurance she needed to turn and walk the few steps that would lead her to her fate; one of which she was both fearful and accepting.

The crowd seemed impossibly quiet as Francine began the ceremony.

"Princess Amira of Velius, successor to the throne and rulership of the island of Cashile, by decree of the angels, with the blessing of the Spirit of the Universe, the time has come for you to claim your rightful authority. Princess Amira, please affirm that you accept and embrace your duty unconditionally."

"I do." She was surprised her voice rang out confidently and didn't waver with her nervousness.

With an encouraging smile, Francine continued, "And do you unreservedly join in the covenant of your forebearers that will permanently bind you to the shielding and sanctuary granted to the Nephilim by the blessed angels?"

"I do."

"Please kneel," Francine instructed with a definitive nod.

Caeden appeared at her side at once to assist her into position. She gave him a grateful smile; she was unsure if she could have done it without help in her gown without embarrassing herself. Once she was settled, he returned to his position at the rear of the stage.

Francine turned to address the crowd.

"By virtue of the council of healers, Vivi will perform the ceremony."

Amira didn't know Vivi well, but she had been chosen for the task because she was the most knowledgeable of the untrained healers. Vivi took Francine's place as her helpers prepared a large circle of white candles surrounding them, and lit them one by one. Once finished, the helpers retreated, leaving Amira and Vivi alone in the circle of light.

"It is my honor to serve you, Princess. Are you ready to continue?" Vivi asked softly.

From her kneeling position, Amira had to tilt her head far backwards to acknowledge her.

"Yes, thank you."

Vivi knelt beside her supplies, retrieving a sharp-looking silver dagger with a shiny black handle. Seeing the blade glinting in the candlelight sent a chill down Amira's spine. She watched closely as Vivi dipped it in what appeared to be water; then she placed the wet tip to the ground and traced a circle around the inside of the candles. Gently placing the dagger down, she began the next step of the sacred ritual, which had been taught to their ancestors by the very angels who had created this safe haven for them. She held a small bundle of white sage to the flame of a yellow candle. When the sage began to smoke, she smoothly blew out the candle. She rose and once again made her way around the circle; three times she went around with the burning sage before stopping in front of Amira and kneeling before her.

"I will bless and cleanse you, Princess," she said softly.

Amira nodded in response. Vivi started at her chest, over her heart, and then brought the herb smoke to Amira's right side before circling to the left until she had been completely covered. The acrid tang of the sage burnt her nose and irritated her eyes, but she was careful not to give any indication of discomfort, aware of the hundreds of eyes upon her. When that was complete, Vivi extinguished the bundle in a small bowl filled with sand. Finally, she grabbed the last bowl and the dagger, returning to Amira. Amira's heart pounded and there was a buzzing in her ears. Vivi must have noticed her apprehension because she smiled reassuringly as she placed the bowl and dagger before Amira. Amira took a deep breath and willed herself to calm; it was almost over.

Vivi stood tall. Confidently raising her arms in the air, she began:

"Spirit of the Universe,
Watchers in the wind,
You who stand in shadows,
And you who reside within."

Lowering her arms, Vivi methodically lit three lavender candles before continuing.

"The covenant that was blessed
Requires a new anchor.
Heavy is this burden,
Exalted is this vessel."

Vivi stood before Amira and placed her hand upon her head.

"Grant her your benediction,
Guide her with your wisdom."

Vivi then picked up the bowl filled with soil and the dagger. She held the dagger out to Amira.

"This must be given freely," she whispered.

Amira's hand shook as she took the dagger in her

right hand and slashed a line across the palm of her left. The wound stung and the blood began to pool. Vivi placed the bowl under her hand, allowing the blood to drip inside.

"Blood to Earth,
This bond is sealed,
Legacy be now fulfilled."

Vivi held the bowl in the air.

"Spirit of the Universe,
Bestower of this rite,
Attest to this new covenant,
Embrace it with your might."

She then purposefully set down the bowl and blew out the lavender candles one by one. Picking up the dagger, she once again dipped it into the water, placed the tip to the ground, and drew a circle around the ring of white candles, but this time going in the opposite direction. When finished, she addressed the crowd.

"By divine merit, I present to you the Queen of Velius and sovereign of Cashile. Arise, Queen Amira."

The crowd cheered joyfully, and Caeden came forward to assist her to her feet. He bowed slightly, and then pressed a possessive kiss to her lips.

By then, Vivi was clearing away the ceremonial paraphernalia and Francine was center stage, smiling at them brightly. She turned to address the audience, who had also witnessed the kiss, and declared, "I am also excited to announce our queen has chosen her king." The crowd went wild. "With your indulgence, we'll make it official," she continued when they began to settle.

A small table was brought forth, containing the supplies needed for the wedding ceremony. A tall, willowy female with long black hair and ivory skin stepped in front of Amira and Caeden.

"I'm Lyra." She bowed respectfully. "It is my honor to perform your wedding ceremony. Please come this way."

She led them over to the table. Amira immediately recognized the sweet vanilla-like scent of burning sweetgrass, deeply breathing in the calming aroma.

Although the ceremony was taking place in public, it was an intimate affair, as the crowd seemed to fade away for Amira. Only she, Caeden, and Lyra existed in that moment.

"I was told there would be no blood bond?" Lyra questioned.

Amira looked down at her still bleeding hand clutching a bandage, but answered in what she hoped was a confident voice.

"Not at this time, you are correct." She met Lyra's eyes and was grateful to find only acceptance and understanding instead of pity or questions. Caeden wrapped his arm around her waist and tugged her body close to his.

"We'll find a way," he whispered against her temple before returning his focus to Lyra.

"Very well, we will proceed as normal except we

will forgo the drawing of blood before you clasp hands." She waited for their nod of understanding before smiling brightly and saying, "Let us begin.

"We are a blessed people, with our strength, resilience, and our longevity, but time is not always our friendly companion. Without love, life is nothing. Without love, death is empty," Lyra began solemnly, lighting a single red candle.

Caeden's arm tightened as a chill swept down her spine. Lyra hesitated until Amira met her eyes. She gave an approving smile as she continued.

"But the truly fortunate among us are those who find the one they are meant to spend eternity with." She then turned to Caeden. "Caeden, it is my honor, but not my right, to bind you to Queen Amira. Only you have this right. If this is your will, declare it at this time."

Amira's heart stopped, and she felt the buzzing in her head from lack of oxygen. She reminded herself to breathe before she passed out and ruined her own wedding. She turned to Caeden as he gave his answer. The intensity and love shining in his eyes brought tears to hers.

"This is my will," he promised her. Amira's tears began to fall in contrast to her brilliant smile.

At that point, he would have sliced his palm with the ceremonial dagger in preparation of the blood bond. Amira refused to allow herself to dwell on what could not be, and focused on her overwhelming joy.

"Queen Amira." Lyra gained her attention. "It is my honor, but not my right, to bind you to Caeden. Only you have this right. If this is your will, declare it at this time."

Amira again met Caeden's eyes; she hoped her voice reflected all of the emotions she tried to convey in the four small words. "It is my will."

"Please join hands," Lyra instructed.

This is where the sacred blood bond would have been sealed, Amira thought.

Lyra grabbed the braided cord of green, gold, and pink silky cloth, and wound it intricately around their arms from elbow to wrist, forming a knot at their clasped hands.

"Let the strength of your will bind you together and the life that courses through your blood make you inseparable in this life and beyond, where you shall meet, remember, and love again."

Lyra bent and blew out the candle. When she straightened, she declared, "Physical restraints are no longer needed, for you are one."

She slid her hands up their combined arms, unexplainably able to slide the cord off as she went without unwinding or untying it.

"Caeden, if it is your will, you may seal this union with a kiss," Lyra said with a knowing grin.

It must have been his will, because Amira found her body pressed tightly to his as his lips slammed to hers before Lyra even finished speaking. The kiss was slow and thorough, full of promise.

"Excuse me, Caeden," Lyra interrupted when the kiss lingered. Caeden gave Amira one last mind-altering kiss before pulling away and giving Lyra his attention. "We have one last detail to attend to before we can all celebrate; your coronation."

He gave her an affirmative nod and she bowed in return before turning to Amira. "Please proceed," she said, handing Amira the dagger and the same bowl used in her coronation, containing soil of the Earth and her own blood.

She stepped in front of Caeden, taking in his serious expression and complete focus. As queen, it was her duty to preside over his coronation.

"Please kneel," she instructed. Once he was in place, she began. "By divine merit, my family was charged with the sacred duty of safeguarding our people and this sanctuary. As my consort, I ask that you join in this covenant and become my king."

Although he had already privately agreed, she trembled with worry, and was almost afraid to ask the next question. "Caeden, what say you?" she asked in a near whisper.

A sexy grin played on his lips, easing her anxiety and causing her to tremble for a completely different reason, before he answered, "It would be my honor, my queen."

She extended the dagger to him. "This must be given freely."

He took the dagger from her hand, his eyes never leaving hers as he slashed his palm and held it over the bowl.

"The covenant is sealed," Amira declared, fighting a huge smile, but losing.

Once complete, Lyra came forth to retrieve and secure the bowl and dagger.

"Please stand," Amira instructed. As he rose, she lowered herself in a deep curtsey, formally addressing him with, "My king."

He bowed in acknowledgement, completing the ceremony. Amira immediately launched herself into his arms, bursting with excitement and overwhelmed with love.

The celebration lasted long into the night: they feasted, they laughed, they danced, and when they finally made it to their chamber, they loved. It was the best night of her life... and then it became the most difficult.

THIRTY-THREE

The demon sat perched unnaturally on the balls of his feet with a sardonic grin, his eyes flickering between black and red, but never leaving Sorin's. He was hungry... empty. The satisfaction of breaking Sorin waned, as it always did. It was never enough, could never be enough. He needed more, always more. But Sorin had nothing left. It was now clear to Sorin how he had been influenced and used by the demon. If he were stronger, better, maybe...

"But you're not. Never were," the demon answered, reading his thoughts.

Sorin refused to respond, determined to give nothing else away. He stared silently, unmoving, as he had since the demon materialized, putting a form to the voice that had always called to him from the darkness; the driving force that had controlled the course of his life.

"Do you really believe that? As much as I'd like to take the credit, the darkness is all yours. I've just given you direction, a purpose, if you will," the demon purred. "We're so close, don't give up on me now. You'll miss all of the fun."

Was he giving up? Or maybe, for the first time he was fighting? Sorin questioned himself.

"Fighting? Fighting?" the demon asked with a chilling laugh, before his features turned to granite. "You think you can defy me?" The demon stood to his full height and spread his magnificent opalescent wings. His deceptive beauty was mesmerizing. Sorin's enthrallment seemed to pacify the demon and he calmed, tucking his massive wings behind himself and clasping his hands behind his back. "I have made you great. I have made you a king. It was your own weakness that you could not hold it for more than a few days. You have failed us both."

He began to pace the small confines of the room, the dream state making it seem endless, his eyes never leaving Sorin. "No matter, it will be over soon." At his prediction, thunder rumbled in the distance, striking fear into Sorin's heart. Still he struggled to show no reaction, to calm his thoughts. He would give nothing more to the wicked creature.

Once again, the demon laughed, the cruel sound echoing in the small confines of his cell. "If you wish to play pretend, you may do so, but we both know the true nature of your character." The demon smirked before crouching back down in his unnatural way. He tilted his head as he closely examined Sorin, looking thoughtful.

"I never could comprehend why the Nephilim were granted sanctuary. Such flawed creatures. Creatures who never should have been, and yet here you are. Protected... cherished even. An accepted deviation, whereas we, the progenitors, were punished, banished, and exposed!" he said on a growl, flaring his pearly white wings. "So fitting that one of the beloved be the determinant of restitution." He smiled savagely.

Sorin didn't understand, but clung to the hope that if he stayed silent and still, he could wake up and it would all cease to exist.

"Soon your desire will be granted. I am a gracious master after all. This sin will be amended and the by-product will perish. This island will cease to exist, along with all of its inhabitants."

Fear permeated Sorin's insides, his mind conjuring the sweetness of Amira's addicting essence and the thought of it being lost forever. The potency of his desire must have drawn her forth, because suddenly she was standing before him. His heart slammed into his chest. Silently she adjusted to her new environment, giving him a questioning look.

"Interesting," the demon drawled, bringing her

attention to his presence. Sorin heard her indrawn breath and her whisper, "Magnificent."

Sorin's eyes shot to the demon. He was standing with his wings spread wide to show their full glory, a peaceful expression on his beautiful face, and his arms stretched before him in a welcoming gesture as he beckoned her with his melodic voice. "Come here, child."

Entranced, she stumbled forward. Sorin gave up his stance and lunged for her, grabbing her around the waist and drawing her body to his. "That's the demon," his unused voice croaked in her ear. He felt her shock as she stiffened. Together they watched the demon drop his facade. His face twisted cruelly and his wicked laughter rang out.

"How touching," he taunted between laughs. "In your own perverse way, you actually care for her. How delightful, for it will be you who destroys everything and everyone she cares for, simply by being you. Apropos, if I must say so myself."

"Who are you?" Amira demanded.

"Why child, don't you recognize your own father?" he answered in a serene tone.

"You are not my father," she returned firmly.

"Oh, but in a way, I am. I am one of the fathers to you all." He paused to smile at her reaction to that revelation. "If you won't call me 'papa'"—he smirked —"you may call me Lahash," he finished regally.

"What do you want?" she demanded, obviously

not wanting to play his games. Sorin noticed her slight shift in stance, which placed her body completely in front of his. Her strength and integrity humbled him.

"What anyone would want. Retribution."

"By destroying Cashile?" Sorin questioned, trying to step around Amira, but she kept her body firmly blocking his.

"By undoing what was never meant to be," he said fiercely, before unnaturally smoothing out his features. "Besides, I'm not destroying Cashile... you are," he reminded Sorin smugly.

Amira's tense body turned to the side, careful not to place Lahash at her back, but enough to look at Sorin.

"He's referring to the storm, isn't he?" she asked, but he could tell she already knew the answer, so he only nodded in agreement. "Can you stop it?" she asked hopefully.

Lahash remained silent, an amused look on his face. He was enjoying Sorin's discomfort. Sorin shook his head, but felt the need to explain. "It's not something I'm doing purposely."

"Of course it's not," Lahash agreed, "it's just who you are... what you are."

The demon knew the words that would cut the deepest, and he never failed to deliver.

"How do we reverse the bond?" Amira asked, her panic evident.

"Darling child, being of 'royal blood,' you of all

people should understand the sanctity of a blood bond. What is done cannot be undone. Sorin controls this bond because you are weak, but his very nature will destroy it. It can do nothing less."

"There has got to be a way!" She looked to Sorin with a pleading expression, desperate for him to reveal a solution, a way to save them all. No one had ever looked at him in such a way before, as if he could be the savior for once... the hero instead of the villain.

"That's because that isn't your role," the demon said contemptuously, once again responding to his thoughts. "You will never be the hero."

If Amira found his statement odd, she didn't show it. Sorin looked at her more closely and realized she had withdrawn inside of herself, probably to re-examine their bond for a hidden solution. Focusing, he followed to where her consciousness was trying to unravel the tangled mess he had created. Odd feelings invaded him... *Could this be what remorse feels like?*

Then it happened. It all clicked into place for Amira. He felt her resolution and as he did, another foreign feeling enveloped him... peace. He braced himself to face what would come; witnessing her courage, he could do no less. He buried all thoughts of her plan deep within himself before emerging. When he opened his eyes, she was gone and he was once again alone with his demon, just as he should be.

∼

Amira jerked awake, the pain inside threatening to consume her. Unyieldingly, she pushed it away. She now understood her purpose. She treated herself to one last look at Caeden before silently slipping from the bed.

"Up," a firm voice demanded, startling Caeden awake. Launching forward, he instinctively reached for his sword only to find it missing.

"Go to her," the voice demanded urgently, echoing throughout the room.

Caeden searched, but to his surprise found no one there. His eyes flew to Amira, only to find the bed beside him empty as well.

"Go now," the voice urged, but Caeden didn't need to be prompted further. He jumped from the bed, and as he hurried from the chamber, he thought he saw a black shimmery form near the corner of the room, but he had no time to consider it further. He rushed out into the night, determined to get to her in time.

She found him right where she knew he'd be. Sorin may once again be active in his dream state, but in the real world, there he sat, unmoving, locked within himself. She scanned the cell. There was no indication of Lahash, but she felt as if his eyes were still upon her. Outside, the wind howled, but she was no longer afraid of the disaster the storm would bring. She paused to look into Sorin's eyes and wondered if she should say something. She discovered his eyes were no longer vacant, and what she saw within them brought a sad smile to her face. No words were needed. She swung the sword just as she had been taught. And then it was over. Her final thought, ironically, was *that wasn't as difficult as I assumed it would be.*

The guards were not at their posts, Caeden noticed absentmindedly as his feet effortlessly and automatically brought him to her. He made it to Sorin's cell just as she was lifting the sword; thankfully, there was still time to stop her. He rushed forward, but before he could reach her, a large dark form materialized in front of him and for a moment time stood still.

"Not yet," the voice he recognized from his chamber said, emanating from the dark form blocking his path. Caeden would figure out the dark creature later; his only concern was Amira.

"Out of my way," he demanded.

The form took solid shape and Caeden was shocked to find himself standing before a beautiful male with massive shimmery obsidian wings. An angel,

Caeden realized. No time to stand in awe, he tried to push past the angel, but he was immovable.

"Let me pass; she will kill herself," Caeden growled in frustration and fear.

"Soon," the angel replied.

"She will die!" Caeden all but yelled.

"It will be an honorable sacrifice," the angel returned calmly.

In slow motion, Caeden watched her swing his sword, her form perfect and her aim true. Unsure where her strength came from, he watched helplessly as Sorin's head was smoothly sliced from his body. Amira stood silently for a moment, before her body collapsed to the unforgiving ground.

"No!" he yelled, but it emerged as a strangled whisper. "Why?" He turned his fury on the angel still blocking his path, anger and grief warring inside of him. "You awoke me to go to her, and yet you prevent me from saving her. Why?"

"It was her destiny," he answered plainly.

"It was *not* her destiny to die here!" Caeden declared firmly.

"No, it was her destiny to become who she is meant to be. Now, King of the Children of the Angels, who will you choose to be?"

"I don't understand," he answered.

And he didn't. He didn't understand what the angel was asking, he didn't understand how the pain in his chest hadn't already strangled the life out of him, and he didn't understand how he was supposed to go on. Numbness began to take over.

"It is a simple choice. The Nephilim, the sanctuary, the kingdom... everything is now all yours or"—the angel stepped to the side, stretching his arm out in Amira's direction—"it can be hers once again."

"Hers?" Caeden's heart stopped.

"She has not yet gone from this world. You can still save her, if that is your wish," the angel said, watching Caeden curiously.

"How?" Caeden demanded, his heart racing frantically.

"Finish the bond that was meant to be," the angel said cryptically, but Caeden understood immediately.

As he knelt at her side and pulled the knife from his belt, uncertainty plagued him. "But her age, she has not reached maturity."

The angel cocked his head, as if listening to silent words only he could hear. His lips twitched, possibly suppressing a smile. After a moment of silence, he announced, "Due to her choices, she is not as she was before."

Panic clawed at Caeden's chest.

"Fear not. All actions bear a consequence, but her motives were pure," the angel assured him. "This form will now sustain a bond, as strength is not determined by time." His ethereal eyes bore into Caeden's, seeing deep down into his soul. "Now, it is time for you to make your choice, but be swift for her time grows short."

Without hesitation, Caeden sliced his palm and then hers. Clasping her hand tightly, he closed his eyes.

"I bind myself to you in this life and the next," he whispered to her fervently. "This is my will and this is my right." As the words left him, sensation pulsated throughout his body and a distracting hum filled his brain.

The angel crouched beside them and laid his hand upon theirs. "You are both as you were meant to be," he declared with a nod.

Amira's eyes fluttered open. Her beautiful silver gaze instantly found Caeden and she softly whispered his name. Relief would have brought him to his knees if he weren't there already.

"Queen Amira, if it is your will to be bound to Caeden, declare it now," the angel interrupted.

Her eyes swung to the angel.

"Who are you?" she asked in a small frightened voice.

In answer he spread his massive wings. To Caeden's confusion, she whispered, "They're black." The angel seemed to understand.

"Only the ones who have deviated from what was meant to be have been exposed and turned white."

His puzzling answer seemed to satisfy her, but led her to another question.

"And the Nephilim? Lahash said we too were not meant to be." Her voice was more confident.

Caeden had no idea what they were talking about, but was extremely grateful for the time it allowed him to collect himself. The pain from almost losing her was too fresh, and the relief of her well-being still unbelievable.

The angel gifted her with a brilliant smile and answered, "You were not of Divine Will, but you are now."

Amira looked as confused as Caeden felt, but before she could ask any more questions, the angel repeated firmly, "If it is your will to be bound to Caeden, declare it now."

"It is my will," her beautiful voice rang out, and Caeden's heart soared.

The angel's eyes closed briefly, and then with a definitive nod he announced, "Your will has been granted."

As the angel opened his otherwordly eyes, the Earth seemed to tremble. The humming in Caeden's ears grew to an unbearable intensity and an immense heaviness overtook him. Vaguely he heard Amira's indrawn breath, but struggled with awareness as he fought through the intense sensations flowing through him. Just when he knew he could bear no more, it suddenly ceased. It all snapped into place, and there she was. Inside him. Connected to him. A part of him.

Amira's silver eyes shot to Caeden's, and he knew she felt the same completeness that filled him.

Their blood bond was complete, but not only was he bonded to her; he felt the solid bond to Cashile, the shield, and all of the Nephilim. The immense responsibility was humbling and exciting at the same time.

"Your tribulation is not yet finished," the angel continued, regaining their attention.

"The demon," Amira guessed, her body tensing with fear.

The angel nodded. Amira's eyes darted to the corner of the cell where she had last seen Lahash. "He is not here, young queen. The dark cannot remain where there is light," he reassured her in his unclear manner.

"What demon?" Caeden asked, regaining his composure and focusing on the present.

"One of the fallen refuses to accept accountability for his misdeeds and seeks to sweep away the manifestation. Full of hatred, he has planted seeds of the vilest nature amongst you: pride, envy, greed, wrath, lust, sloth, and gluttony. Surely you can feel this within the bond that ties you to your sanctuary and your people."

The angel paused, seemingly to allow them time to evaluate the truth within his words. All of it was new for Caeden. He closed his eyes and sought the beauty that was their miraculous union. Not allowing himself to be caught up in the wonder of it all, he searched for and found the corruption the angel spoke of.

Amira's appalled expression mirrored his emotions.

"The fallen one has wrought much damage," the angel stated, discerning their horror.

"How did my father not perceive this?" Amira asked in confusion.

"The former king was blinded by his grief."

"Why can't you stop the demon?" Caeden asked.

"I can, but that is not my destiny," the angel informed them matter-of-factly.

"What does that mean?"

The angel gave a knowing look, but continued without answering. "The Nephilim must understand their purpose and reach their potential. Balance must be restored. Strength in leadership will be needed to succeed. You are worthy," he addressed them both, "and with assistance from your trusted companions, you will set right what is wrong."

With that, the angel moved to take his leave.

"Wait!" Amira reached out to stop him. "Will you be here to help us?"

"When I am able," he answered solemnly.

"Thank you..."

"Briathos," he introduced himself with a slight bow.

"Thank you, Briathos."

"Be well." And then he was gone.

Caeden pulled Amira into his arms, needing the physical bond as reassurance that he hadn't lost her.

"Never again will you sacrifice yourself." His voice was stern, but his fingers were gentle as they caressed her hair.

She buried her face in the crook of his neck; apparently, she was still shaken from the experience as well.

"I'm so—" she began to apologize, but he interrupted.

"You did what you thought was right, never be sorry for that. But in the future, we face our problems together. Where you go, I go, in this life and the next," he promised.

She lifted her head, bestowing a glorious smile upon him.

"Together," she affirmed.

"Always."

EPILOGUE

The brilliant colors in the sky emerged with the rising of the sun. It had always been Amira's favorite time of day, but a chill swept through her as a cold wind blew in through the open window.

Strong arms circled her waist as Caeden's heat pressed against her back, drawing her into his embrace.

"The storm has passed," he assured her, staring over her shoulder out to the horizon.

"For now, but Lahash is still out there," she whispered. She feared saying his name too loudly would draw the demon to them.

Caeden's arms tightened around her and he pressed a tender kiss to her neck. It was the only comfort he could give; he too felt the swirling turmoil within the bond.

"We cannot predict the future, nor defend against the unknown. We must live in the moment and face our difficulties as they come," he reminded her softly.

Amira knew he was right, but fear still threatened to overwhelm her. "Inaya should reach the border of Ammon by day's end, don't you think?"

"If all goes as planned," he agreed.

"I worry about what she'll find and the reception she'll receive. There is no way to know how many are left of Sorin's loyal followers. And those who were not loyal were treated so badly. Maybe we should have gone ourselves?" She turned in his arms to look up at him as she asked the same question she had asked many times since Inaya's departure.

He bent and kissed her forehead as he patiently answered one more time, "Amira, you cannot keep second-guessing your decisions. We are needed here, and Inaya is the perfect emissary. She is strong, but nonthreatening in nature, and an excellent judge of character. Besides, Trevin will not allow harm to come to her; you know this."

"You're right." She nodded. "But should we have sent more soldiers with them?"

"If we did, there would be no reserves left to send to Levi's aid, should he need."

Which brought to mind another of her major concerns, but before she could voice it, he pulled her close and whispered, "Soon. We'll hear something soon."

The adventure continues in DIVINE GRACE!

ACKNOWLEDGMENTS

There are so many lovely people who have supported me and encouraged me to follow my passion and reach for my dreams, but there are a few who have gone above and beyond, and I would have never made it this far without each and every one of them. Words are inadequate to express my gratitude and what you ladies mean to me, but I'm gonna try.

Martha Pecenka, thank you for making me give myself permission to dream and prompting me to take this journey. I wouldn't be here without you. Thank you for helping me find myself.

Jacqueline Flanders, you are an amazing woman. You're selfless and giving, and I am blessed to have you as my friend and biggest supporter. I can never thank you enough.

Jenn McCoy, thank you for helping to make not one, but two of my dreams come true. You are an inspiration to me.

Justine Littleton, I owe you my sanity. Thank you for being the Melissa to my Sandra. Your friendship means the world to me.

Becky Johnson, thank you for taking a chance on

me and allowing me to live my dream. Your beautiful spirit can be felt from oceans away.

Thank you to my family, who puts up with my quirks and absentmindedness.

To my beautiful girl, Jacobi, I hope this proves to you that dreams do come true and it's okay to dream big.

About the Author

Virginia's greatest passion has always been fiction, particularly romance. The innocent in her loves the idea of a happily ever after, but she has a massive soft spot for the bad boys. If you ask her, she'll tell you she's living her dream—getting paid to read and helping indie authors to create beauty by working as an editor for Hot Tree Editing. She's inspired by the many amazing indie authors she has met and has (finally) found the courage to follow her other dream by becoming a published author.

facebook.com/V.Cantrell.Author

About the Publisher

Hot Tree Publishing loves love. Publishing adult romantic fiction, HTPubs are all about diverse reads featuring heroes and heroines to swoon over. Since opening in 2015, HTPubs have published more than 300 titles across the wide and diverse range of romantic genres. If you're chasing a happily ever after in your favourite subgenre, HTPubs have you covered.

Interested in discovering more amazing reads brought to you by Hot Tree Publishing? Head over to the website for information:

WWW.HOTTREEPUBLISHING.COM

facebook.com/hottreepublishing

twitter.com/hottreepubs

instagram.com/hottreepublishing

www.ingramcontent.com/pod-product-compliance
Lightning Source LLC
Chambersburg PA
CBHW061615210726
48287CB00001B/148